NANCY DREW
girl detective ®

PAPERCUTZ™

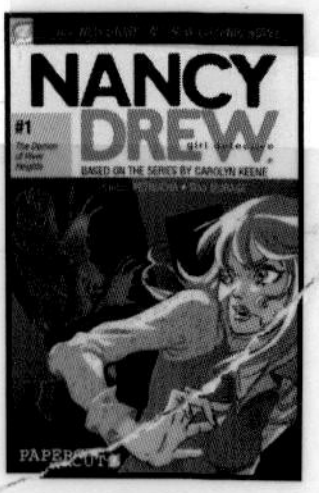
NANCY DREW
girl detective
#1
BASED ON THE SERIES BY CAROLYN KEENE
PAPERCUTZ

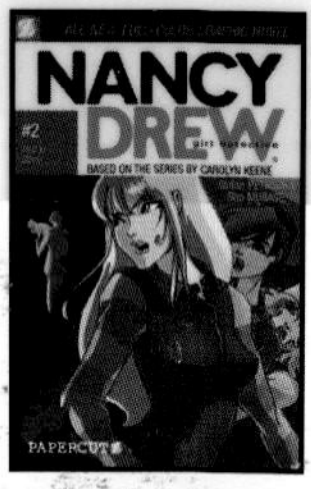
NANCY DREW
girl detective
#2
BASED ON THE SERIES BY CAROLYN KEENE
PAPERCUTZ

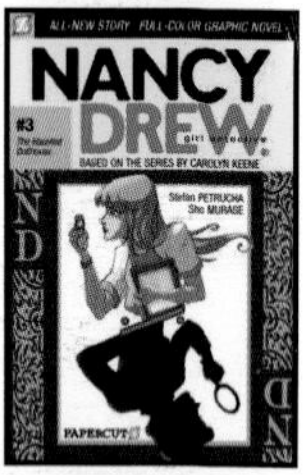
ALL-NEW STORY FULL-COLOR GRAPHIC NOVEL
NANCY DREW
girl detective
#3
BASED ON THE SERIES BY CAROLYN KEENE
Stefan PETRUCHA
Sho MURASE
PAPERCUTZ

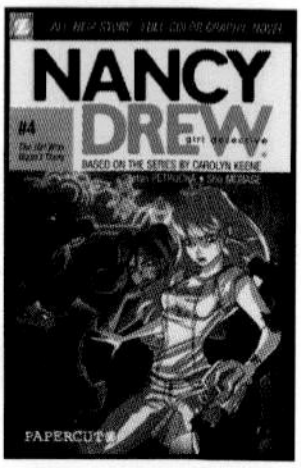
NANCY DREW
girl detective
#4
BASED ON THE SERIES BY CAROLYN KEENE
PAPERCUTZ

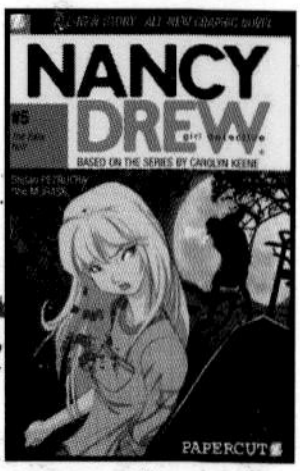
NANCY DREW
girl detective
#5
BASED ON THE SERIES BY CAROLYN KEENE
PAPERCUTZ

NANCY DREW
#4 DREW girl detective ®

The Girl Who Wasn't There

STEFAN PETRUCHA • Writer
SHO MURASE • Artist
with 3D CG elements by RACHEL ITO
preview art by VAUGHN ROSS

PAPERCUTZ™
New York

The Girl Who Wasn't There
STEFAN PETRUCHA – Writer
SHO MURASE – Artist
with 3D CG elements by RACHEL ITO
BRYAN SENKA – Letterer
CARLOS JOSE GUZMAN
SHO MURASE
Colorists
JIM SALICRUP
Editor-in-Chief

ISBN 10: 1-59707-012-2 paperback edition
ISBN 13: 978-1-59707-012-6 paperback edition
ISBN 10: 1-59707-013-0 hardcover edition
ISBN 13: 978-1-59707-013-3 hardcover edition

Printed in China.

10   9   8   7   6   5   4   3   2   1

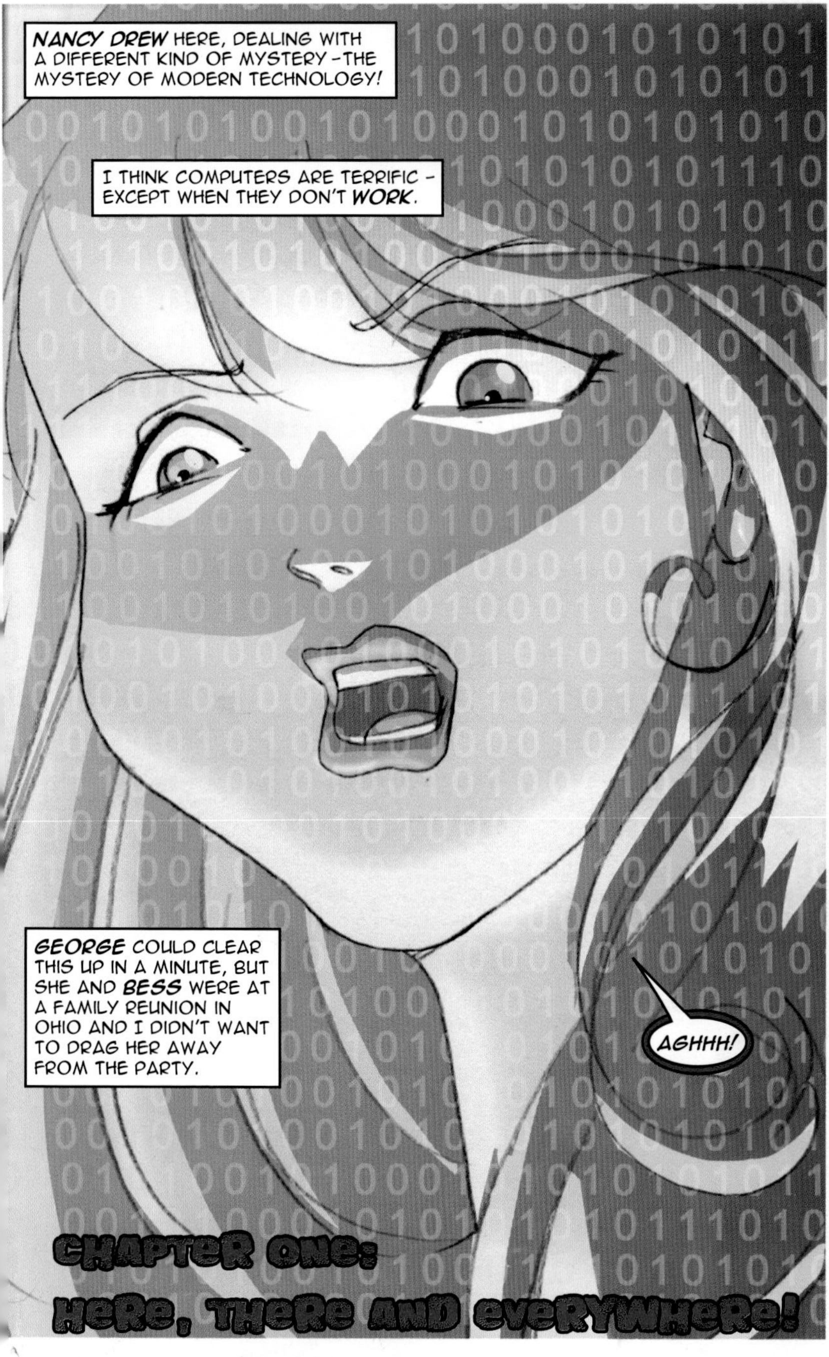
NANCY DREW HERE, DEALING WITH A DIFFERENT KIND OF MYSTERY –THE MYSTERY OF MODERN TECHNOLOGY!
I THINK COMPUTERS ARE TERRIFIC – EXCEPT WHEN THEY DON'T WORK.
GEORGE COULD CLEAR THIS UP IN A MINUTE, BUT SHE AND BESS WERE AT A FAMILY REUNION IN OHIO AND I DIDN'T WANT TO DRAG HER AWAY FROM THE PARTY.
AGHHH!
CHAPTER ONE:
HERE, THERE AND EVERYWHERE!

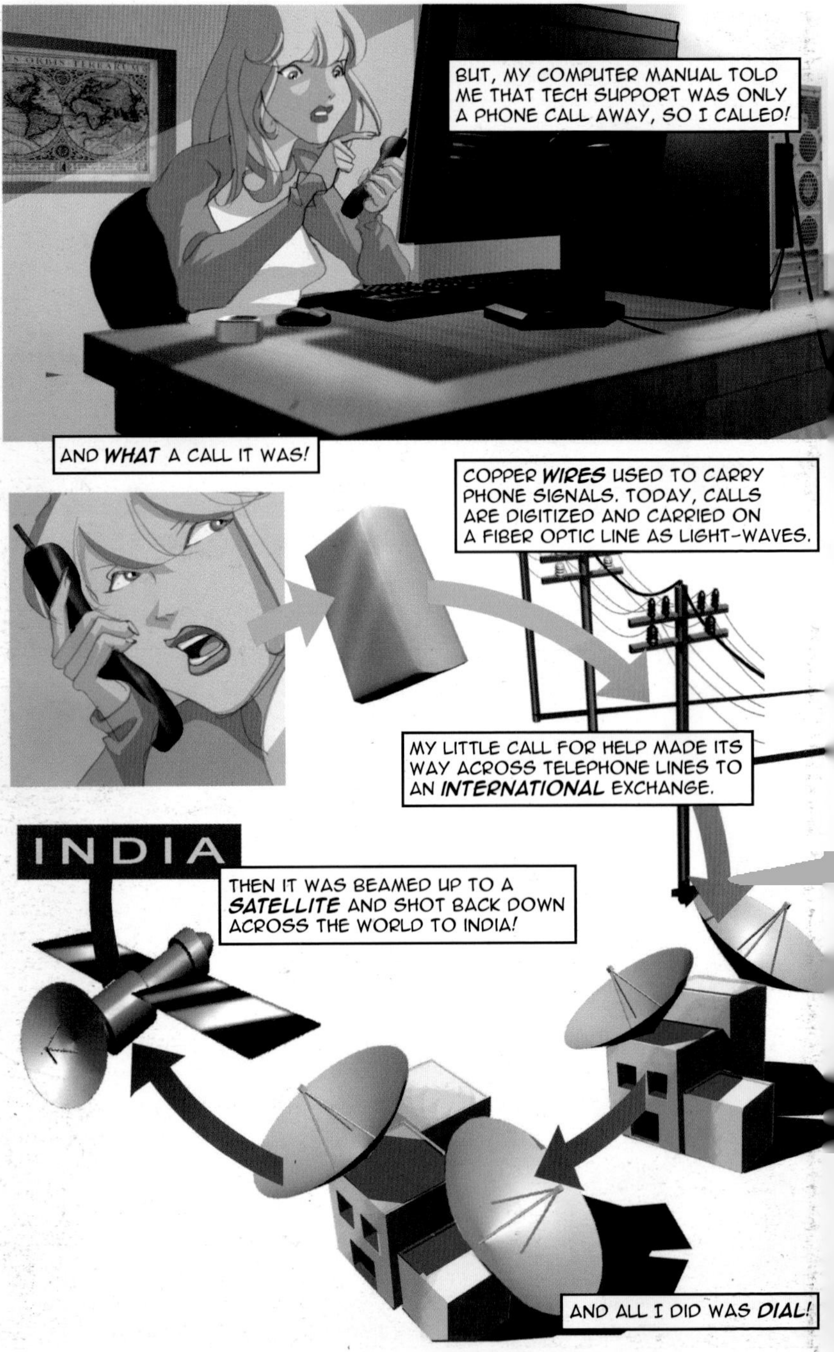
BUT, MY COMPUTER MANUAL TOLD ME THAT TECH SUPPORT WAS ONLY A PHONE CALL AWAY, SO I CALLED!
AND *WHAT* A CALL IT WAS!
COPPER *WIRES* USED TO CARRY PHONE SIGNALS. TODAY, CALLS ARE DIGITIZED AND CARRIED ON A FIBER OPTIC LINE AS LIGHT-WAVES.
MY LITTLE CALL FOR HELP MADE ITS WAY ACROSS TELEPHONE LINES TO AN *INTERNATIONAL* EXCHANGE.
INDIA
THEN IT WAS BEAMED UP TO A *SATELLITE* AND SHOT BACK DOWN ACROSS THE WORLD TO INDIA!
AND ALL I DID WAS *DIAL!*

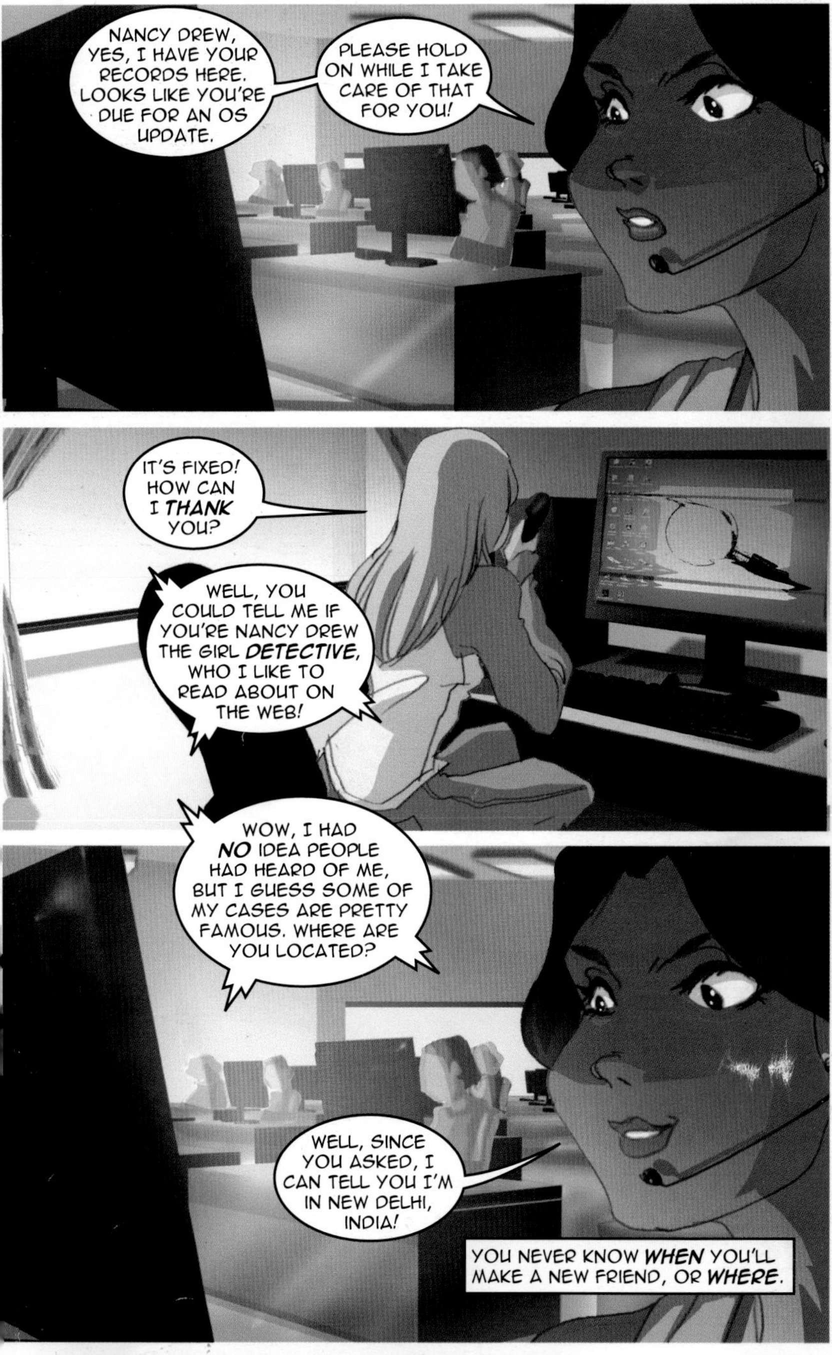
NANCY DREW, YES, I HAVE YOUR RECORDS HERE. LOOKS LIKE YOU'RE DUE FOR AN OS UPDATE.
PLEASE HOLD ON WHILE I TAKE CARE OF THAT FOR YOU!
IT'S FIXED! HOW CAN I THANK YOU?
WELL, YOU COULD TELL ME IF YOU'RE NANCY DREW THE GIRL DETECTIVE, WHO I LIKE TO READ ABOUT ON THE WEB!
WOW, I HAD NO IDEA PEOPLE HAD HEARD OF ME, BUT I GUESS SOME OF MY CASES ARE PRETTY FAMOUS. WHERE ARE YOU LOCATED?
WELL, SINCE YOU ASKED, I CAN TELL YOU I'M IN NEW DELHI, INDIA!
YOU NEVER KNOW WHEN YOU'LL MAKE A NEW FRIEND, OR WHERE.

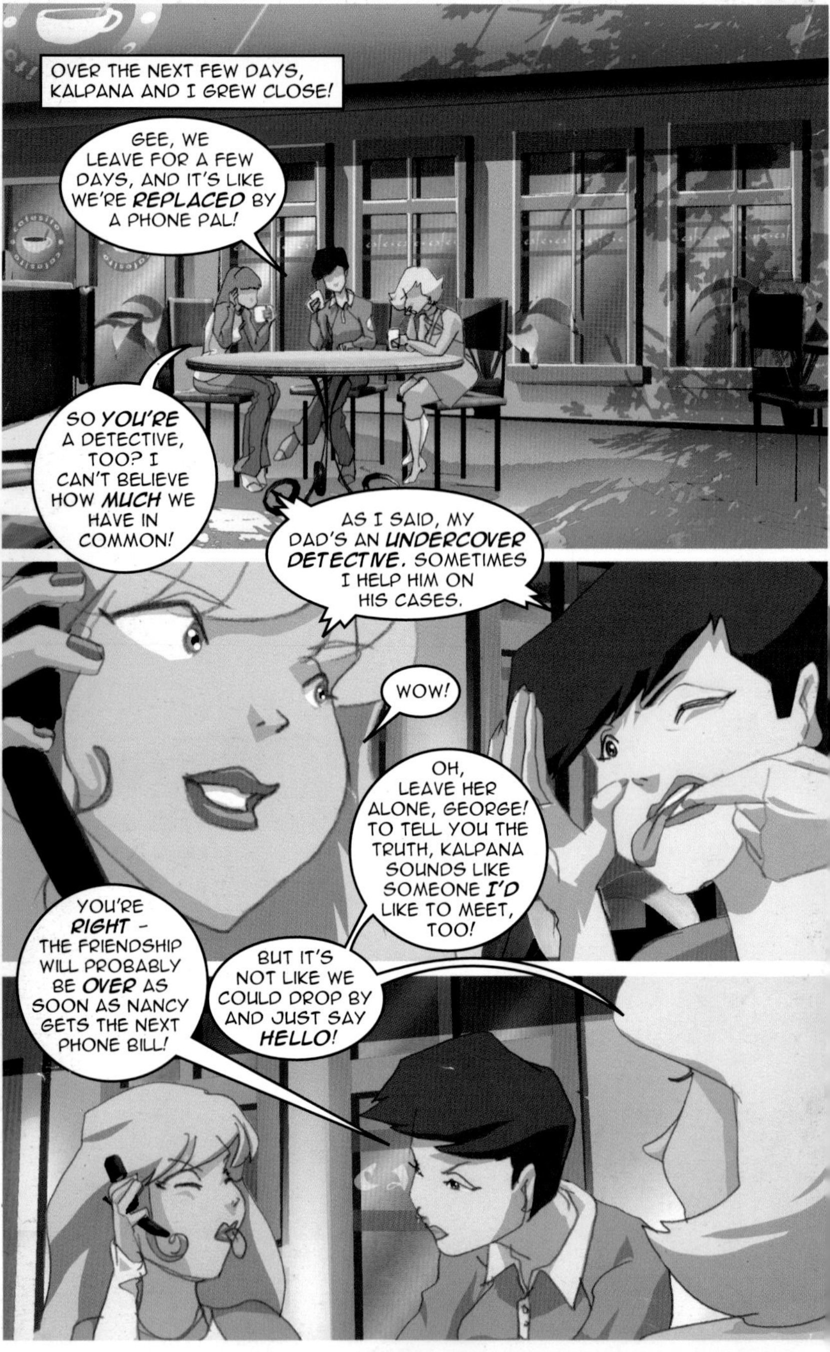
OVER THE NEXT FEW DAYS, KALPANA AND I GREW CLOSE!
GEE, WE LEAVE FOR A FEW DAYS, AND IT'S LIKE WE'RE REPLACED BY A PHONE PAL!
SO YOU'RE A DETECTIVE, TOO? I CAN'T BELIEVE HOW MUCH WE HAVE IN COMMON!
AS I SAID, MY DAD'S AN UNDERCOVER DETECTIVE. SOMETIMES I HELP HIM ON HIS CASES.
WOW!
OH, LEAVE HER ALONE, GEORGE! TO TELL YOU THE TRUTH, KALPANA SOUNDS LIKE SOMEONE I'D LIKE TO MEET, TOO!
YOU'RE RIGHT - THE FRIENDSHIP WILL PROBABLY BE OVER AS SOON AS NANCY GETS THE NEXT PHONE BILL!
BUT IT'S NOT LIKE WE COULD DROP BY AND JUST SAY HELLO!

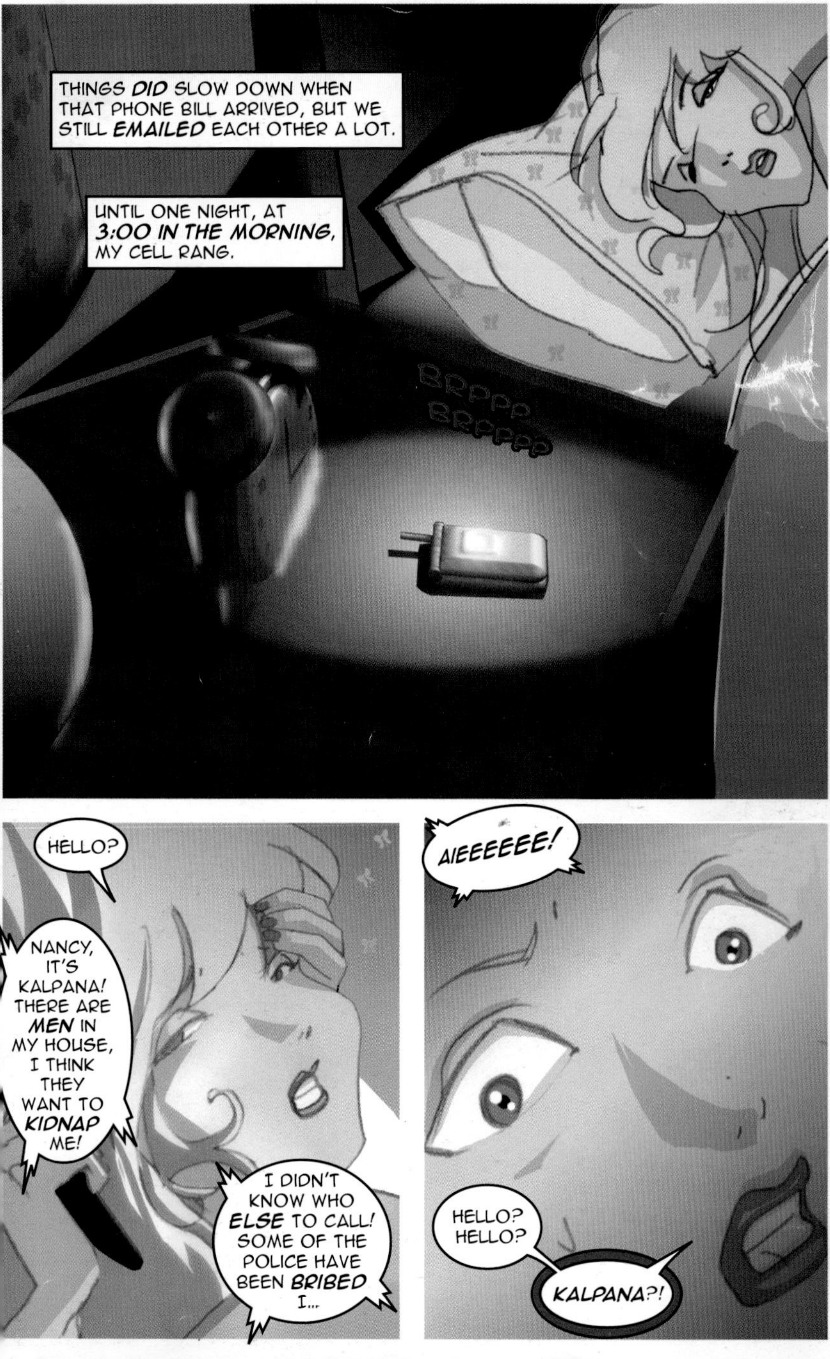
THINGS DID SLOW DOWN WHEN THAT PHONE BILL ARRIVED, BUT WE STILL EMAILED EACH OTHER A LOT.
UNTIL ONE NIGHT, AT 3:00 IN THE MORNING, MY CELL RANG.
BRPPPP BRPPPPP
HELLO?
NANCY, IT'S KALPANA! THERE ARE MEN IN MY HOUSE, I THINK THEY WANT TO KIDNAP ME!
I DIDN'T KNOW WHO ELSE TO CALL! SOME OF THE POLICE HAVE BEEN BRIBED I...
AIEEEEEE!
HELLO? HELLO?
KALPANA?!

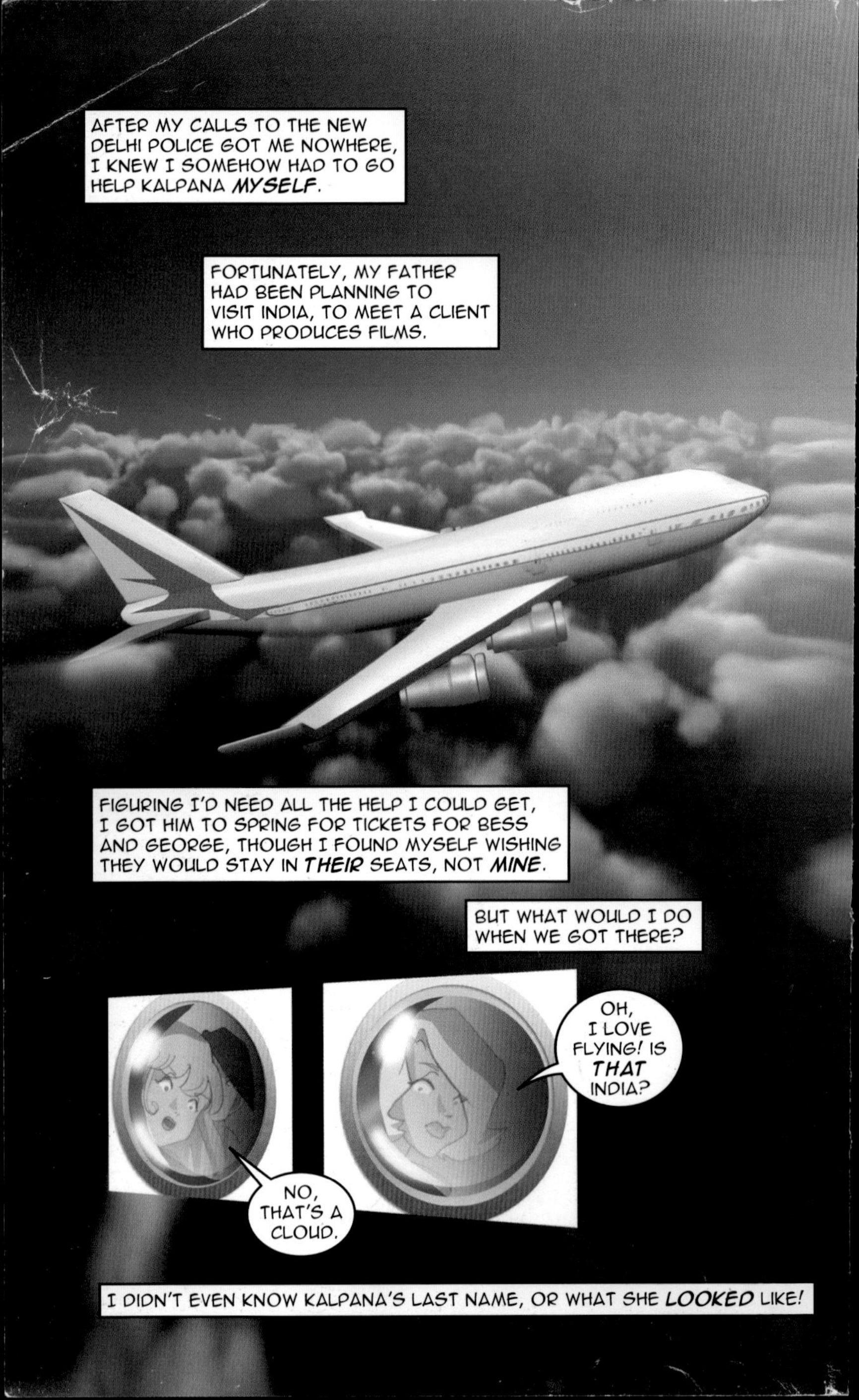
AFTER MY CALLS TO THE NEW DELHI POLICE GOT ME NOWHERE, I KNEW I SOMEHOW HAD TO GO HELP KALPANA *MYSELF*.
FORTUNATELY, MY FATHER HAD BEEN PLANNING TO VISIT INDIA, TO MEET A CLIENT WHO PRODUCES FILMS.
FIGURING I'D NEED ALL THE HELP I COULD GET, I GOT HIM TO SPRING FOR TICKETS FOR BESS AND GEORGE, THOUGH I FOUND MYSELF WISHING THEY WOULD STAY IN *THEIR* SEATS, NOT *MINE*.
BUT WHAT WOULD I DO WHEN WE GOT THERE?
OH, I LOVE FLYING! IS *THAT* INDIA?
NO, THAT'S A CLOUD.
I DIDN'T EVEN KNOW KALPANA'S LAST NAME, OR WHAT SHE *LOOKED* LIKE!

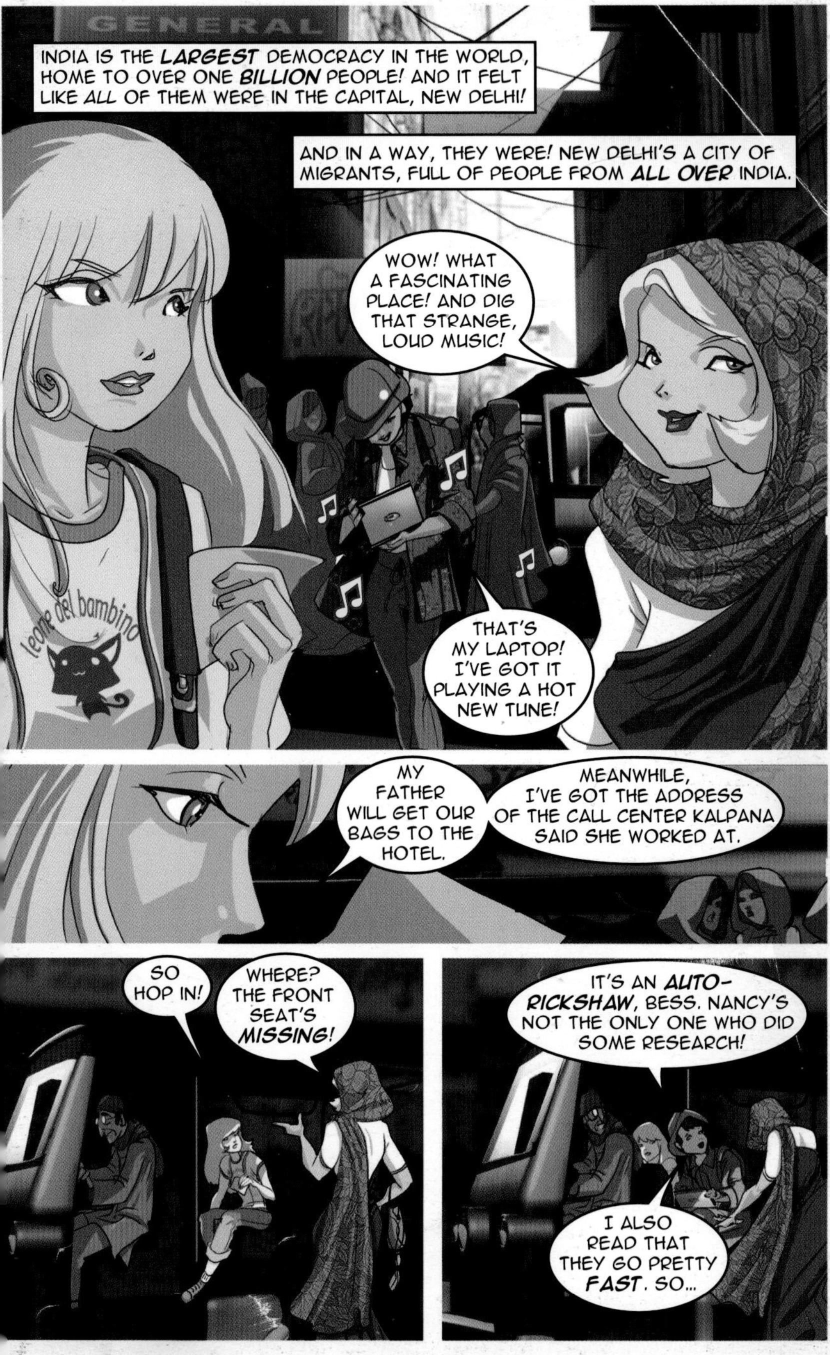
GENERAL
INDIA IS THE LARGEST DEMOCRACY IN THE WORLD, HOME TO OVER ONE BILLION PEOPLE! AND IT FELT LIKE ALL OF THEM WERE IN THE CAPITAL, NEW DELHI!
AND IN A WAY, THEY WERE! NEW DELHI'S A CITY OF MIGRANTS, FULL OF PEOPLE FROM ALL OVER INDIA.
WOW! WHAT A FASCINATING PLACE! AND DIG THAT STRANGE, LOUD MUSIC!
leone del bambino
THAT'S MY LAPTOP! I'VE GOT IT PLAYING A HOT NEW TUNE!
MY FATHER WILL GET OUR BAGS TO THE HOTEL.
MEANWHILE, I'VE GOT THE ADDRESS OF THE CALL CENTER KALPANA SAID SHE WORKED AT.
SO HOP IN!
WHERE? THE FRONT SEAT'S MISSING!
IT'S AN AUTO-RICKSHAW, BESS. NANCY'S NOT THE ONLY ONE WHO DID SOME RESEARCH!
I ALSO READ THAT THEY GO PRETTY FAST. SO...

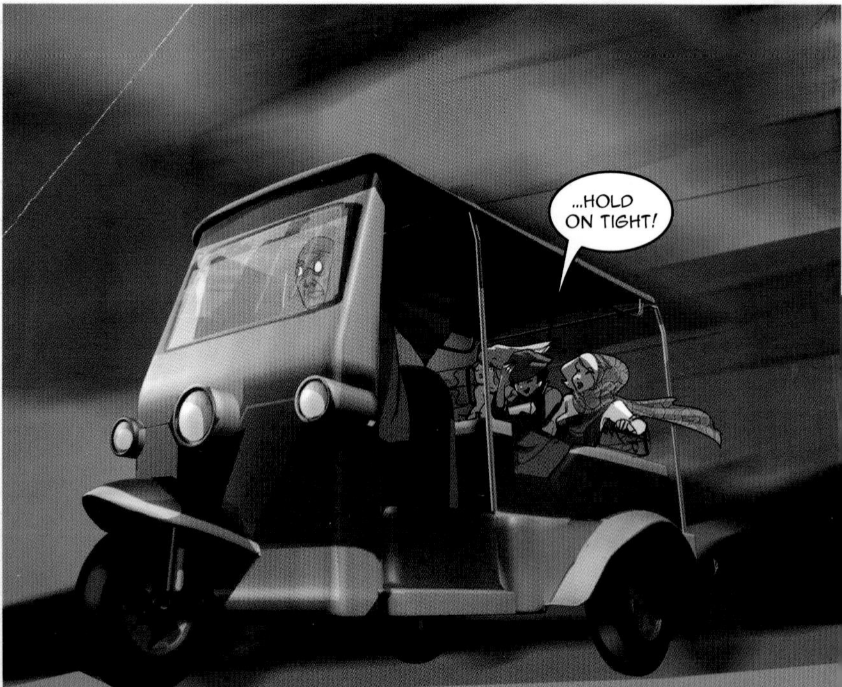
...HOLD ON TIGHT!

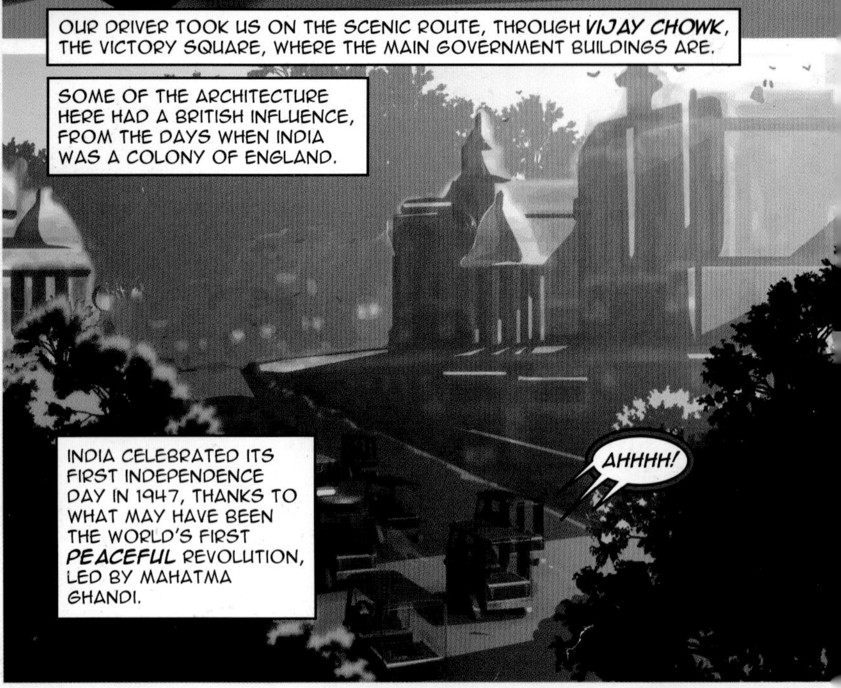
OUR DRIVER TOOK US ON THE SCENIC ROUTE, THROUGH *VIJAY CHOWK*, THE VICTORY SQUARE, WHERE THE MAIN GOVERNMENT BUILDINGS ARE.
SOME OF THE ARCHITECTURE HERE HAD A BRITISH INFLUENCE, FROM THE DAYS WHEN INDIA WAS A COLONY OF ENGLAND.
INDIA CELEBRATED ITS FIRST INDEPENDENCE DAY IN 1947, THANKS TO WHAT MAY HAVE BEEN THE WORLD'S FIRST ***PEACEFUL*** REVOLUTION, LED BY MAHATMA GHANDI.
AHHHH!

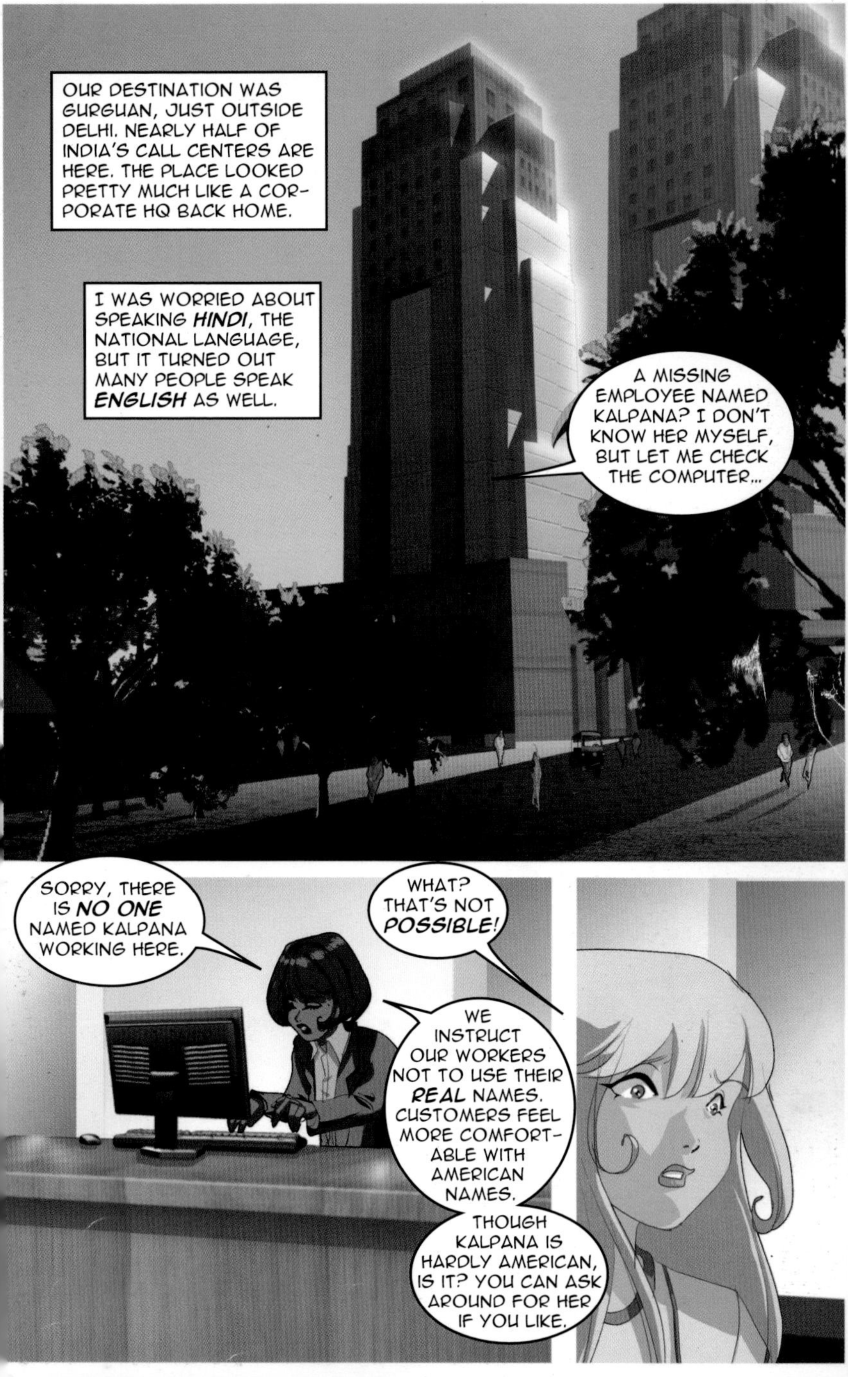
OUR DESTINATION WAS GURGUAN, JUST OUTSIDE DELHI. NEARLY HALF OF INDIA'S CALL CENTERS ARE HERE. THE PLACE LOOKED PRETTY MUCH LIKE A CORPORATE HQ BACK HOME.
I WAS WORRIED ABOUT SPEAKING *HINDI*, THE NATIONAL LANGUAGE, BUT IT TURNED OUT MANY PEOPLE SPEAK *ENGLISH* AS WELL.
A MISSING EMPLOYEE NAMED KALPANA? I DON'T KNOW HER MYSELF, BUT LET ME CHECK THE COMPUTER...
SORRY, THERE IS **NO ONE** NAMED KALPANA WORKING HERE.
WHAT? THAT'S NOT ***POSSIBLE***!
WE INSTRUCT OUR WORKERS NOT TO USE THEIR ***REAL*** NAMES. CUSTOMERS FEEL MORE COMFORTABLE WITH AMERICAN NAMES.
THOUGH KALPANA IS HARDLY AMERICAN, IS IT? YOU CAN ASK AROUND FOR HER IF YOU LIKE.

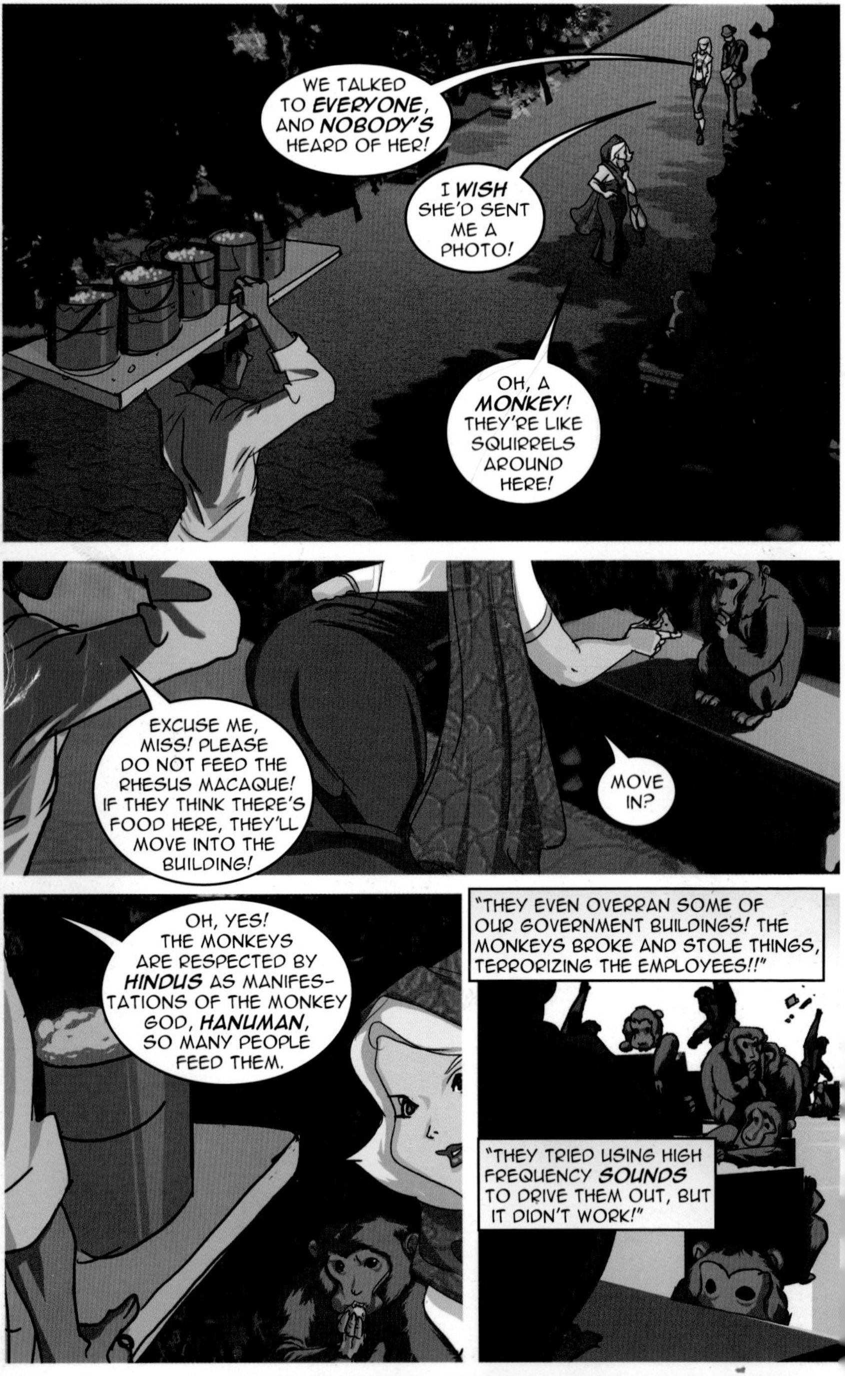
WE TALKED TO EVERYONE, AND NOBODY'S HEARD OF HER!
I WISH SHE'D SENT ME A PHOTO!
OH, A MONKEY! THEY'RE LIKE SQUIRRELS AROUND HERE!
EXCUSE ME, MISS! PLEASE DO NOT FEED THE RHESUS MACAQUE! IF THEY THINK THERE'S FOOD HERE, THEY'LL MOVE INTO THE BUILDING!
MOVE IN?
OH, YES! THE MONKEYS ARE RESPECTED BY HINDUS AS MANIFESTATIONS OF THE MONKEY GOD, HANUMAN, SO MANY PEOPLE FEED THEM.
"THEY EVEN OVERRAN SOME OF OUR GOVERNMENT BUILDINGS! THE MONKEYS BROKE AND STOLE THINGS, TERRORIZING THE EMPLOYEES!!"
"THEY TRIED USING HIGH FREQUENCY SOUNDS TO DRIVE THEM OUT, BUT IT DIDN'T WORK!"

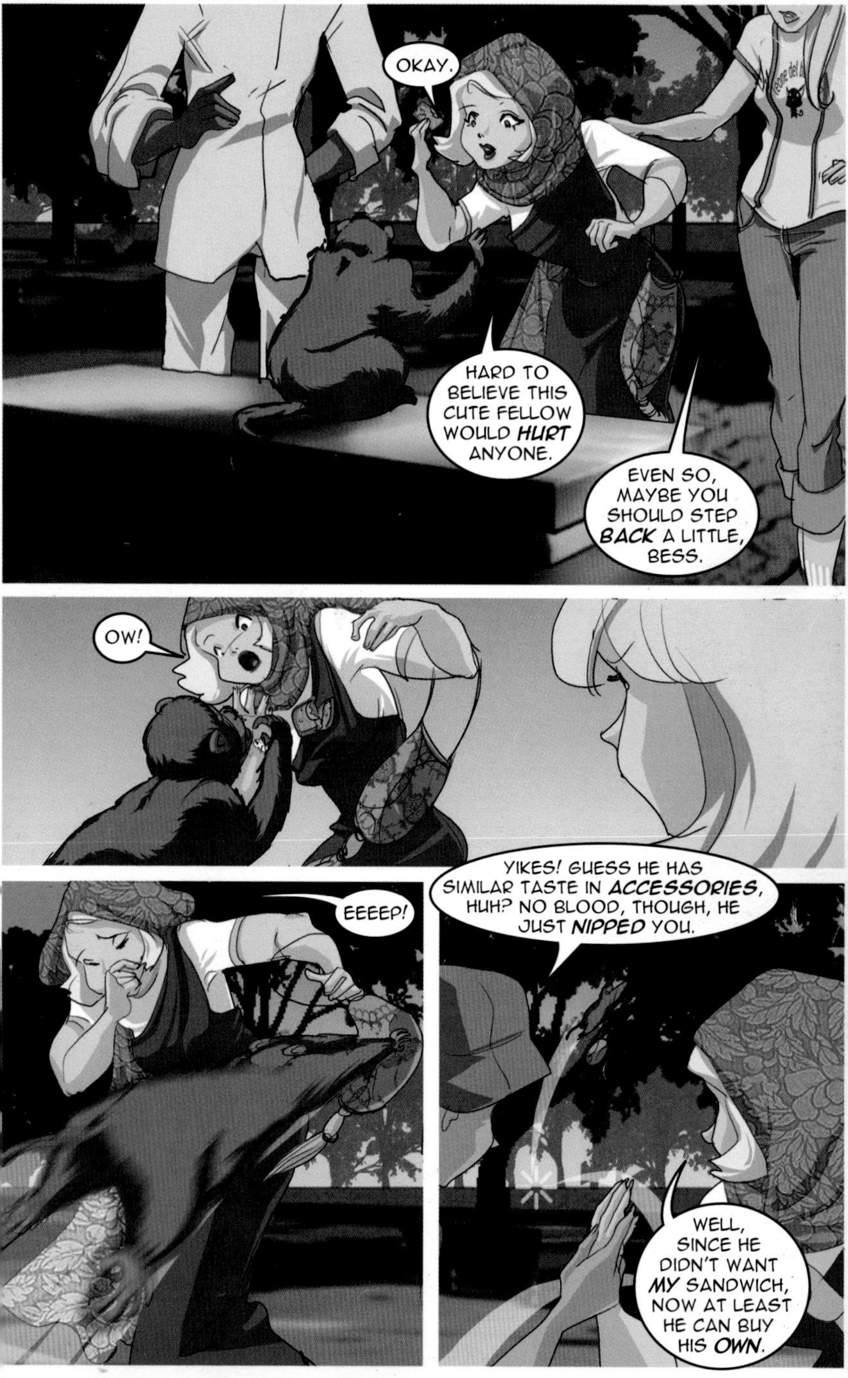
OKAY.
HARD TO BELIEVE THIS CUTE FELLOW WOULD HURT ANYONE.
EVEN SO, MAYBE YOU SHOULD STEP BACK A LITTLE, BESS.
OW!
EEEEP!
YIKES! GUESS HE HAS SIMILAR TASTE IN ACCESSORIES, HUH? NO BLOOD, THOUGH, HE JUST NIPPED YOU.
WELL, SINCE HE DIDN'T WANT MY SANDWICH, NOW AT LEAST HE CAN BUY HIS OWN.

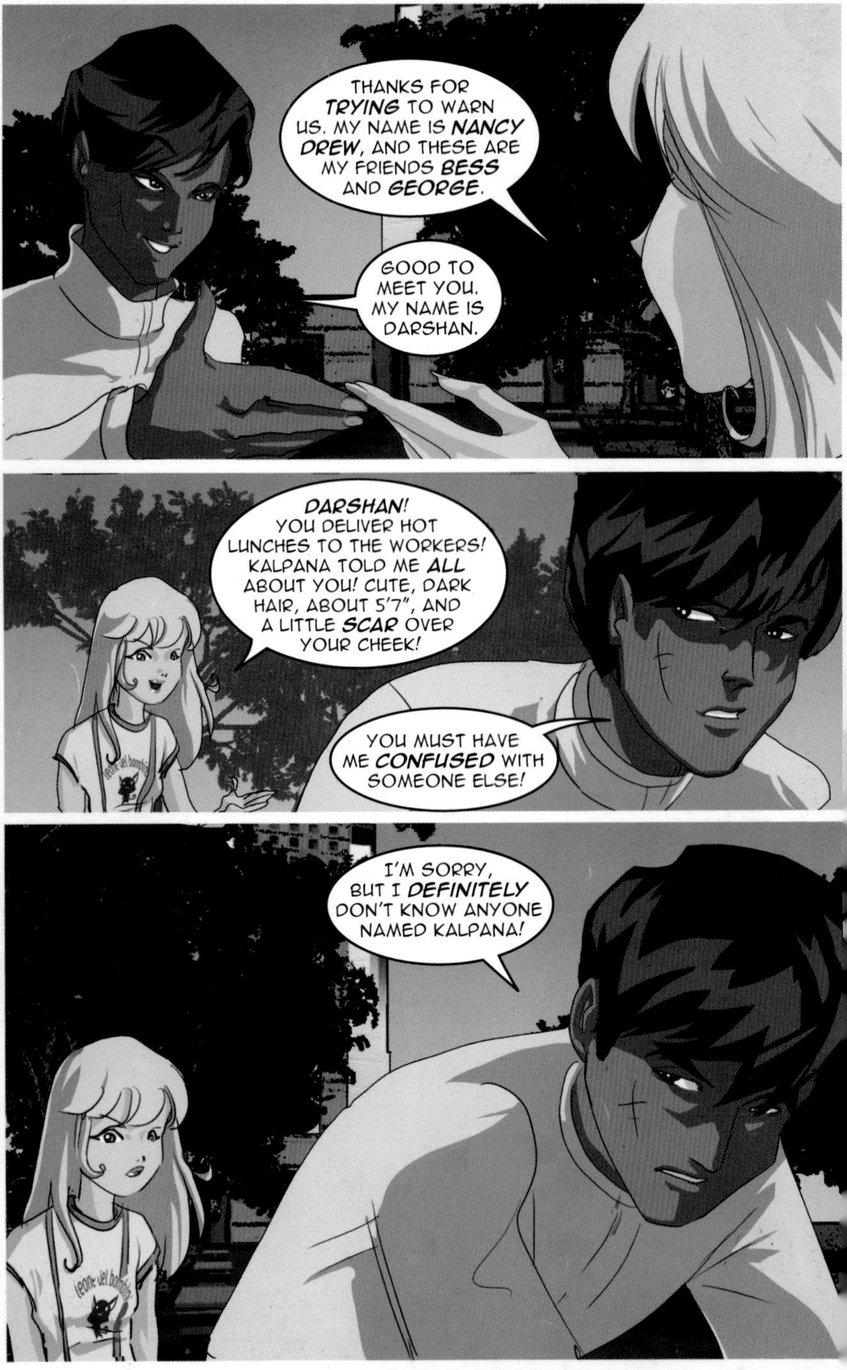
THANKS FOR TRYING TO WARN US. MY NAME IS NANCY DREW, AND THESE ARE MY FRIENDS BESS AND GEORGE.
GOOD TO MEET YOU. MY NAME IS DARSHAN.
DARSHAN! YOU DELIVER HOT LUNCHES TO THE WORKERS! KALPANA TOLD ME ALL ABOUT YOU! CUTE, DARK HAIR, ABOUT 5'7", AND A LITTLE SCAR OVER YOUR CHEEK!
YOU MUST HAVE ME CONFUSED WITH SOMEONE ELSE!
I'M SORRY, BUT I DEFINITELY DON'T KNOW ANYONE NAMED KALPANA!

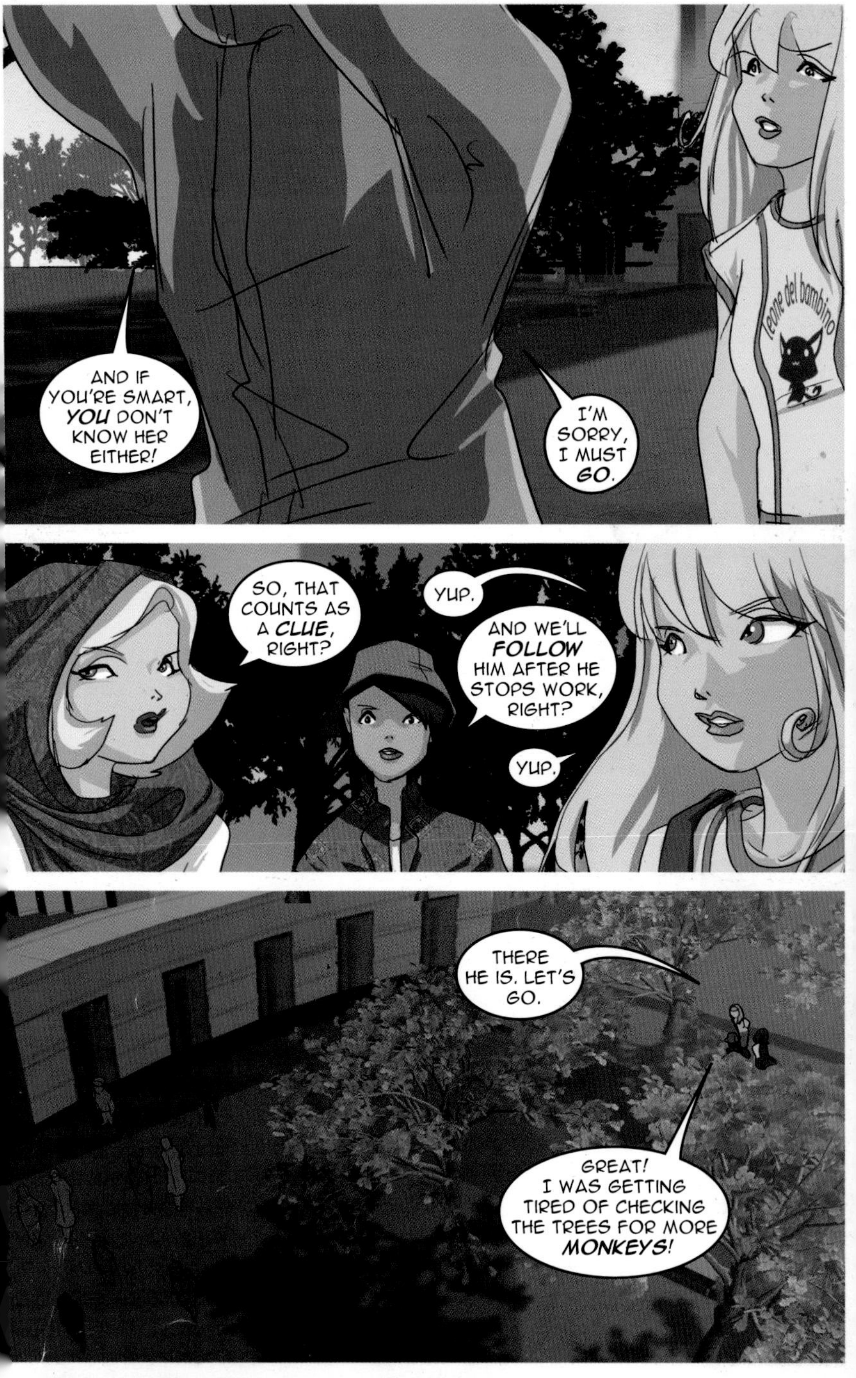
AND IF YOU'RE SMART, *YOU* DON'T KNOW HER EITHER!
leone del bambino
I'M SORRY, I MUST *GO*.
SO, THAT COUNTS AS A *CLUE*, RIGHT?
YUP.
AND WE'LL *FOLLOW* HIM AFTER HE STOPS WORK, RIGHT?
YUP.
THERE HE IS. LET'S GO.
GREAT! I WAS GETTING TIRED OF CHECKING THE TREES FOR MORE *MONKEYS*!

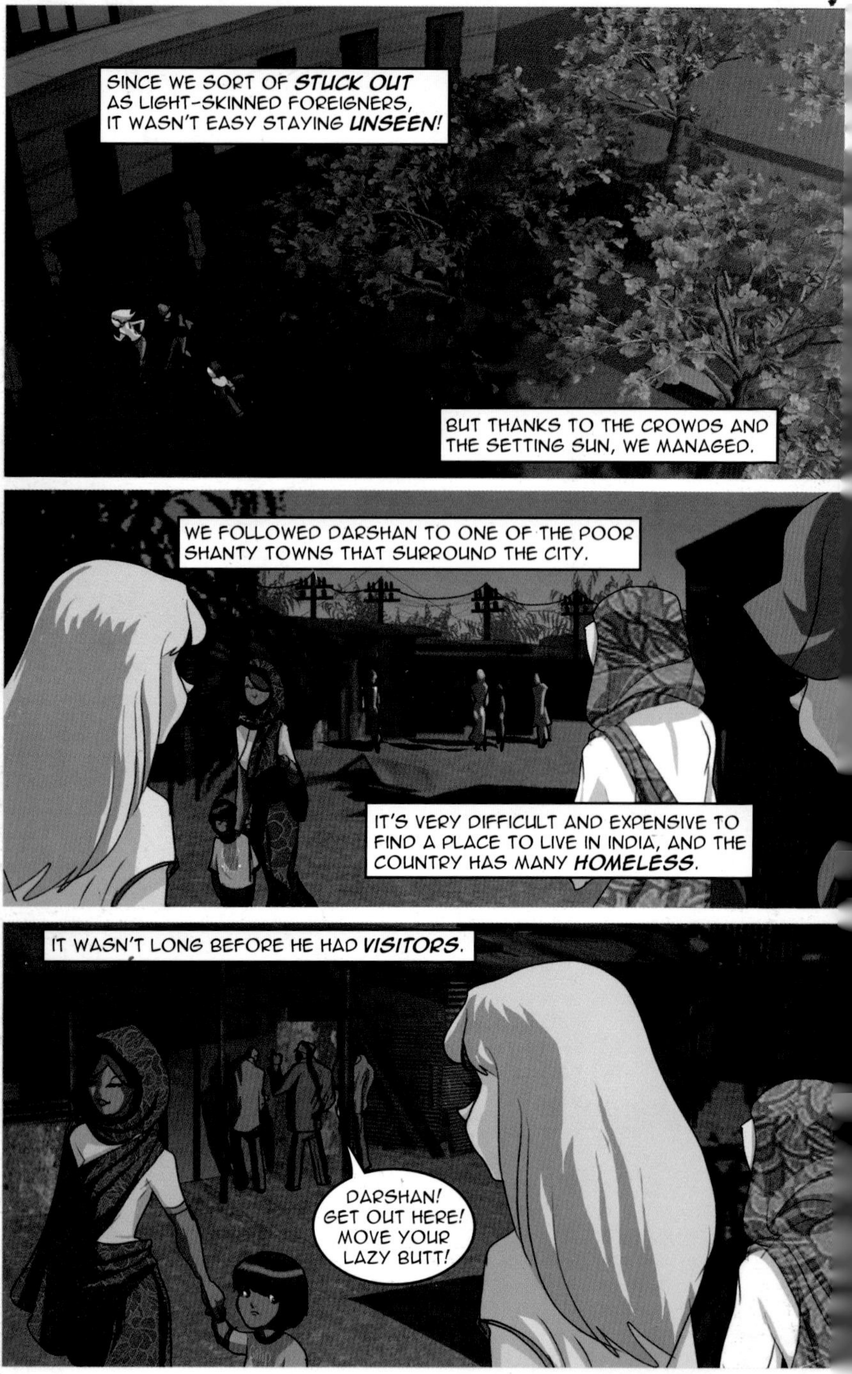
SINCE WE SORT OF STUCK OUT AS LIGHT-SKINNED FOREIGNERS, IT WASN'T EASY STAYING UNSEEN!
BUT THANKS TO THE CROWDS AND THE SETTING SUN, WE MANAGED.
WE FOLLOWED DARSHAN TO ONE OF THE POOR SHANTY TOWNS THAT SURROUND THE CITY.
IT'S VERY DIFFICULT AND EXPENSIVE TO FIND A PLACE TO LIVE IN INDIA, AND THE COUNTRY HAS MANY HOMELESS.
IT WASN'T LONG BEFORE HE HAD VISITORS.
DARSHAN! GET OUT HERE! MOVE YOUR LAZY BUTT!

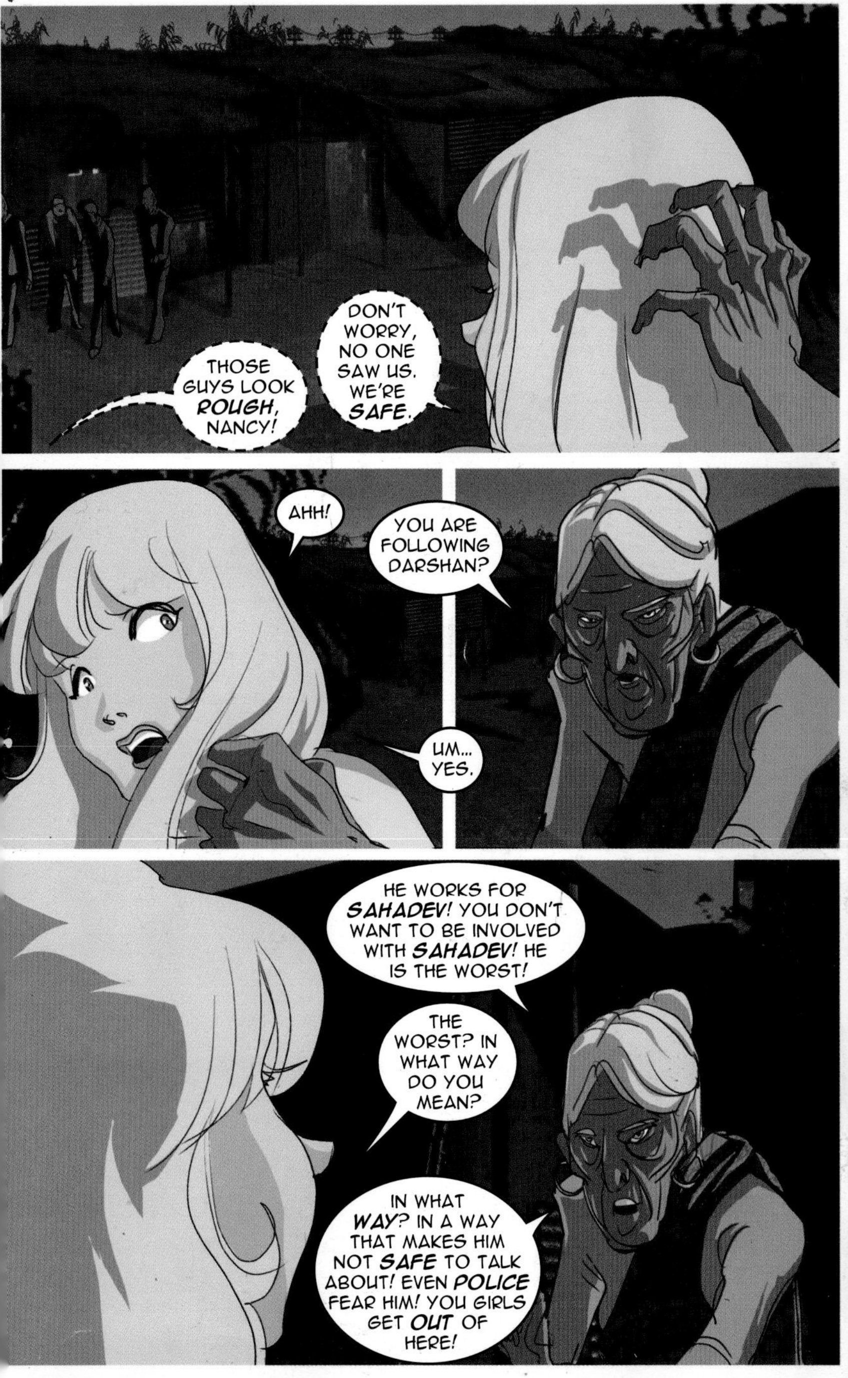
THOSE GUYS LOOK ROUGH, NANCY!
DON'T WORRY, NO ONE SAW US. WE'RE SAFE.
AHH!
YOU ARE FOLLOWING DARSHAN?
UM... YES.
HE WORKS FOR SAHADEV! YOU DON'T WANT TO BE INVOLVED WITH SAHADEV! HE IS THE WORST!
THE WORST? IN WHAT WAY DO YOU MEAN?
IN WHAT WAY? IN A WAY THAT MAKES HIM NOT SAFE TO TALK ABOUT! EVEN POLICE FEAR HIM! YOU GIRLS GET OUT OF HERE!

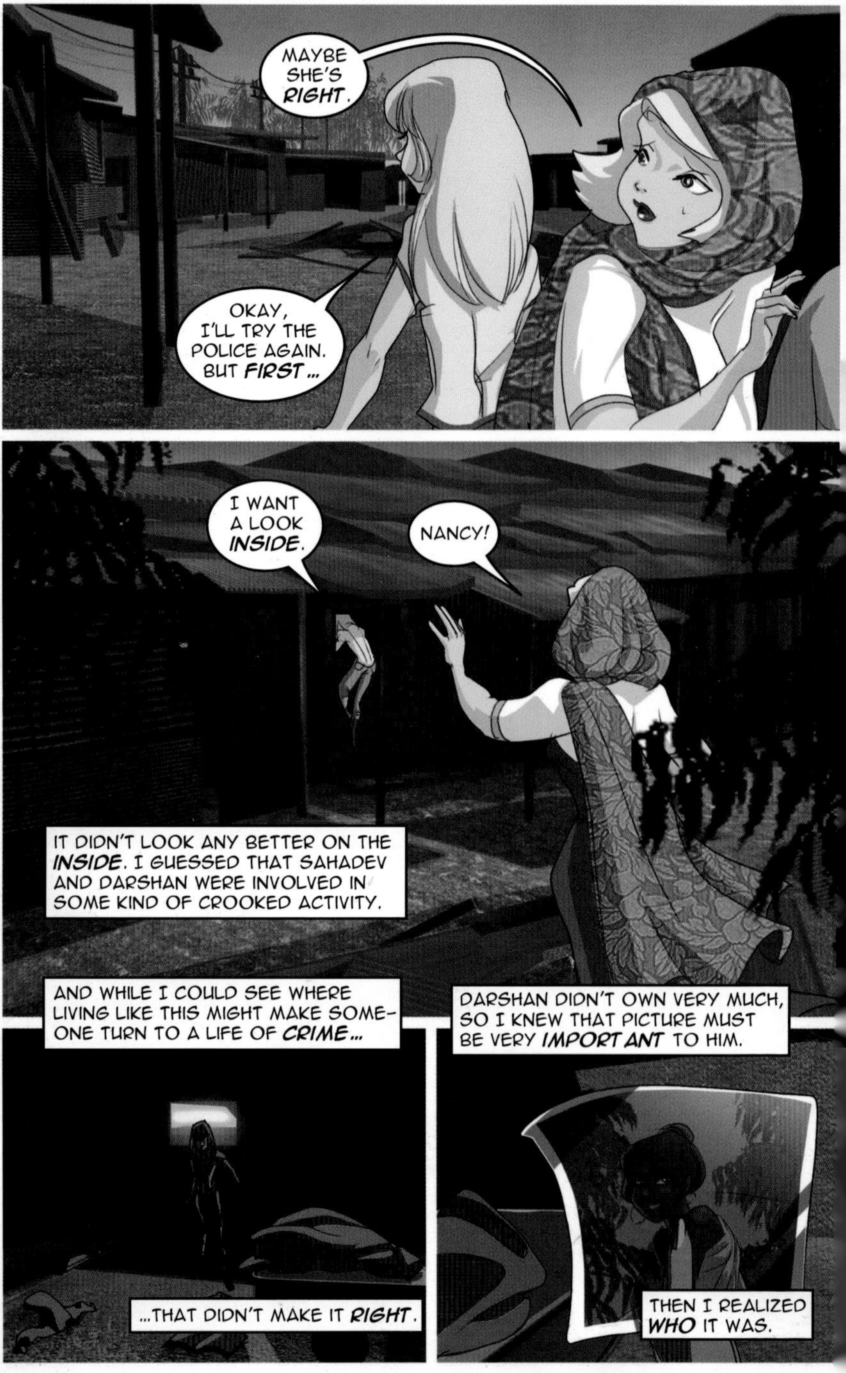
MAYBE SHE'S RIGHT.
OKAY, I'LL TRY THE POLICE AGAIN. BUT FIRST...
I WANT A LOOK INSIDE.
NANCY!
IT DIDN'T LOOK ANY BETTER ON THE INSIDE. I GUESSED THAT SAHADEV AND DARSHAN WERE INVOLVED IN SOME KIND OF CROOKED ACTIVITY.
AND WHILE I COULD SEE WHERE LIVING LIKE THIS MIGHT MAKE SOME-ONE TURN TO A LIFE OF CRIME...
...THAT DIDN'T MAKE IT RIGHT.
DARSHAN DIDN'T OWN VERY MUCH, SO I KNEW THAT PICTURE MUST BE VERY IMPORTANT TO HIM.
THEN I REALIZED WHO IT WAS.

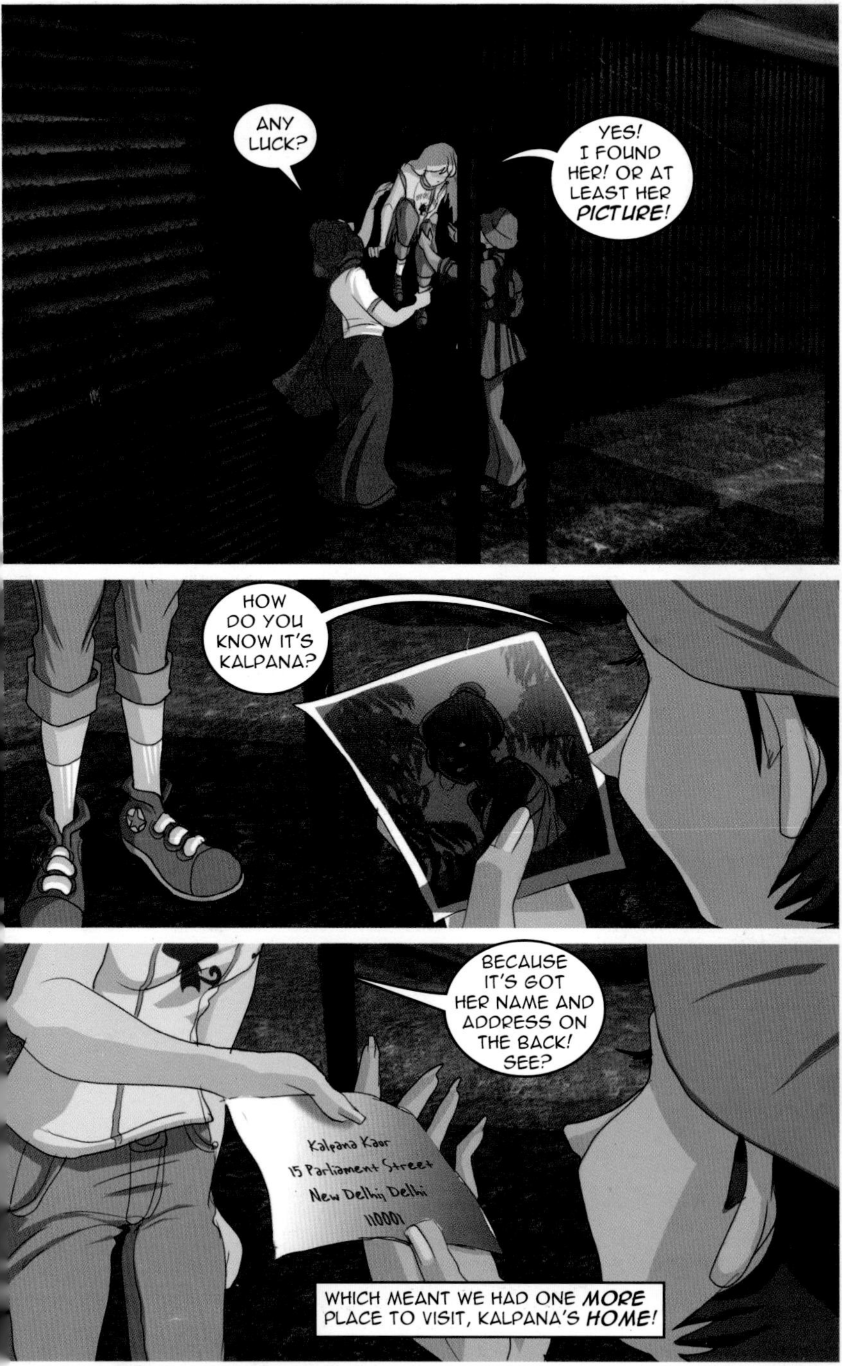
ANY LUCK?
YES! I FOUND HER! OR AT LEAST HER *PICTURE*!
HOW DO YOU KNOW IT'S KALPANA?
BECAUSE IT'S GOT HER NAME AND ADDRESS ON THE BACK! SEE?
Kalpana Kaur
15 Parliament Street
New Delhi, Delhi
110001
WHICH MEANT WE HAD ONE *MORE* PLACE TO VISIT, KALPANA'S *HOME*!

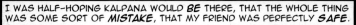

I WAS HALF-HOPING KALPANA WOULD *BE* THERE, THAT THE WHOLE THING WAS SOME SORT OF *MISTAKE*, THAT MY FRIEND WAS PERFECTLY *SAFE*.

NO SUCH LUCK. THE HOUSE WAS TOTALLY *ABANDONED.*

HOW ABOUT THOSE POLICE *NOW*?

NOT YET!

YOU HEARD WHAT THAT WOMAN SAID, THE POLICE ARE *AFRAID* OF THIS SAHADEV.

I'VE A HUNCH *HE'S* BEHIND WHAT HAPPENED TO KALPANA, AND IF HE IS, I NEED MORE EVIDENCE FOR THE POLICE.

THE PHOTO *ALONE* DOESN'T TELL US WHAT HAPPENED. FOR STARTERS, I NEED TO FIND PROOF SHE LIVED *HERE*!

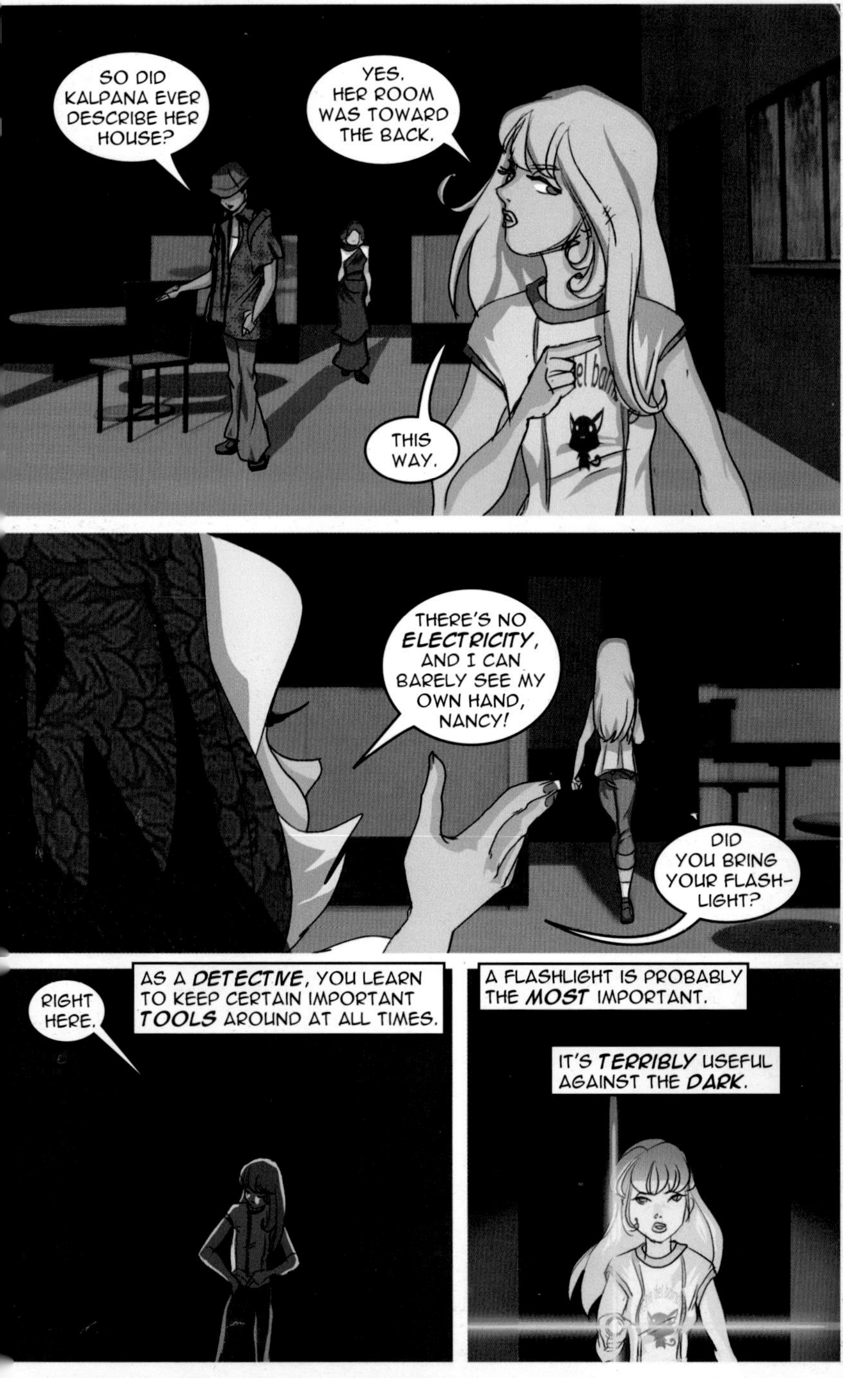
SO DID KALPANA EVER DESCRIBE HER HOUSE?
YES. HER ROOM WAS TOWARD THE BACK.
THIS WAY.
THERE'S NO ELECTRICITY, AND I CAN BARELY SEE MY OWN HAND, NANCY!
DID YOU BRING YOUR FLASH-LIGHT?
AS A DETECTIVE, YOU LEARN TO KEEP CERTAIN IMPORTANT TOOLS AROUND AT ALL TIMES.
RIGHT HERE.
A FLASHLIGHT IS PROBABLY THE MOST IMPORTANT.
IT'S TERRIBLY USEFUL AGAINST THE DARK.

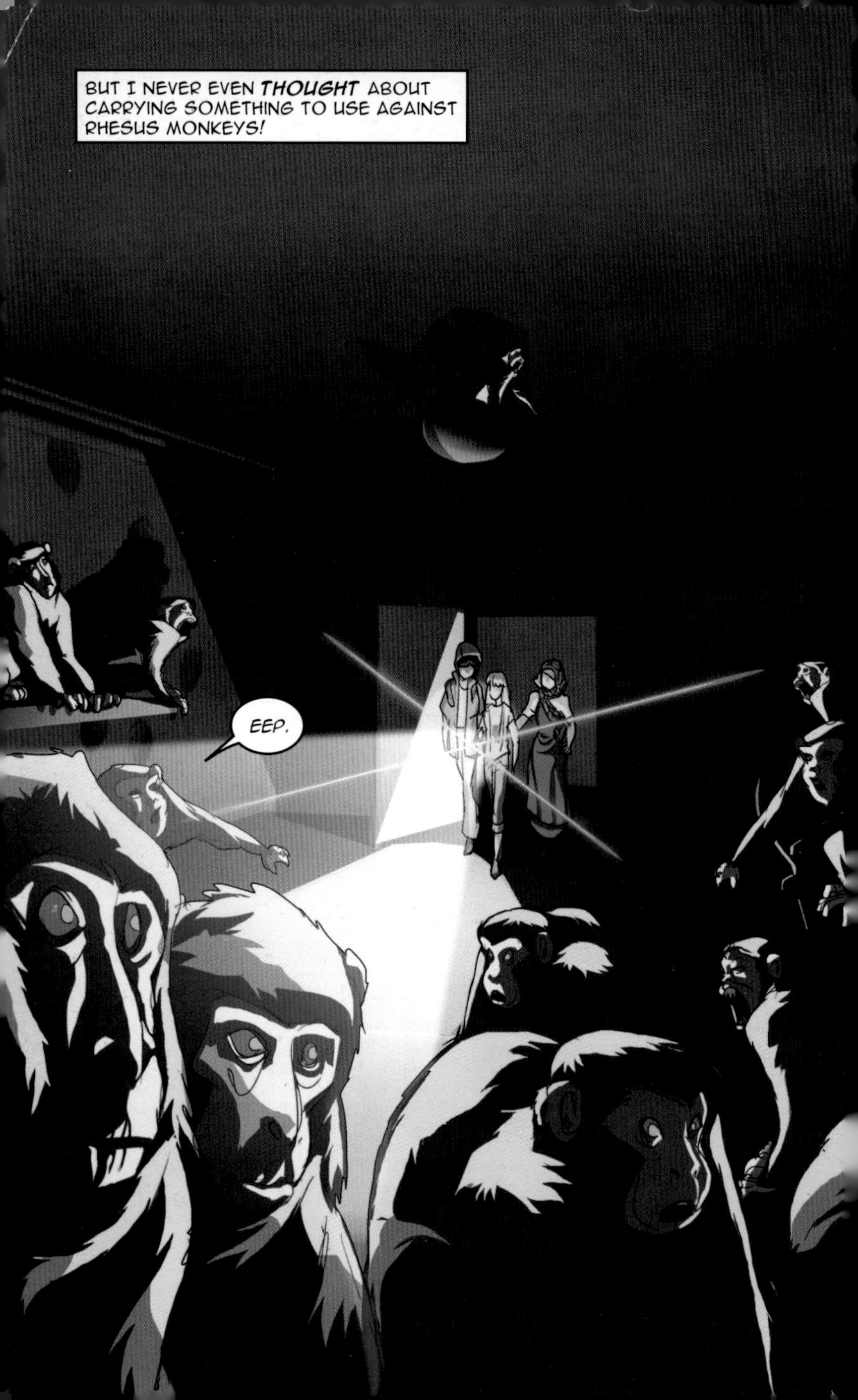
BUT I NEVER EVEN THOUGHT ABOUT CARRYING SOMETHING TO USE AGAINST RHESUS MONKEYS!
EEP.

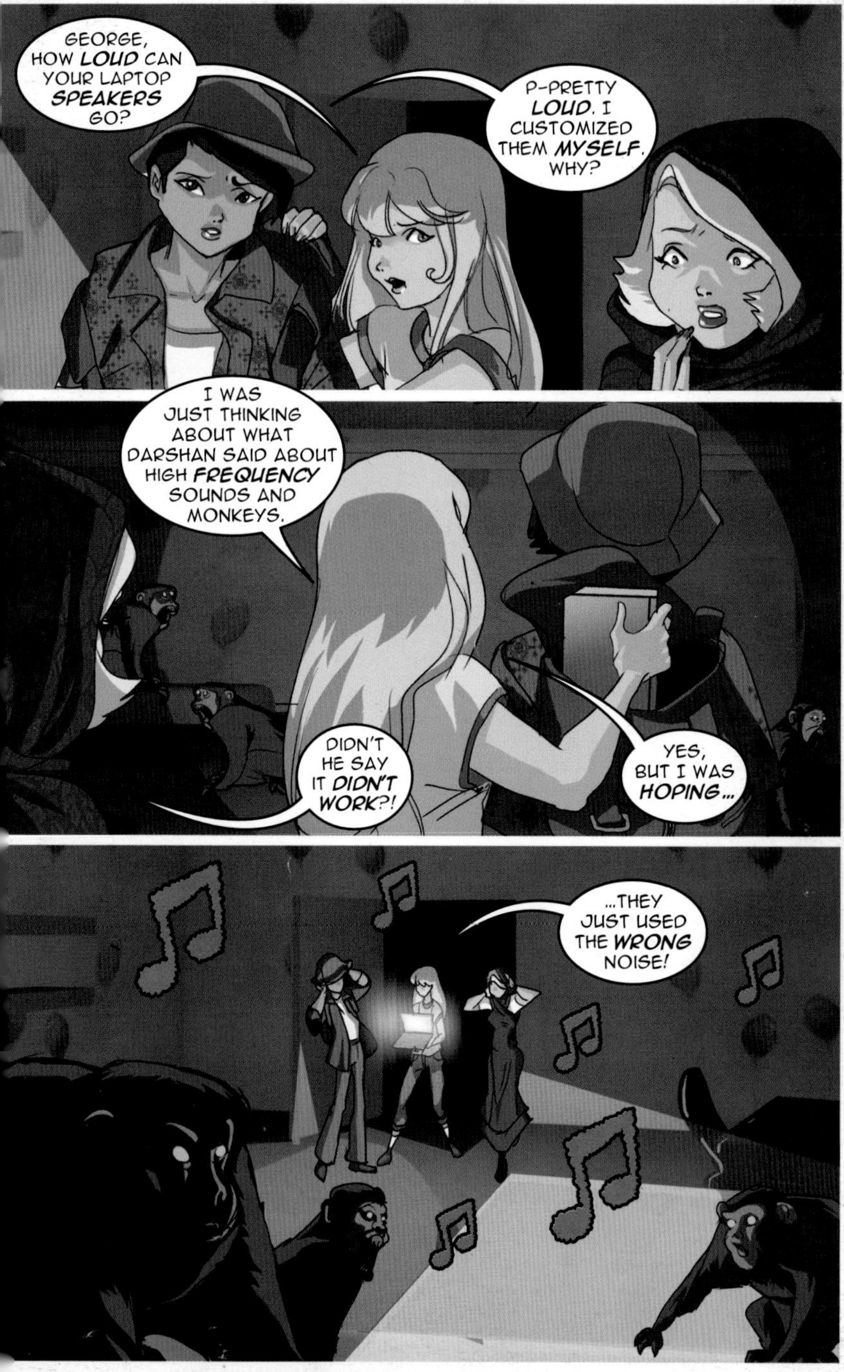
GEORGE, HOW LOUD CAN YOUR LAPTOP SPEAKERS GO?
P-PRETTY LOUD. I CUSTOMIZED THEM MYSELF. WHY?
I WAS JUST THINKING ABOUT WHAT DARSHAN SAID ABOUT HIGH FREQUENCY SOUNDS AND MONKEYS.
DIDN'T HE SAY IT DIDN'T WORK?!
YES, BUT I WAS HOPING...
...THEY JUST USED THE WRONG NOISE!

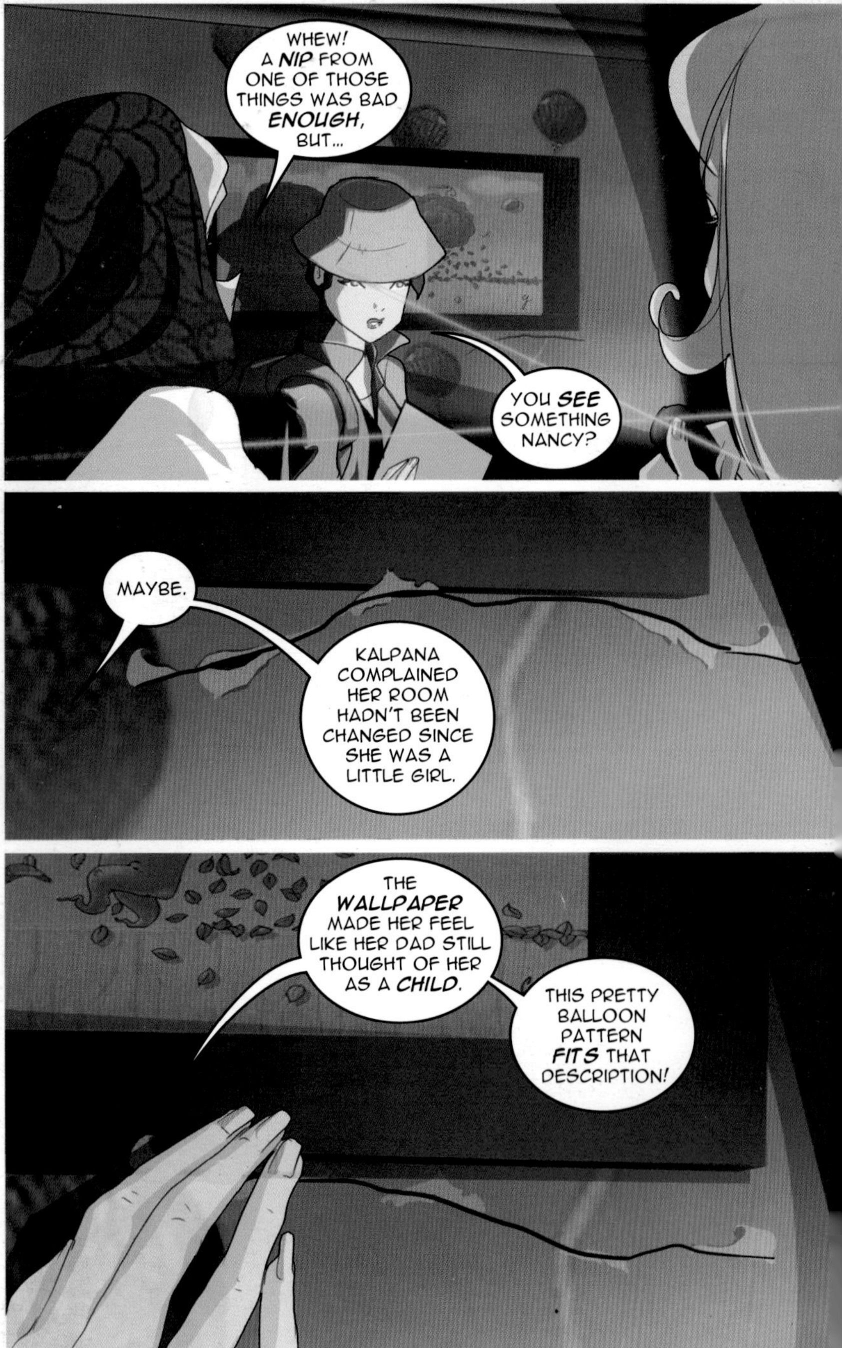
WHEW! A NIP FROM ONE OF THOSE THINGS WAS BAD ENOUGH, BUT...
YOU SEE SOMETHING NANCY?
MAYBE.
KALPANA COMPLAINED HER ROOM HADN'T BEEN CHANGED SINCE SHE WAS A LITTLE GIRL.
THE WALLPAPER MADE HER FEEL LIKE HER DAD STILL THOUGHT OF HER AS A CHILD.
THIS PRETTY BALLOON PATTERN FITS THAT DESCRIPTION!

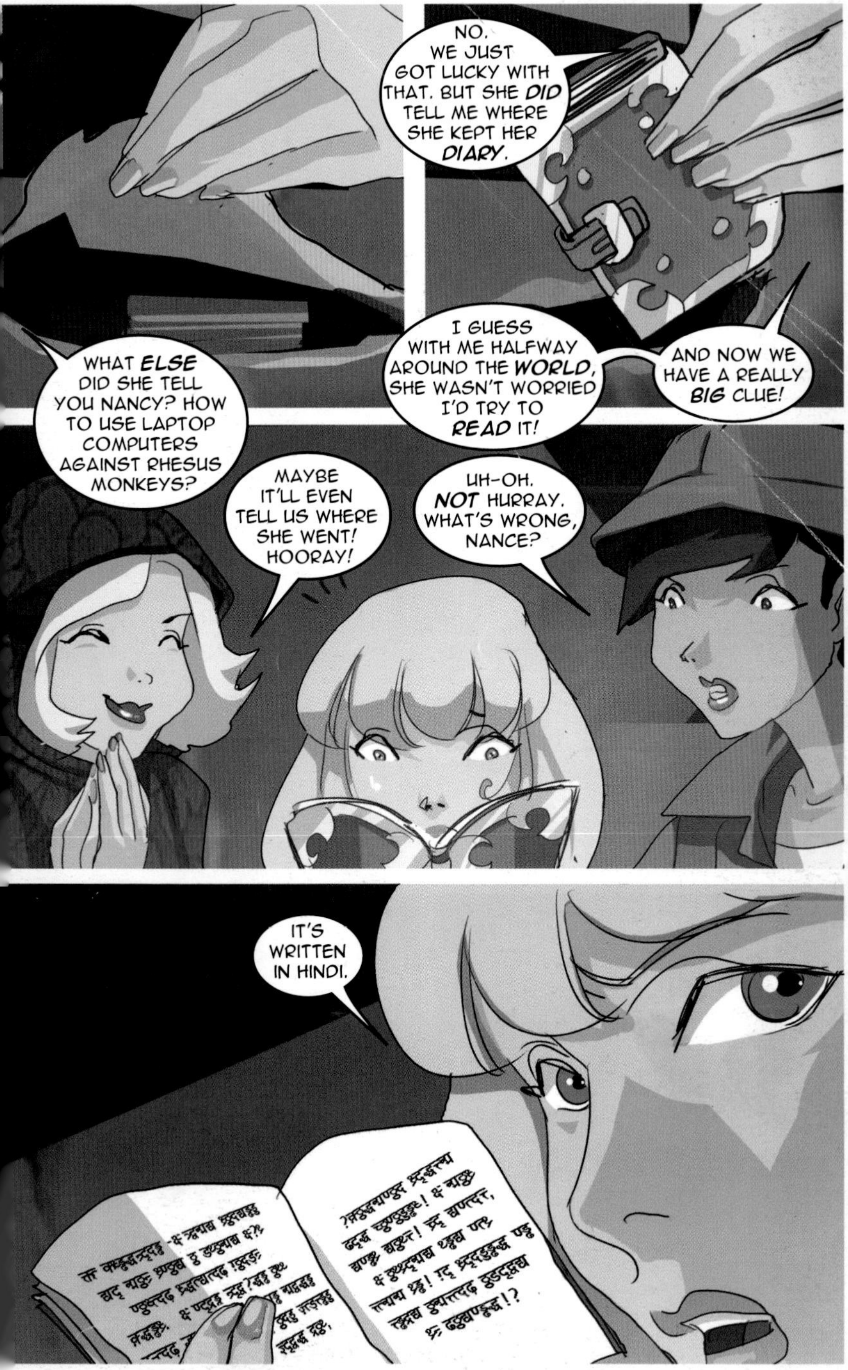

WHAT ELSE DID SHE TELL YOU NANCY? HOW TO USE LAPTOP COMPUTERS AGAINST RHESUS MONKEYS?
NO. WE JUST GOT LUCKY WITH THAT. BUT SHE DID TELL ME WHERE SHE KEPT HER DIARY.
I GUESS WITH ME HALFWAY AROUND THE WORLD, SHE WASN'T WORRIED I'D TRY TO READ IT!
AND NOW WE HAVE A REALLY BIG CLUE!
MAYBE IT'LL EVEN TELL US WHERE SHE WENT! HOORAY!
UH-OH. NOT HURRAY. WHAT'S WRONG, NANCE?
IT'S WRITTEN IN HINDI.

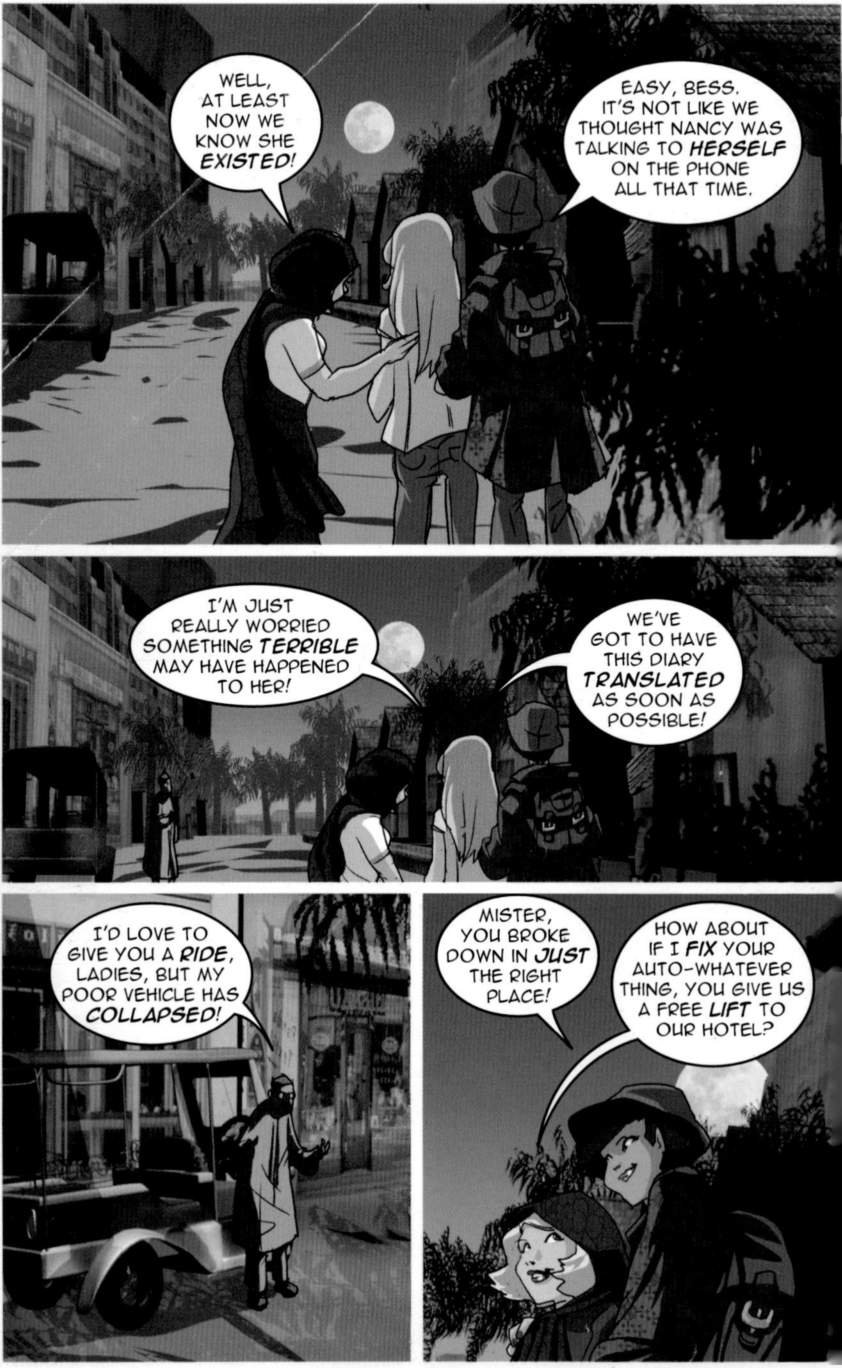
WELL, AT LEAST NOW WE KNOW SHE *EXISTED!*
EASY, BESS. IT'S NOT LIKE WE THOUGHT NANCY WAS TALKING TO *HERSELF* ON THE PHONE ALL THAT TIME.
I'M JUST REALLY WORRIED SOMETHING *TERRIBLE* MAY HAVE HAPPENED TO HER!
WE'VE GOT TO HAVE THIS DIARY *TRANSLATED* AS SOON AS POSSIBLE!
I'D LOVE TO GIVE YOU A *RIDE*, LADIES, BUT MY POOR VEHICLE HAS *COLLAPSED!*
MISTER, YOU BROKE DOWN IN *JUST* THE RIGHT PLACE!
HOW ABOUT IF I *FIX* YOUR AUTO-WHATEVER THING, YOU GIVE US A FREE *LIFT* TO OUR HOTEL?

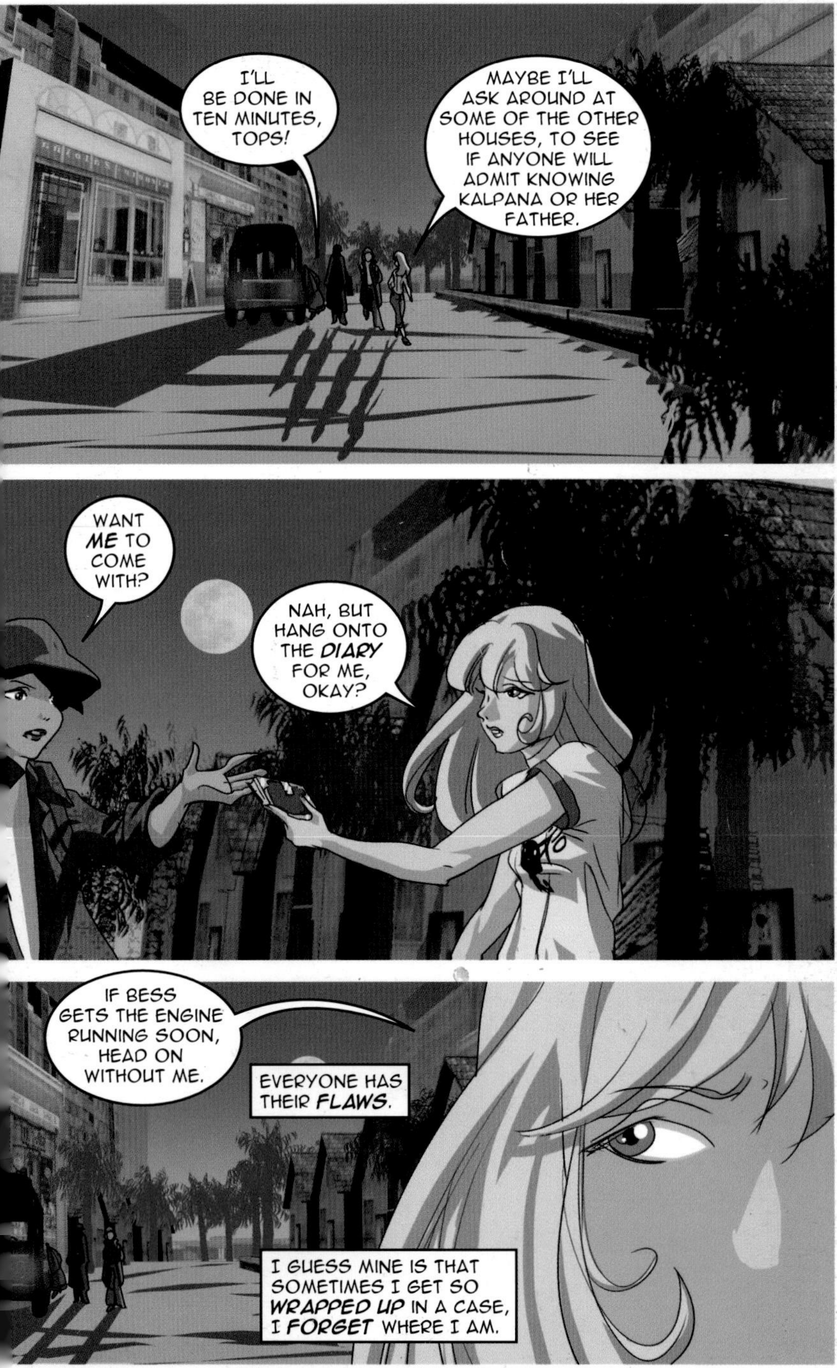
I'LL BE DONE IN TEN MINUTES, TOPS!
MAYBE I'LL ASK AROUND AT SOME OF THE OTHER HOUSES, TO SEE IF ANYONE WILL ADMIT KNOWING KALPANA OR HER FATHER.
WANT ME TO COME WITH?
NAH, BUT HANG ONTO THE DIARY FOR ME, OKAY?
IF BESS GETS THE ENGINE RUNNING SOON, HEAD ON WITHOUT ME.
EVERYONE HAS THEIR FLAWS.
I GUESS MINE IS THAT SOMETIMES I GET SO WRAPPED UP IN A CASE, I FORGET WHERE I AM.

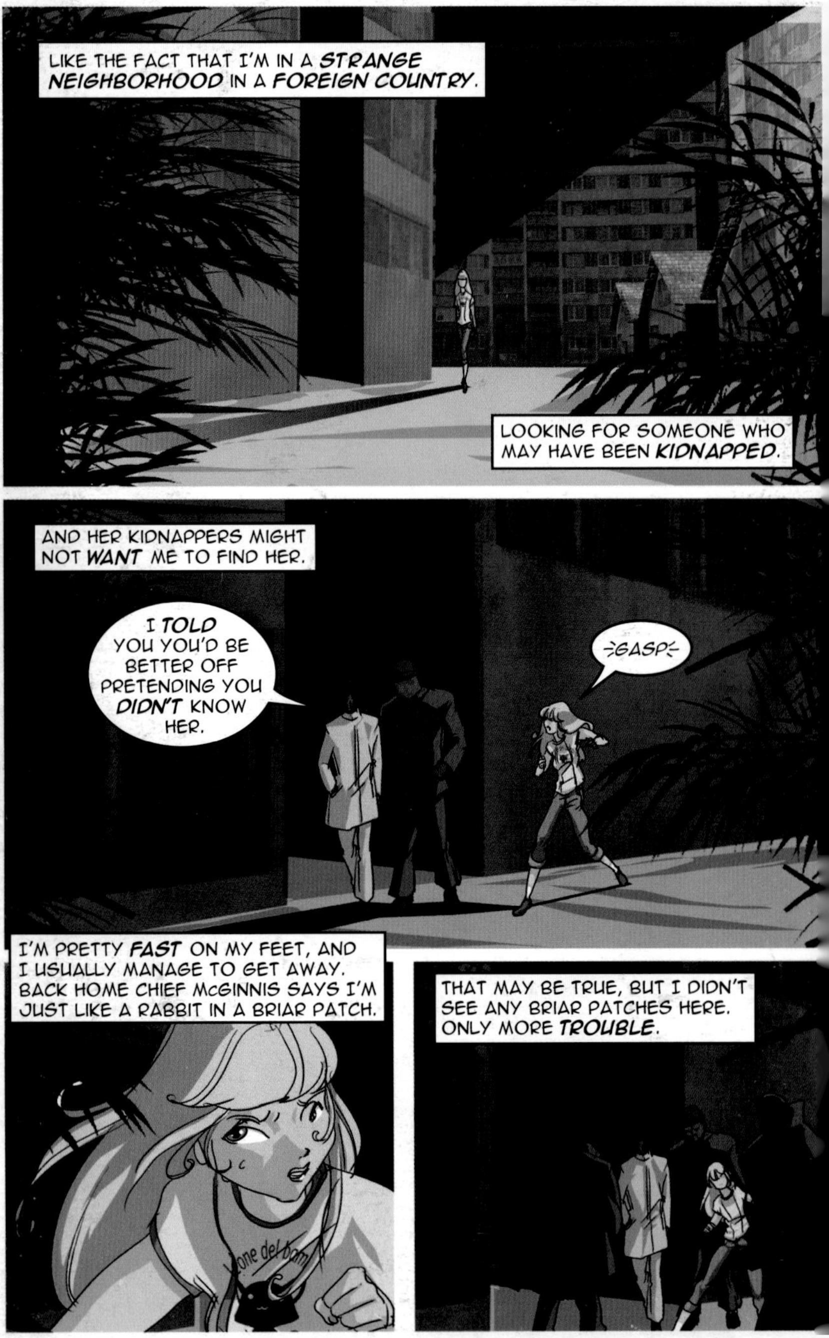
LIKE THE FACT THAT I'M IN A STRANGE NEIGHBORHOOD IN A FOREIGN COUNTRY.
LOOKING FOR SOMEONE WHO MAY HAVE BEEN KIDNAPPED.
AND HER KIDNAPPERS MIGHT NOT WANT ME TO FIND HER.
I TOLD YOU YOU'D BE BETTER OFF PRETENDING YOU DIDN'T KNOW HER.
GASP
I'M PRETTY FAST ON MY FEET, AND I USUALLY MANAGE TO GET AWAY. BACK HOME CHIEF McGINNIS SAYS I'M JUST LIKE A RABBIT IN A BRIAR PATCH.
THAT MAY BE TRUE, BUT I DIDN'T SEE ANY BRIAR PATCHES HERE. ONLY MORE TROUBLE.

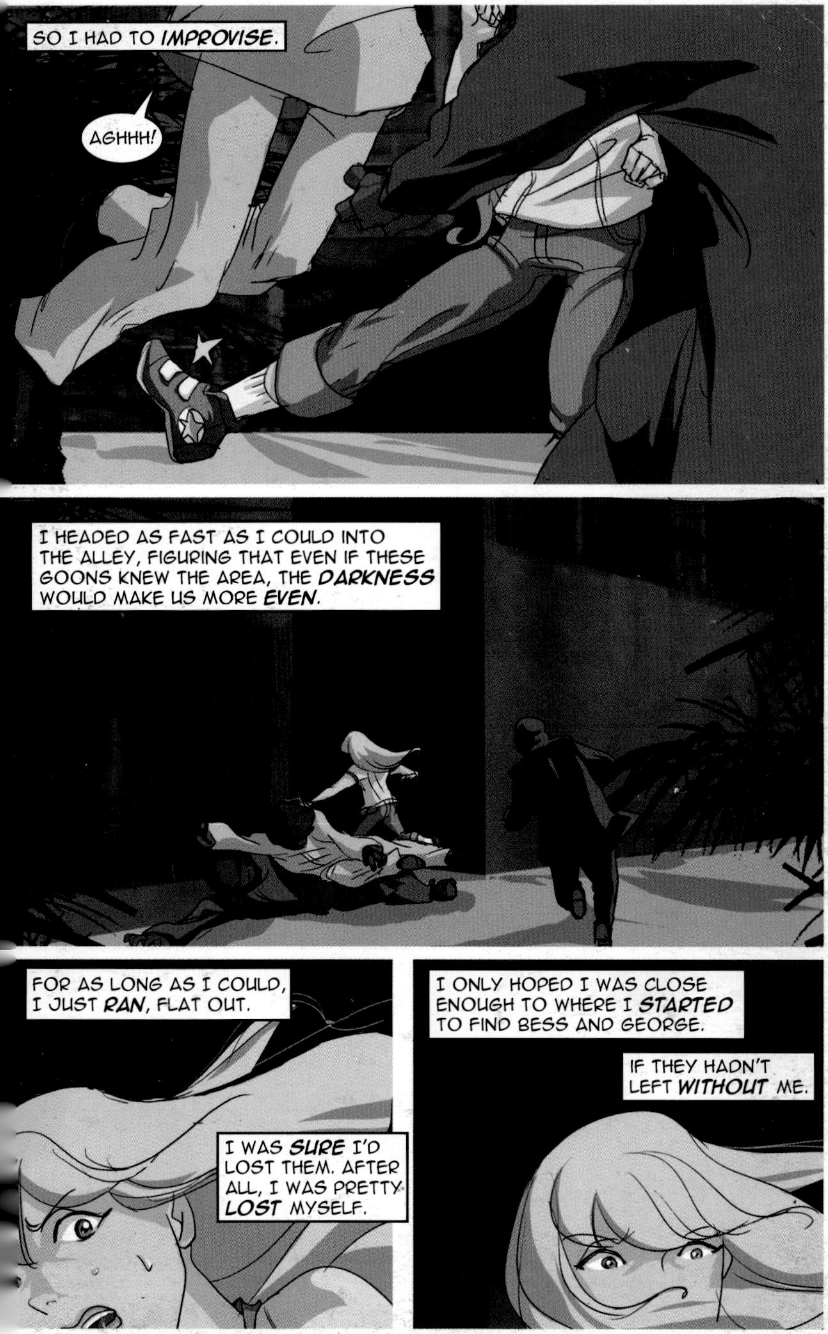
SO I HAD TO *IMPROVISE*.
AGHHH!
I HEADED AS FAST AS I COULD INTO THE ALLEY, FIGURING THAT EVEN IF THESE GOONS KNEW THE AREA, THE *DARKNESS* WOULD MAKE US MORE *EVEN*.
FOR AS LONG AS I COULD, I JUST *RAN*, FLAT OUT.
I WAS *SURE* I'D LOST THEM. AFTER ALL, I WAS PRETTY *LOST* MYSELF.
I ONLY HOPED I WAS CLOSE ENOUGH TO WHERE I *STARTED* TO FIND BESS AND GEORGE.
IF THEY HADN'T LEFT *WITHOUT* ME.

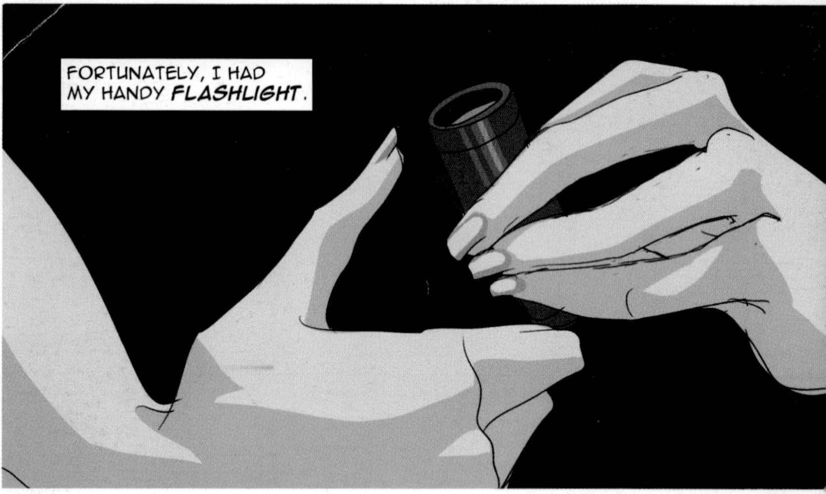
FORTUNATELY, I HAD
MY HANDY FLASHLIGHT.

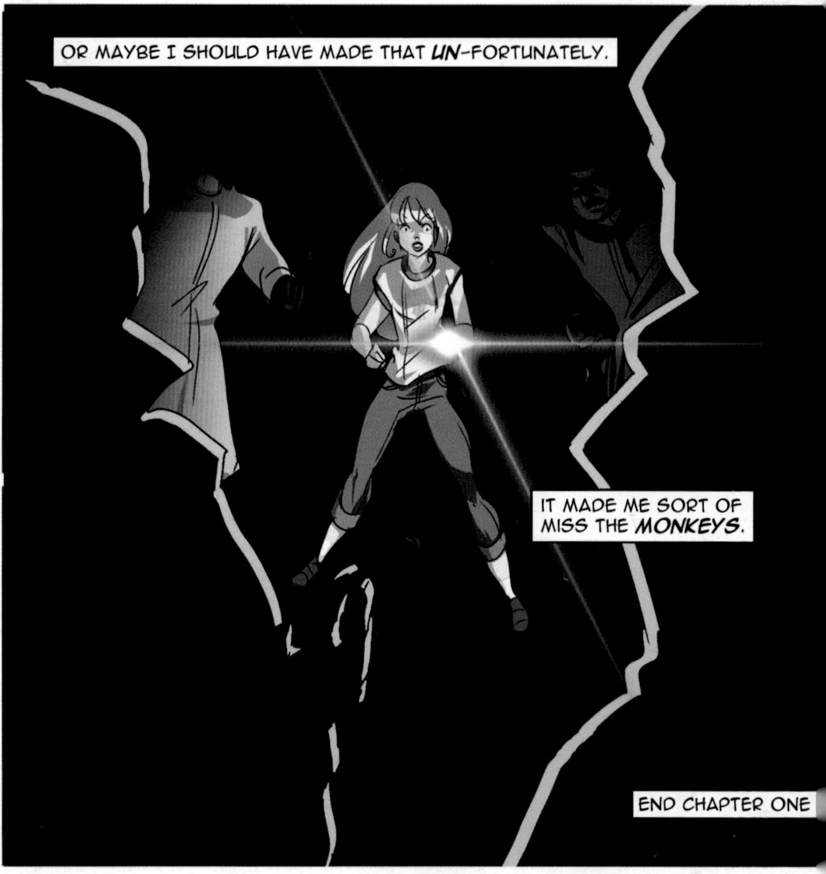
OR MAYBE I SHOULD HAVE MADE THAT UN-FORTUNATELY.
IT MADE ME SORT OF
MISS THE MONKEYS.
END CHAPTER ONE

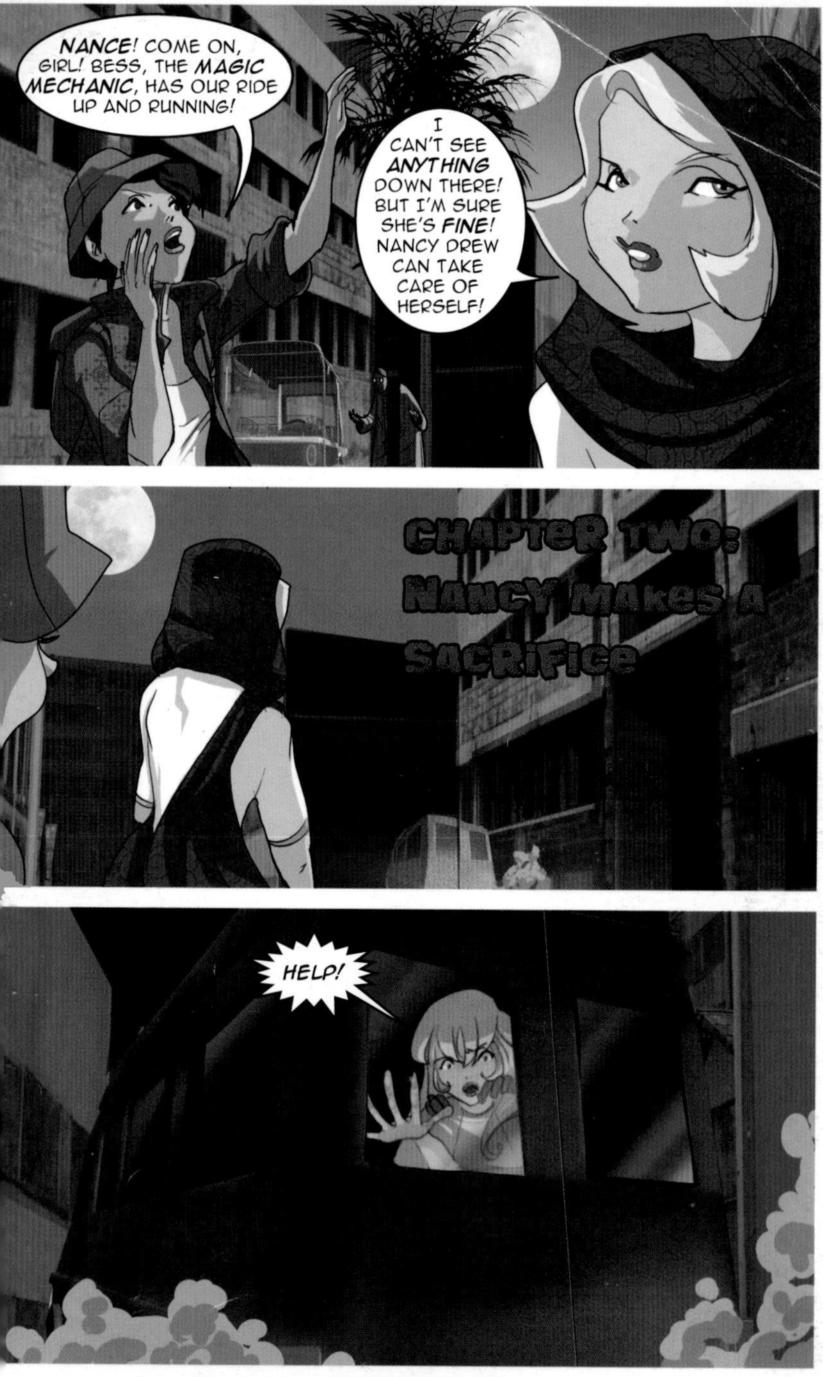

NANCE! COME ON, GIRL! BESS, THE MAGIC MECHANIC, HAS OUR RIDE UP AND RUNNING!
I CAN'T SEE ANYTHING DOWN THERE! BUT I'M SURE SHE'S FINE! NANCY DREW CAN TAKE CARE OF HERSELF!
CHAPTER TWO: NANCY MAKES A SACRIFICE
HELP!

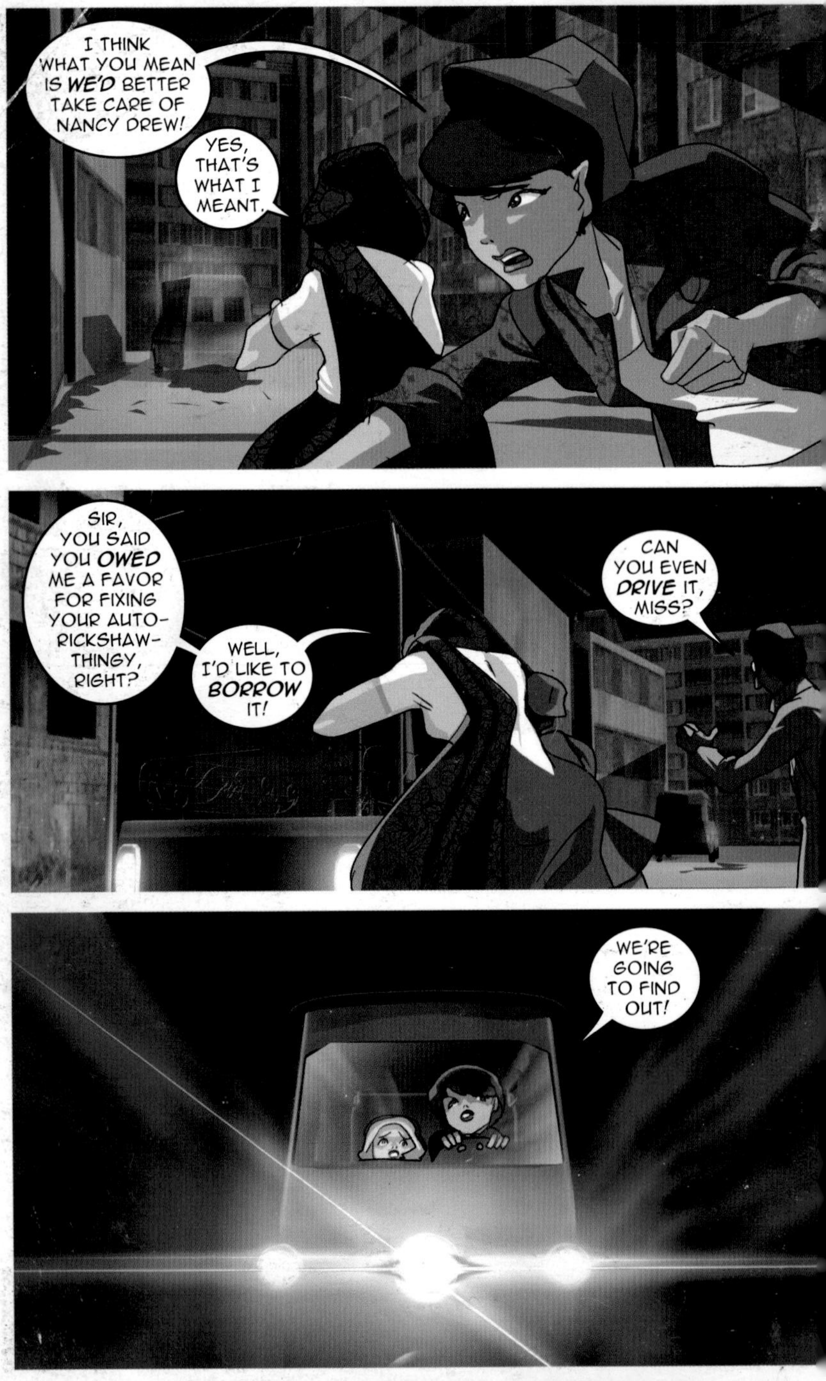
I THINK WHAT YOU MEAN IS *WE'D* BETTER TAKE CARE OF NANCY DREW!
YES, THAT'S WHAT I MEANT.
SIR, YOU SAID YOU *OWED* ME A FAVOR FOR FIXING YOUR AUTO-RICKSHAW-THINGY, RIGHT?
WELL, I'D LIKE TO *BORROW* IT!
CAN YOU EVEN *DRIVE* IT, MISS?
WE'RE GOING TO FIND OUT!

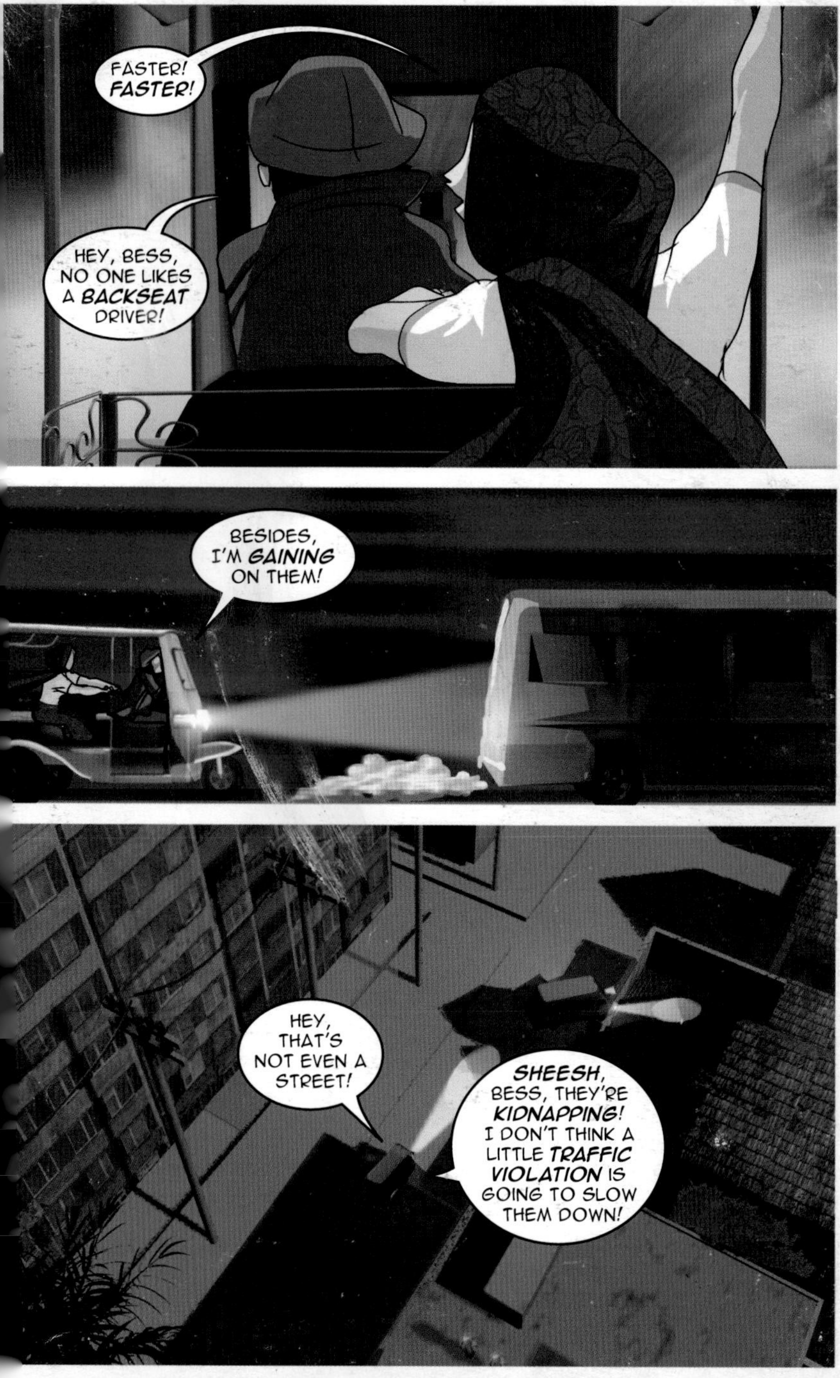
FASTER! FASTER!
HEY, BESS, NO ONE LIKES A BACKSEAT DRIVER!
BESIDES, I'M GAINING ON THEM!
HEY, THAT'S NOT EVEN A STREET!
SHEESH, BESS, THEY'RE KIDNAPPING! I DON'T THINK A LITTLE TRAFFIC VIOLATION IS GOING TO SLOW THEM DOWN!

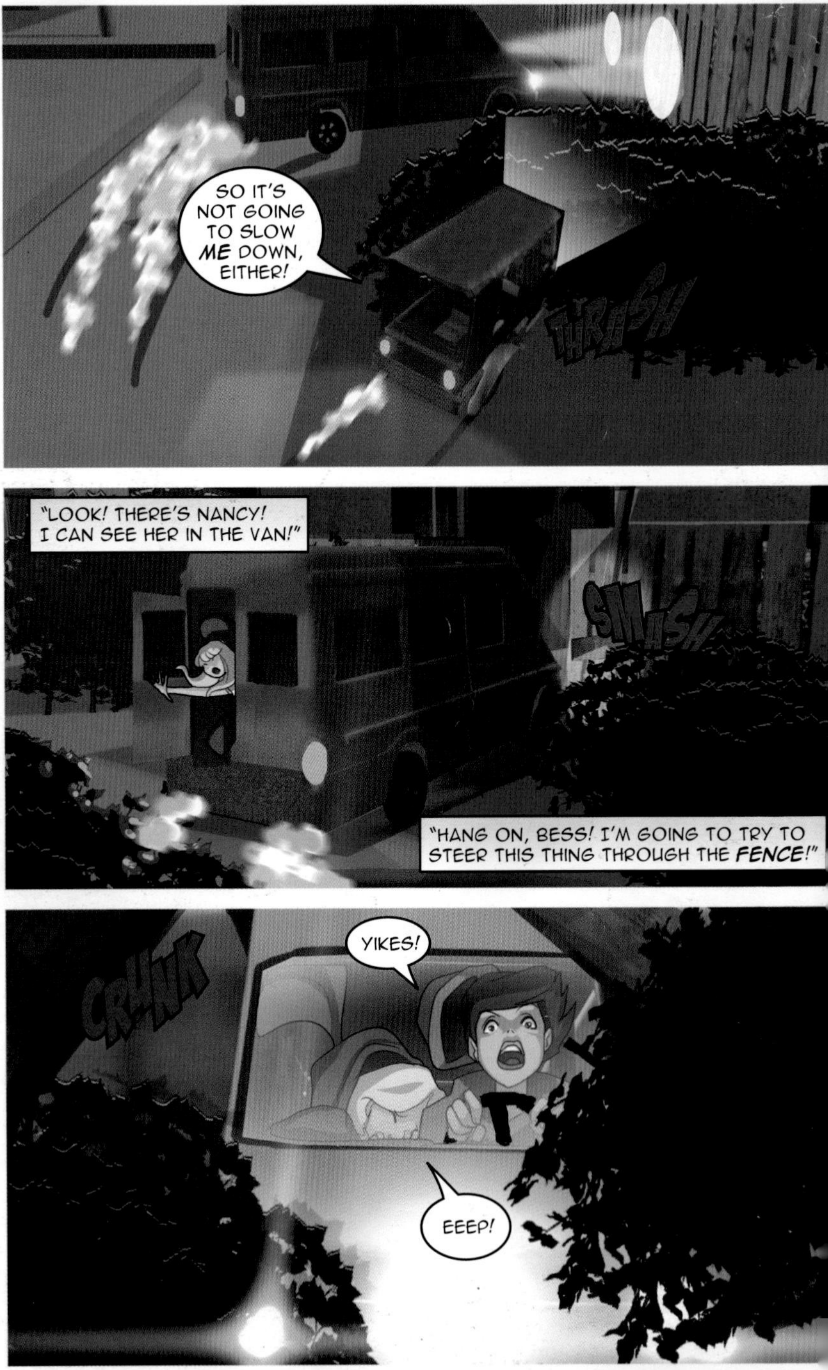
SO IT'S NOT GOING TO SLOW *ME* DOWN, EITHER!
THRUSH
"LOOK! THERE'S NANCY! I CAN SEE HER IN THE VAN!"
SMASH
"HANG ON, BESS! I'M GOING TO TRY TO STEER THIS THING THROUGH THE *FENCE*!"
CRUNK
YIKES!
EEEP!

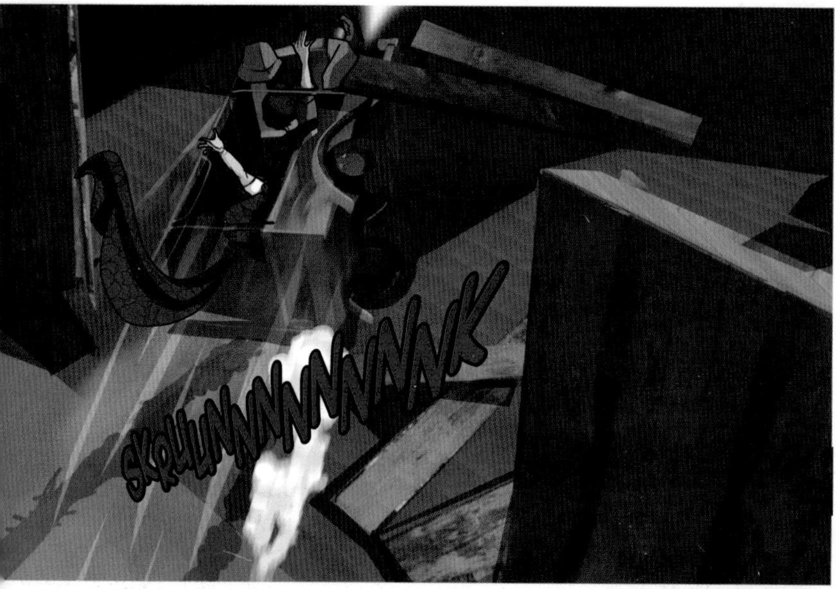
SKRUUNNNNNNNNNNK

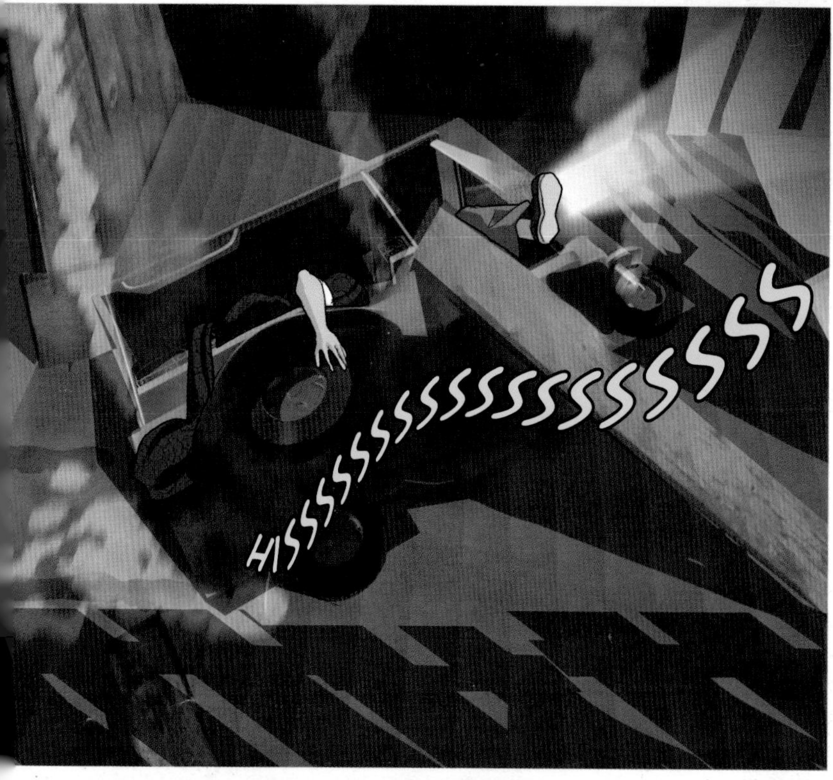
HISSSSSSSSSSSSSSSSSSSS

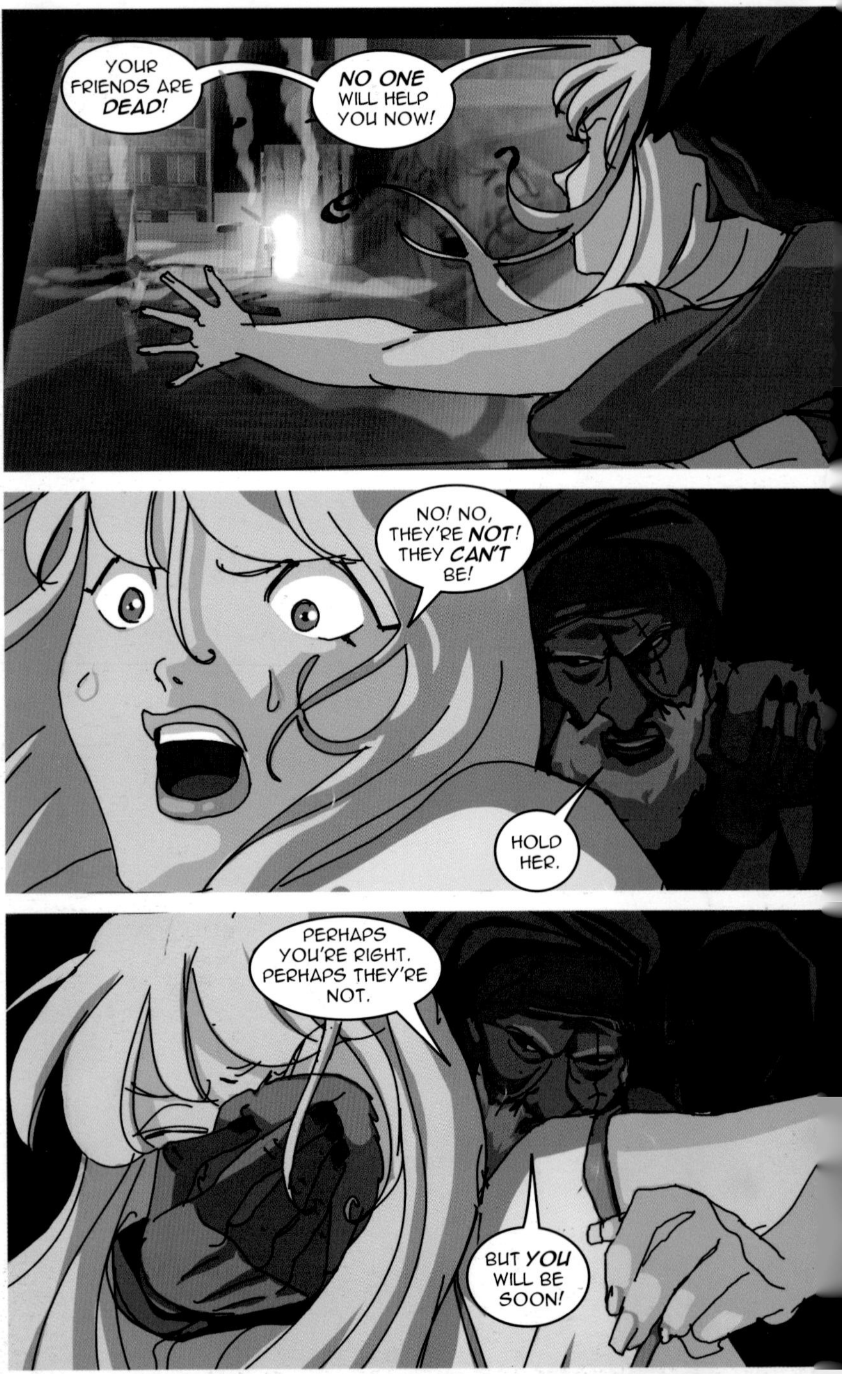
YOUR FRIENDS ARE DEAD!
NO ONE WILL HELP YOU NOW!
NO! NO, THEY'RE NOT! THEY CAN'T BE!
HOLD HER.
PERHAPS YOU'RE RIGHT. PERHAPS THEY'RE NOT.
BUT YOU WILL BE SOON!

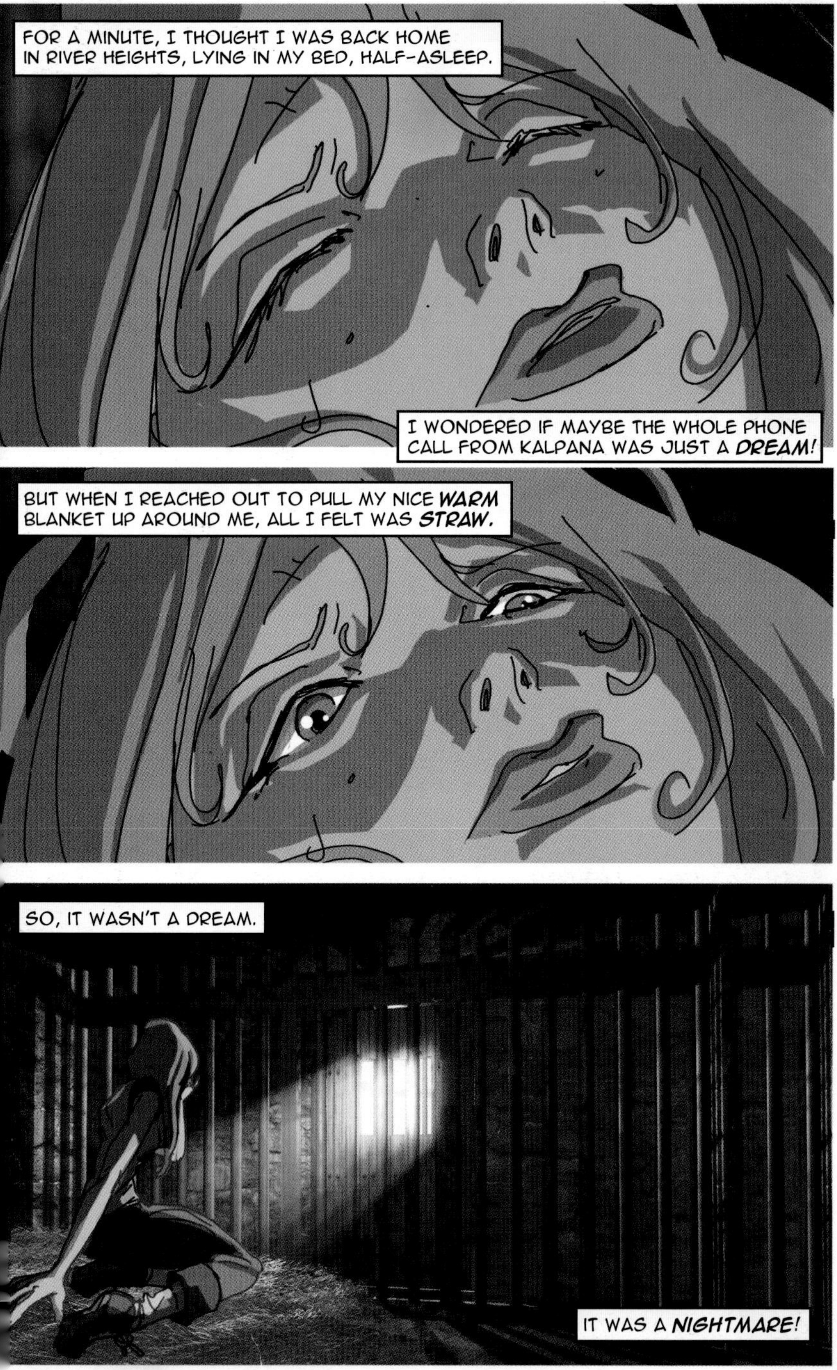
FOR A MINUTE, I THOUGHT I WAS BACK HOME IN RIVER HEIGHTS, LYING IN MY BED, HALF-ASLEEP.
I WONDERED IF MAYBE THE WHOLE PHONE CALL FROM KALPANA WAS JUST A DREAM!
BUT WHEN I REACHED OUT TO PULL MY NICE WARM BLANKET UP AROUND ME, ALL I FELT WAS STRAW.
SO, IT WASN'T A DREAM.
IT WAS A NIGHTMARE!

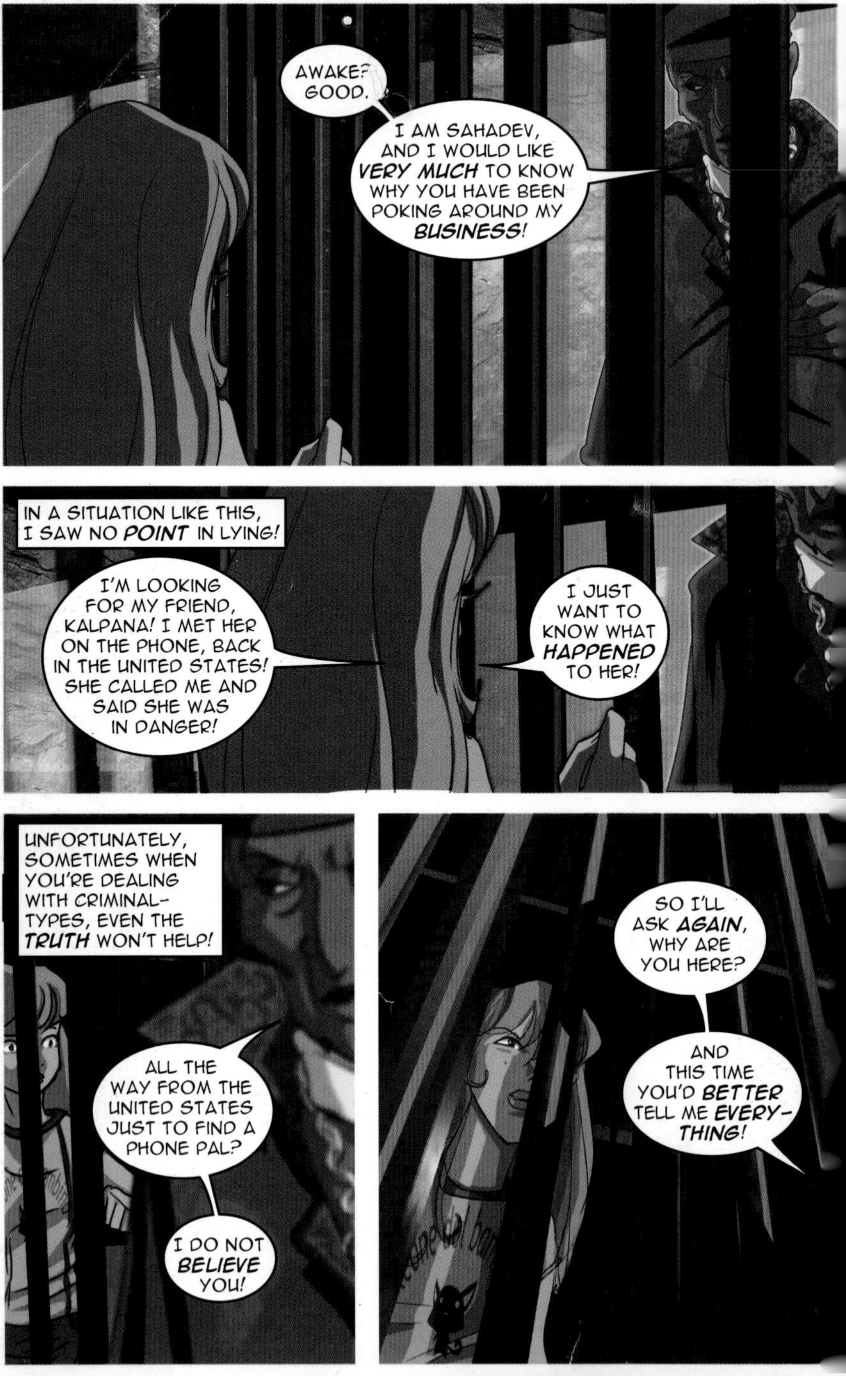
AWAKE? GOOD.
I AM SAHADEV, AND I WOULD LIKE VERY MUCH TO KNOW WHY YOU HAVE BEEN POKING AROUND MY BUSINESS!
IN A SITUATION LIKE THIS, I SAW NO POINT IN LYING!
I'M LOOKING FOR MY FRIEND, KALPANA! I MET HER ON THE PHONE, BACK IN THE UNITED STATES! SHE CALLED ME AND SAID SHE WAS IN DANGER!
I JUST WANT TO KNOW WHAT HAPPENED TO HER!
UNFORTUNATELY, SOMETIMES WHEN YOU'RE DEALING WITH CRIMINAL-TYPES, EVEN THE TRUTH WON'T HELP!
ALL THE WAY FROM THE UNITED STATES JUST TO FIND A PHONE PAL?
I DO NOT BELIEVE YOU!
SO I'LL ASK AGAIN, WHY ARE YOU HERE?
AND THIS TIME YOU'D BETTER TELL ME EVERY-THING!

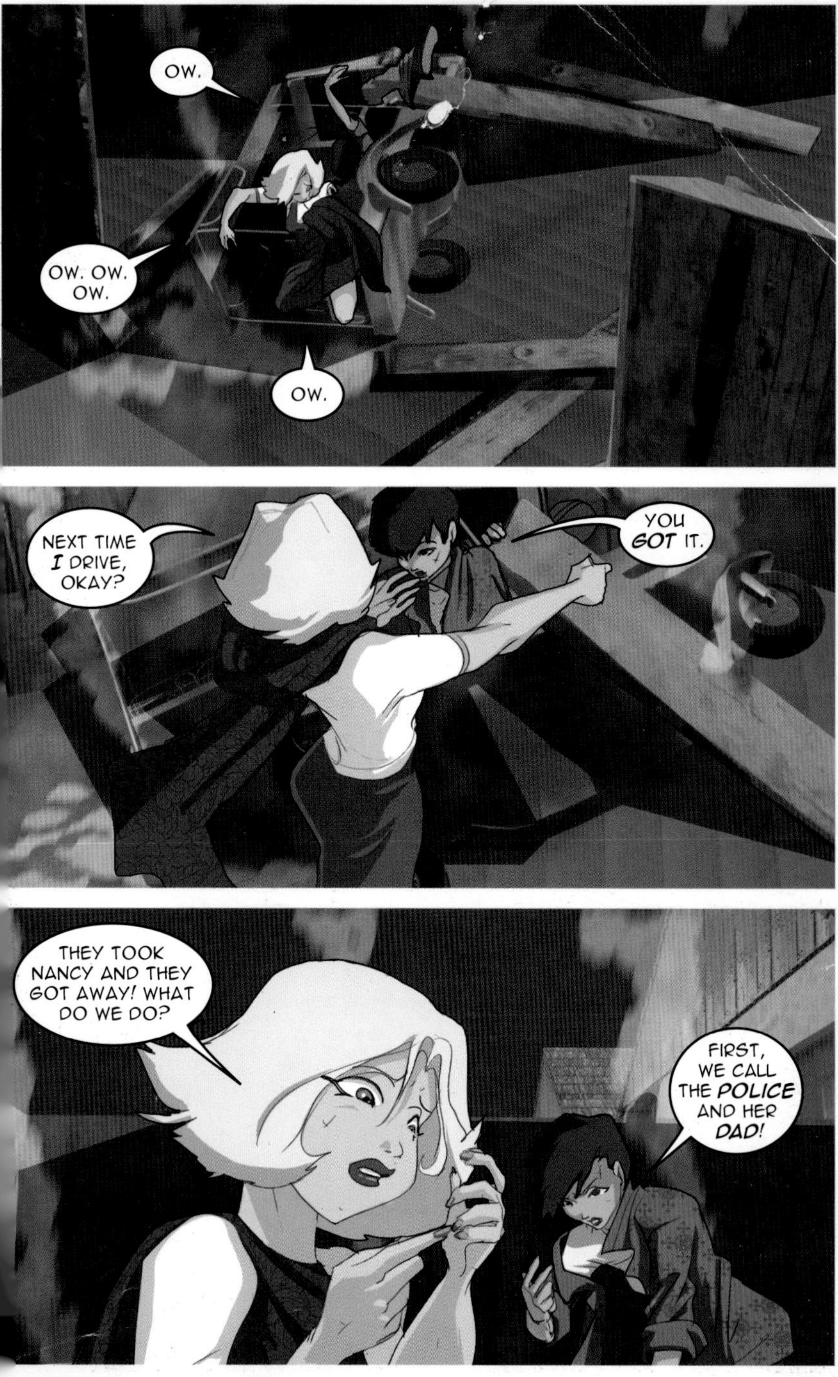
OW.
OW. OW. OW.
OW.
NEXT TIME I DRIVE, OKAY?
YOU GOT IT.
THEY TOOK NANCY AND THEY GOT AWAY! WHAT DO WE DO?
FIRST, WE CALL THE POLICE AND HER DAD!

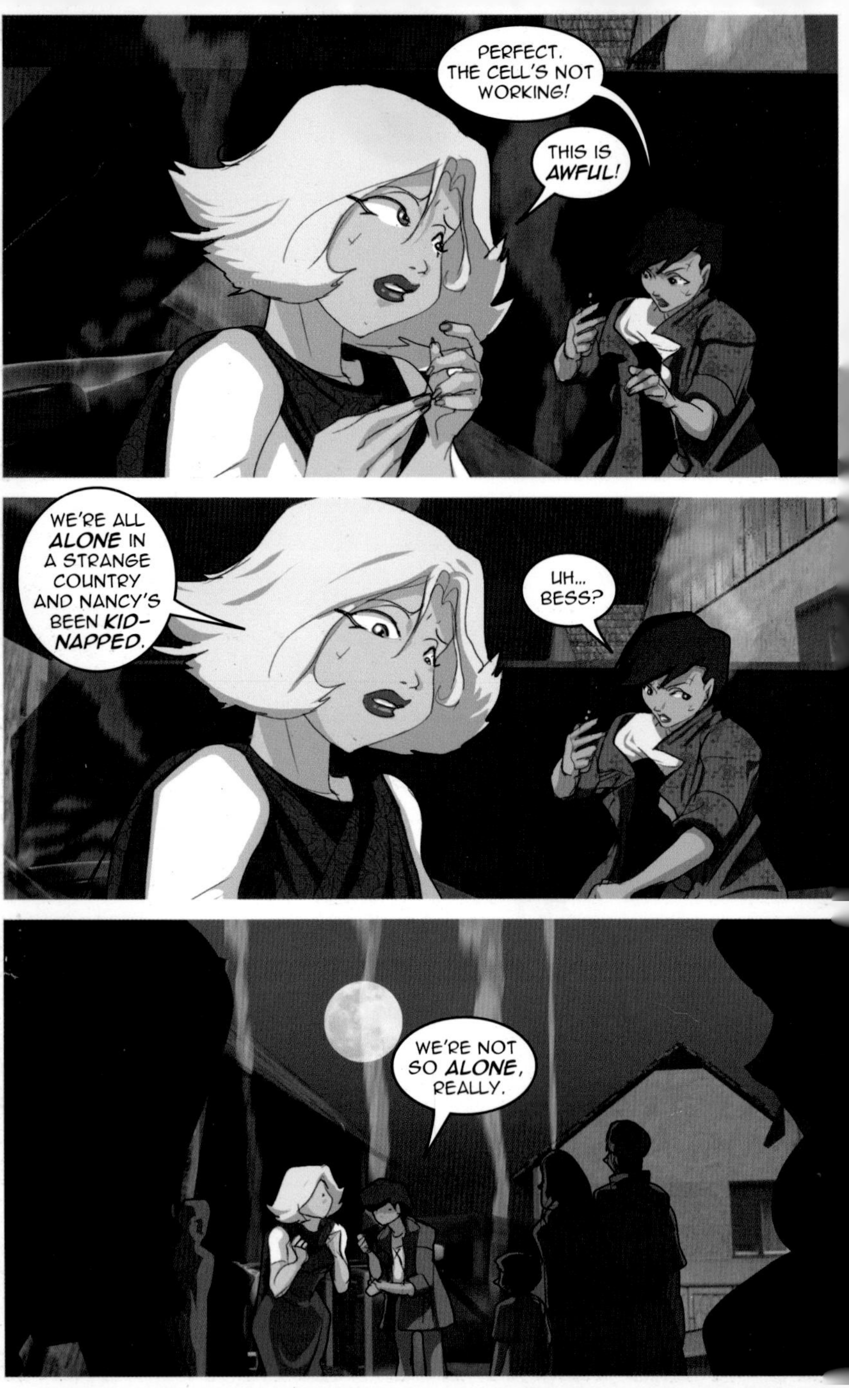
PERFECT. THE CELL'S NOT WORKING!
THIS IS AWFUL!
WE'RE ALL ALONE IN A STRANGE COUNTRY AND NANCY'S BEEN KID-NAPPED.
UH... BESS?
WE'RE NOT SO ALONE, REALLY.

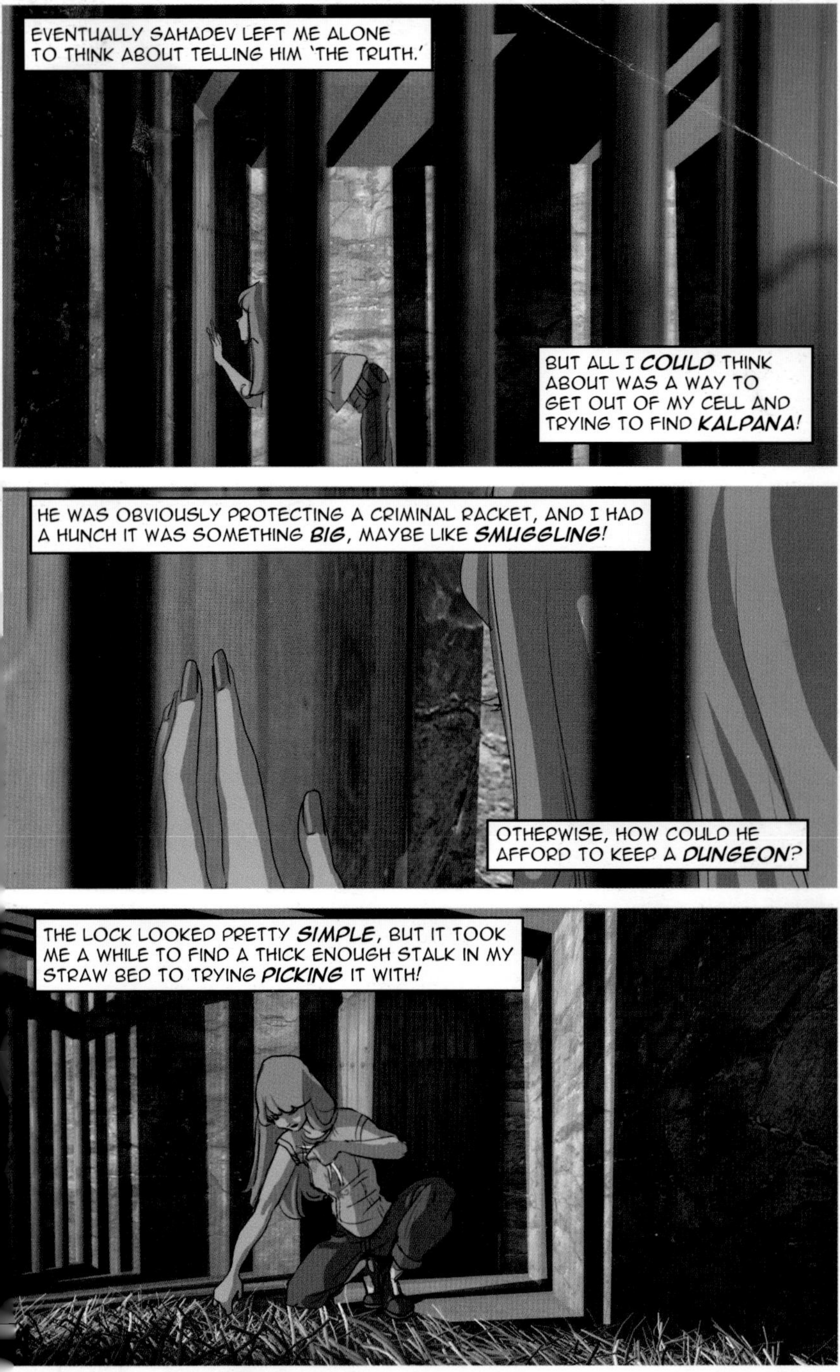
EVENTUALLY SAHADEV LEFT ME ALONE TO THINK ABOUT TELLING HIM 'THE TRUTH.'
BUT ALL I *COULD* THINK ABOUT WAS A WAY TO GET OUT OF MY CELL AND TRYING TO FIND *KALPANA*!
HE WAS OBVIOUSLY PROTECTING A CRIMINAL RACKET, AND I HAD A HUNCH IT WAS SOMETHING *BIG*, MAYBE LIKE *SMUGGLING*!
OTHERWISE, HOW COULD HE AFFORD TO KEEP A *DUNGEON*?
THE LOCK LOOKED PRETTY *SIMPLE*, BUT IT TOOK ME A WHILE TO FIND A THICK ENOUGH STALK IN MY STRAW BED TO TRYING *PICKING* IT WITH!

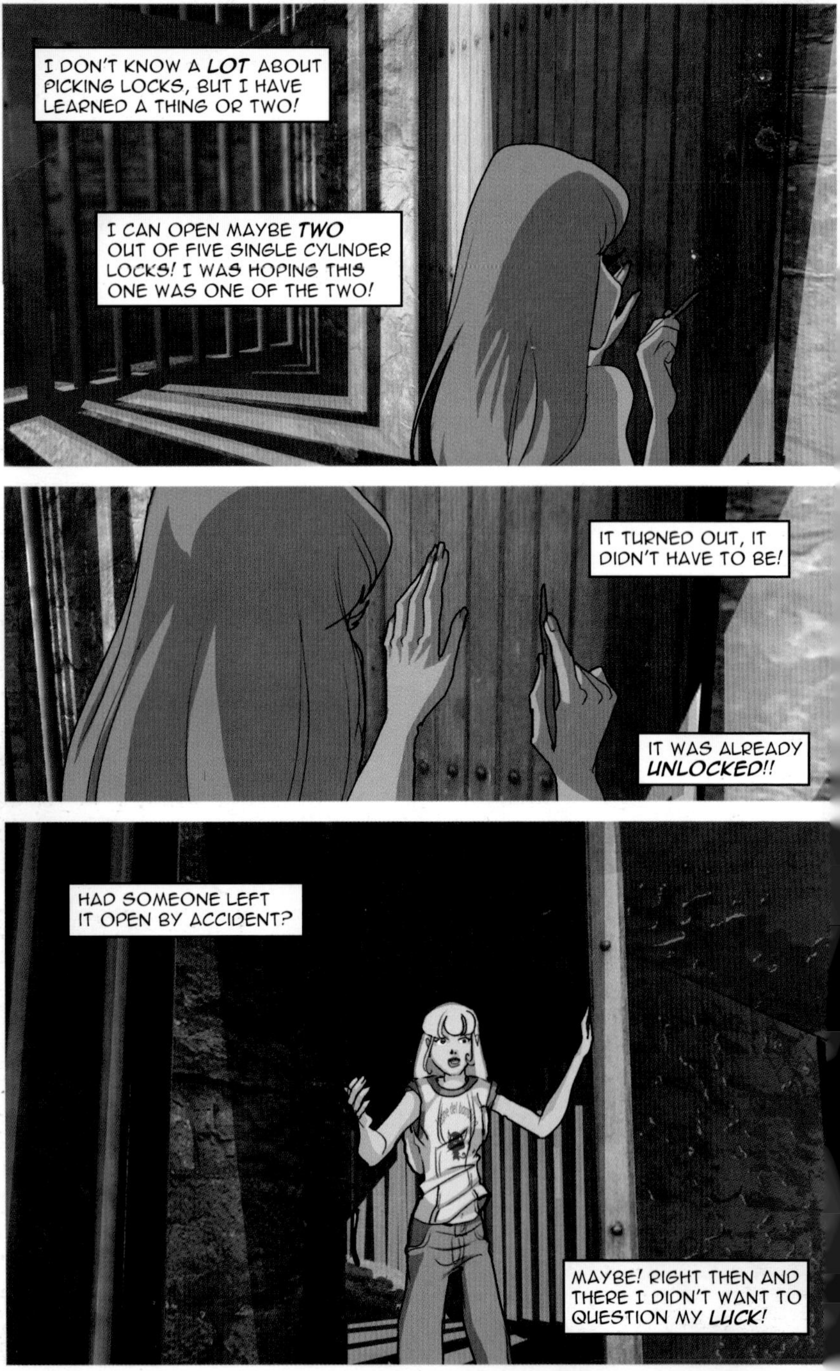
I DON'T KNOW A *LOT* ABOUT PICKING LOCKS, BUT I HAVE LEARNED A THING OR TWO!
I CAN OPEN MAYBE *TWO* OUT OF FIVE SINGLE CYLINDER LOCKS! I WAS HOPING THIS ONE WAS ONE OF THE TWO!
IT TURNED OUT, IT DIDN'T HAVE TO BE!
IT WAS ALREADY *UNLOCKED*!!
HAD SOMEONE LEFT IT OPEN BY ACCIDENT?
MAYBE! RIGHT THEN AND THERE I DIDN'T WANT TO QUESTION MY *LUCK*!

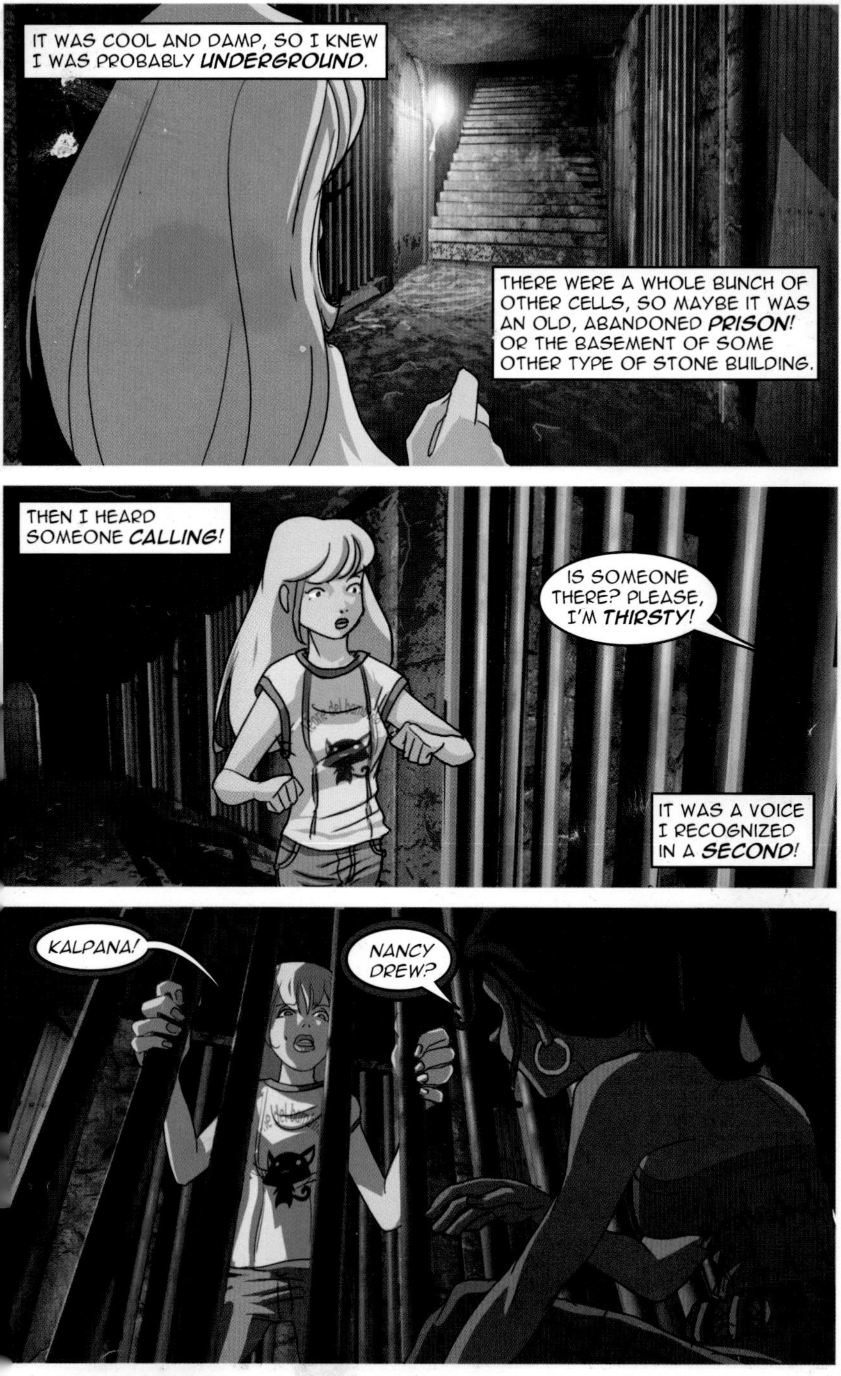
IT WAS COOL AND DAMP, SO I KNEW I WAS PROBABLY UNDERGROUND.
THERE WERE A WHOLE BUNCH OF OTHER CELLS, SO MAYBE IT WAS AN OLD, ABANDONED PRISON! OR THE BASEMENT OF SOME OTHER TYPE OF STONE BUILDING.
THEN I HEARD SOMEONE CALLING!
IS SOMEONE THERE? PLEASE, I'M THIRSTY!
IT WAS A VOICE I RECOGNIZED IN A SECOND!
KALPANA!
NANCY DREW?

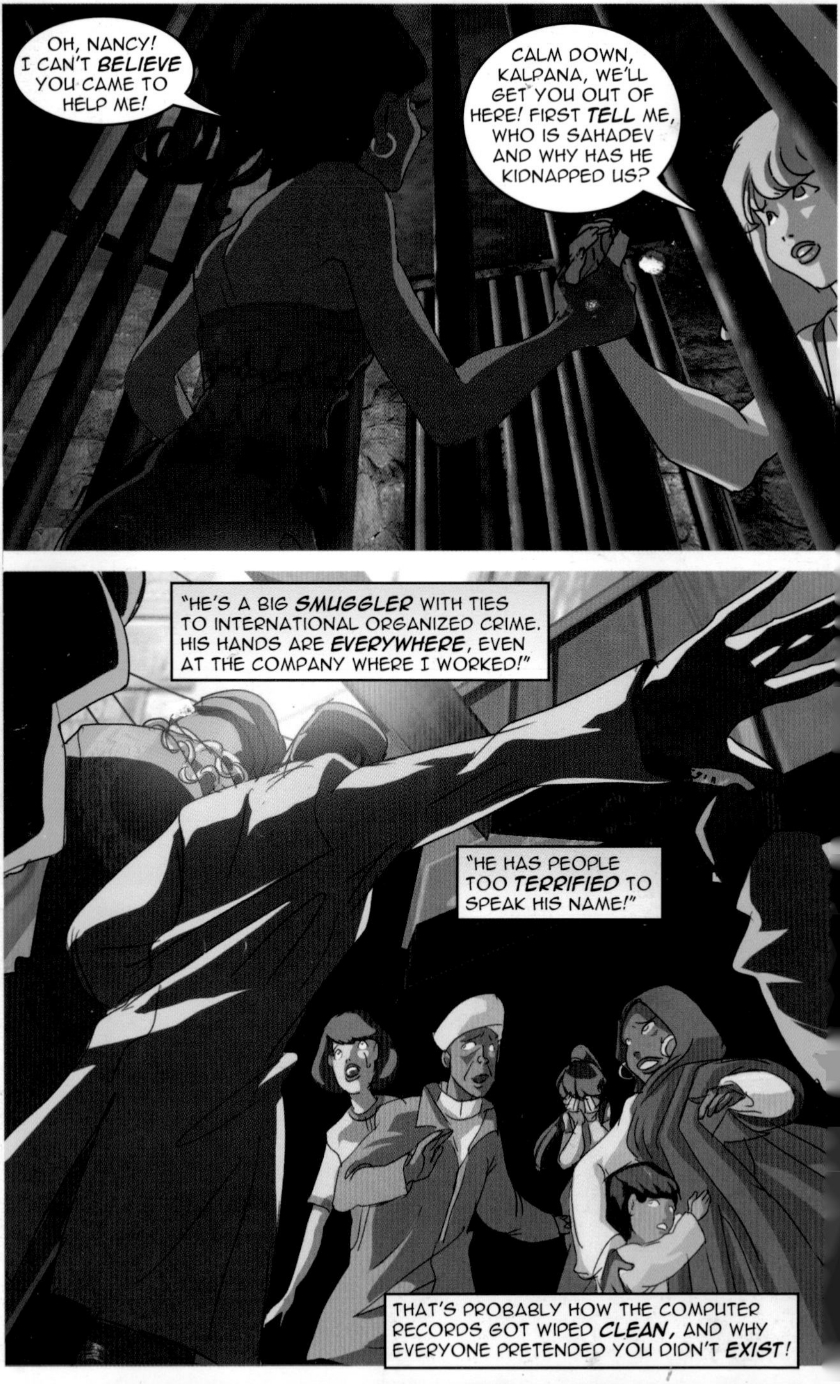

OH, NANCY! I CAN'T BELIEVE YOU CAME TO HELP ME!
CALM DOWN, KALPANA, WE'LL GET YOU OUT OF HERE! FIRST TELL ME, WHO IS SAHADEV AND WHY HAS HE KIDNAPPED US?
"HE'S A BIG SMUGGLER WITH TIES TO INTERNATIONAL ORGANIZED CRIME. HIS HANDS ARE EVERYWHERE, EVEN AT THE COMPANY WHERE I WORKED!"
"HE HAS PEOPLE TOO TERRIFIED TO SPEAK HIS NAME!"
THAT'S PROBABLY HOW THE COMPUTER RECORDS GOT WIPED CLEAN, AND WHY EVERYONE PRETENDED YOU DIDN'T EXIST!

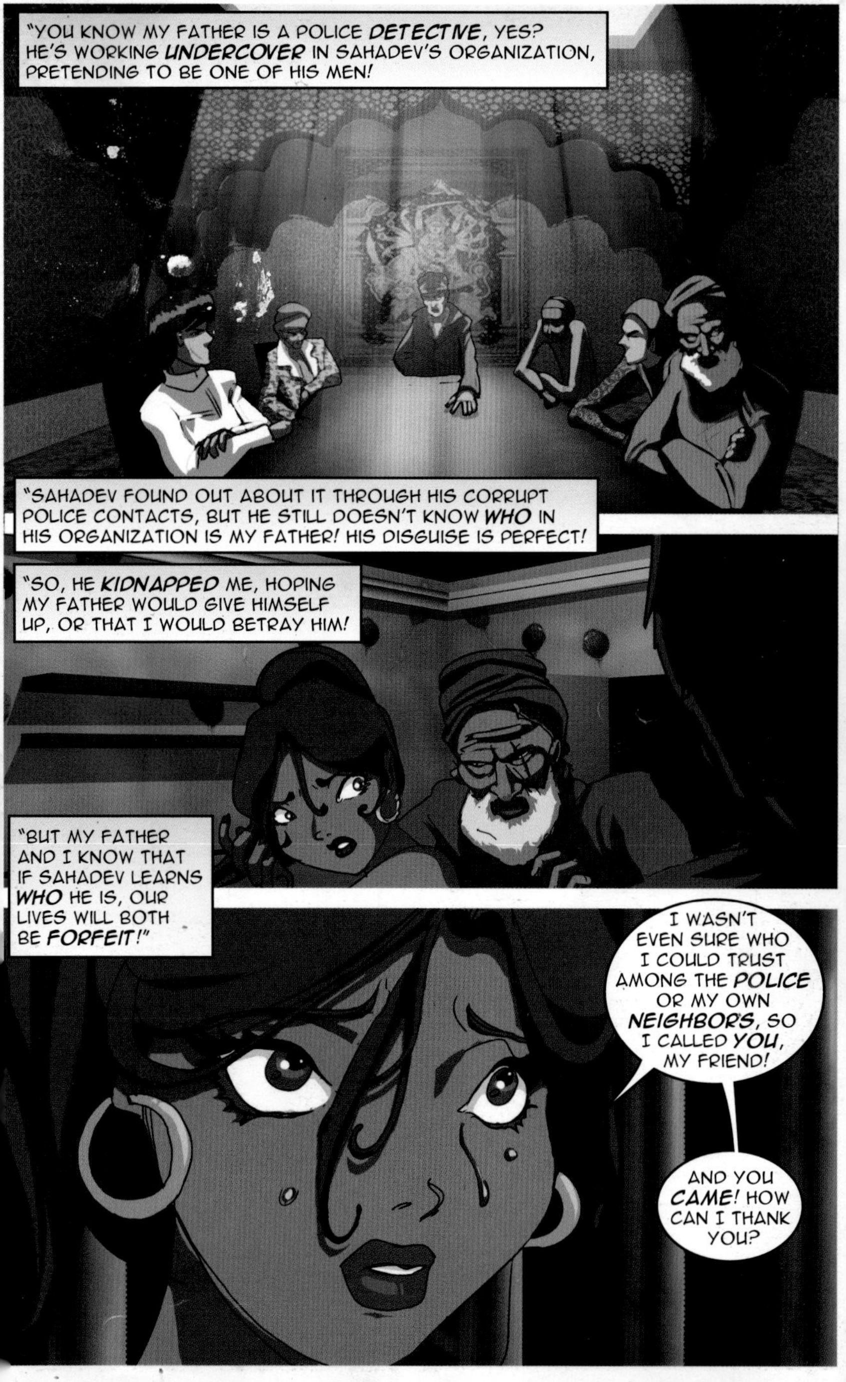
"YOU KNOW MY FATHER IS A POLICE DETECTIVE, YES? HE'S WORKING UNDERCOVER IN SAHADEV'S ORGANIZATION, PRETENDING TO BE ONE OF HIS MEN!
"SAHADEV FOUND OUT ABOUT IT THROUGH HIS CORRUPT POLICE CONTACTS, BUT HE STILL DOESN'T KNOW WHO IN HIS ORGANIZATION IS MY FATHER! HIS DISGUISE IS PERFECT!
"SO, HE KIDNAPPED ME, HOPING MY FATHER WOULD GIVE HIMSELF UP, OR THAT I WOULD BETRAY HIM!
"BUT MY FATHER AND I KNOW THAT IF SAHADEV LEARNS WHO HE IS, OUR LIVES WILL BOTH BE FORFEIT!"
I WASN'T EVEN SURE WHO I COULD TRUST AMONG THE POLICE OR MY OWN NEIGHBORS, SO I CALLED YOU, MY FRIEND!
AND YOU CAME! HOW CAN I THANK YOU?

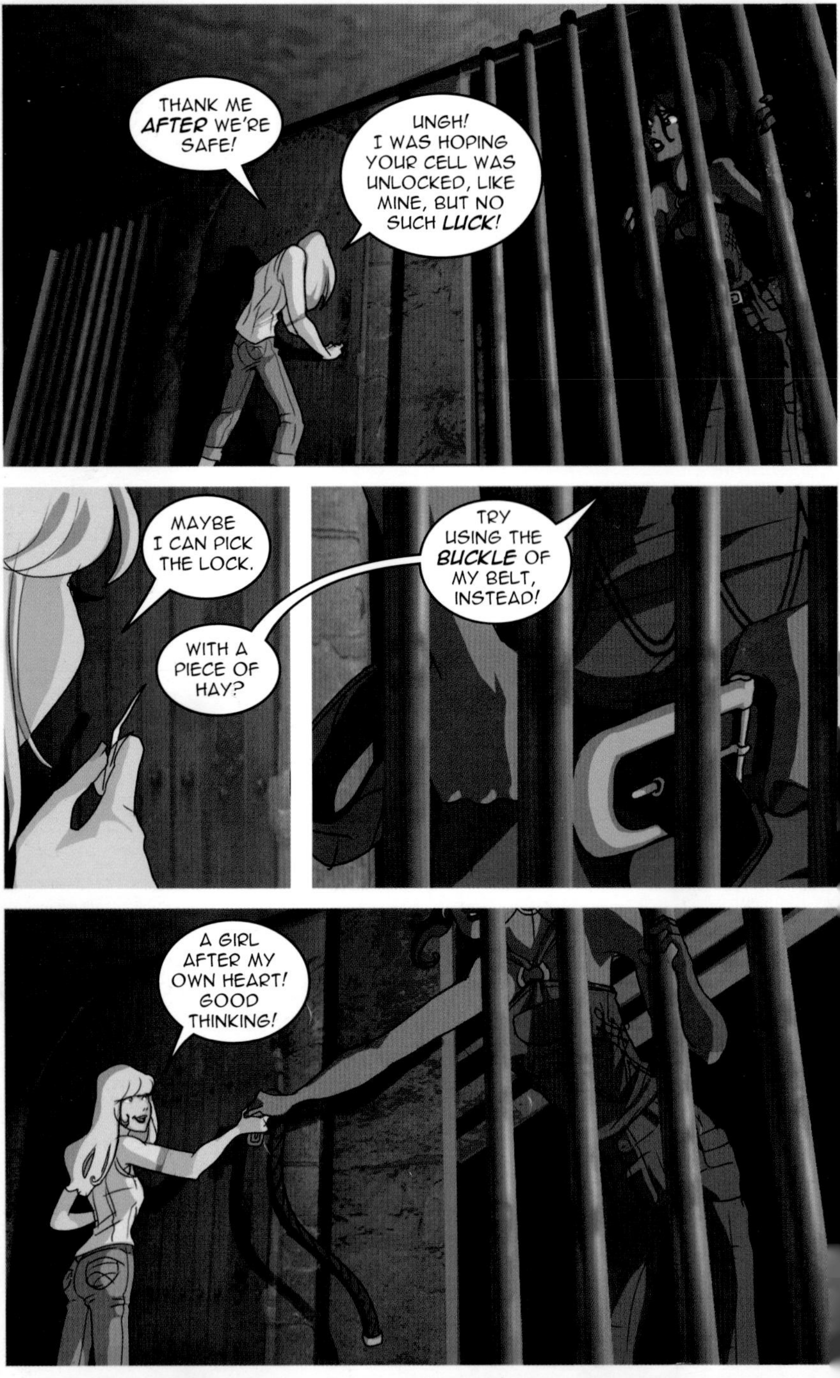
THANK ME AFTER WE'RE SAFE!
UNGH! I WAS HOPING YOUR CELL WAS UNLOCKED, LIKE MINE, BUT NO SUCH LUCK!
MAYBE I CAN PICK THE LOCK.
WITH A PIECE OF HAY?
TRY USING THE BUCKLE OF MY BELT, INSTEAD!
A GIRL AFTER MY OWN HEART! GOOD THINKING!

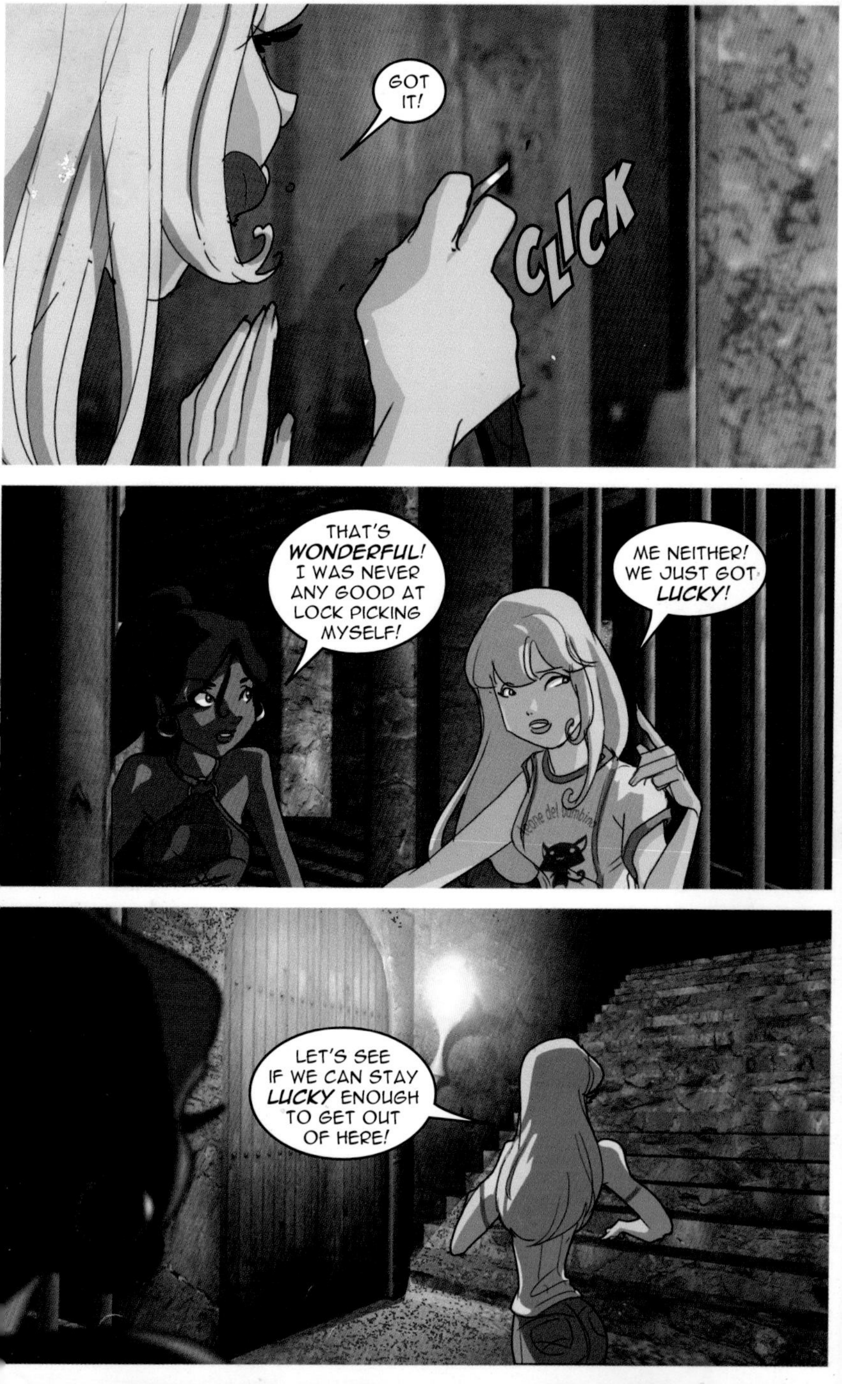
GOT IT!
CLICK
THAT'S *WONDERFUL!* I WAS NEVER ANY GOOD AT LOCK PICKING MYSELF!
ME NEITHER! WE JUST GOT *LUCKY!*
LET'S SEE IF WE CAN STAY *LUCKY* ENOUGH TO GET OUT OF HERE!

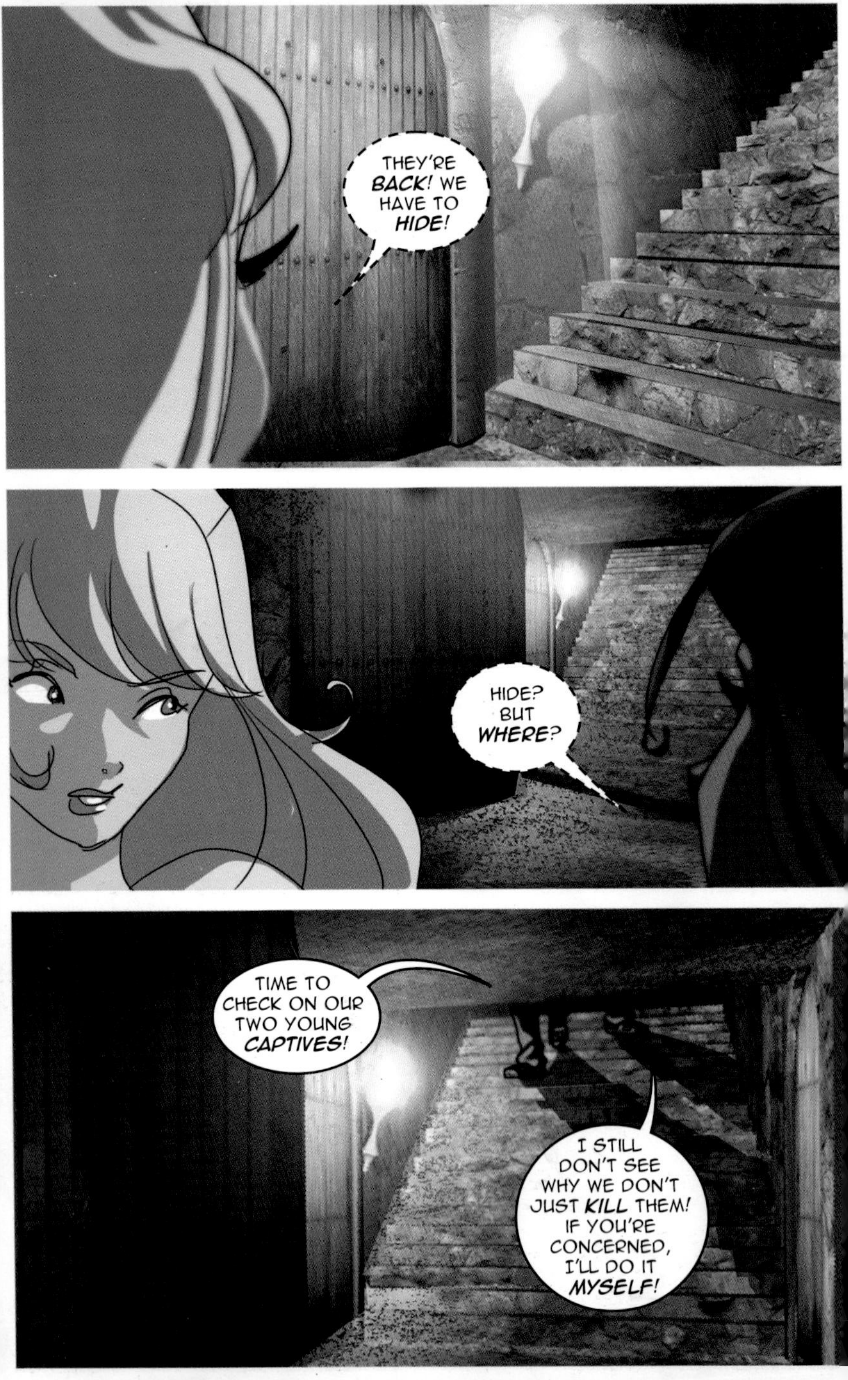
THEY'RE BACK! WE HAVE TO HIDE!
HIDE? BUT WHERE?
TIME TO CHECK ON OUR TWO YOUNG CAPTIVES!
I STILL DON'T SEE WHY WE DON'T JUST KILL THEM! IF YOU'RE CONCERNED, I'LL DO IT MYSELF!

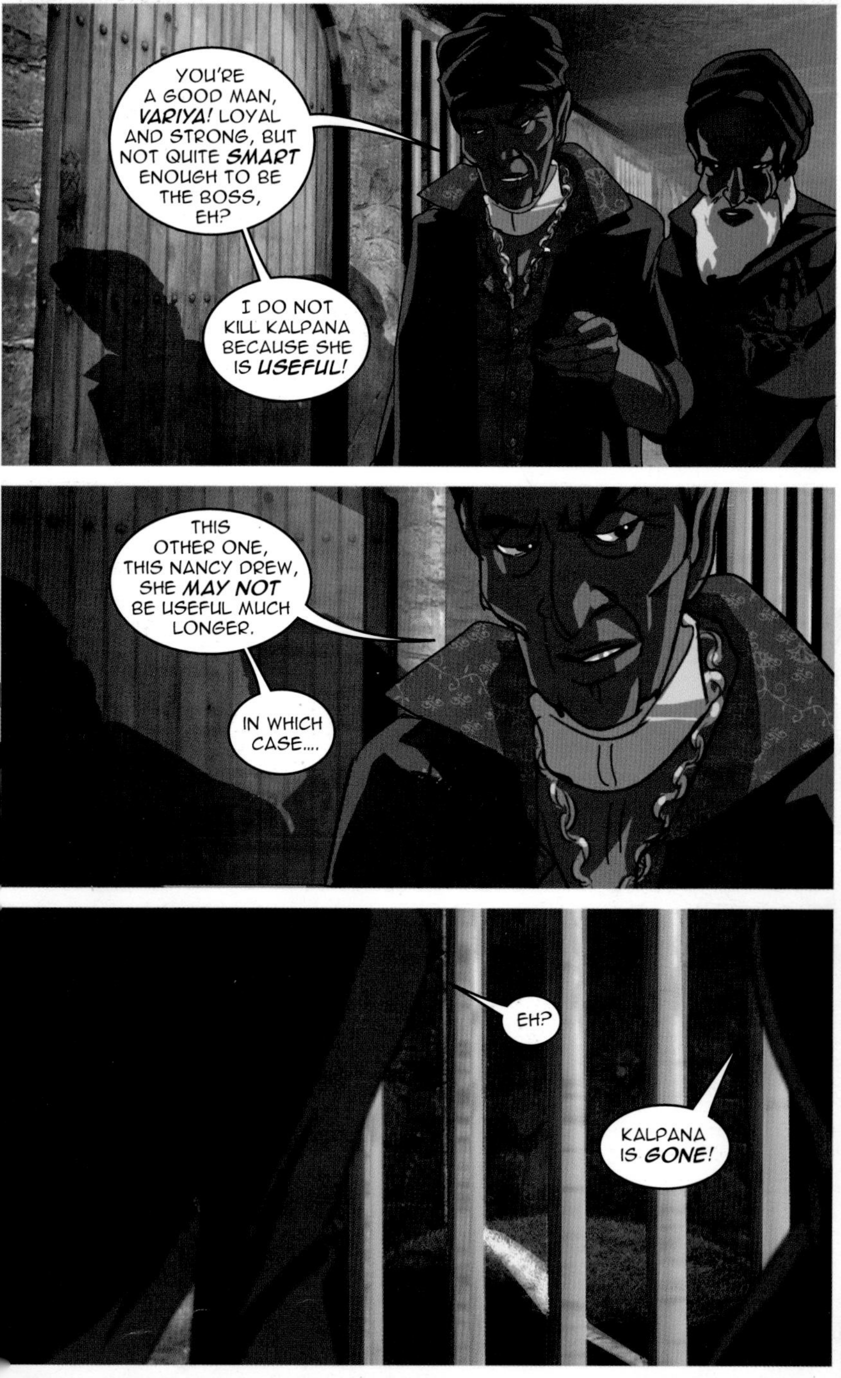
YOU'RE A GOOD MAN, VARIYA! LOYAL AND STRONG, BUT NOT QUITE SMART ENOUGH TO BE THE BOSS, EH?
I DO NOT KILL KALPANA BECAUSE SHE IS USEFUL!
THIS OTHER ONE, THIS NANCY DREW, SHE MAY NOT BE USEFUL MUCH LONGER.
IN WHICH CASE....
EH?
KALPANA IS GONE!

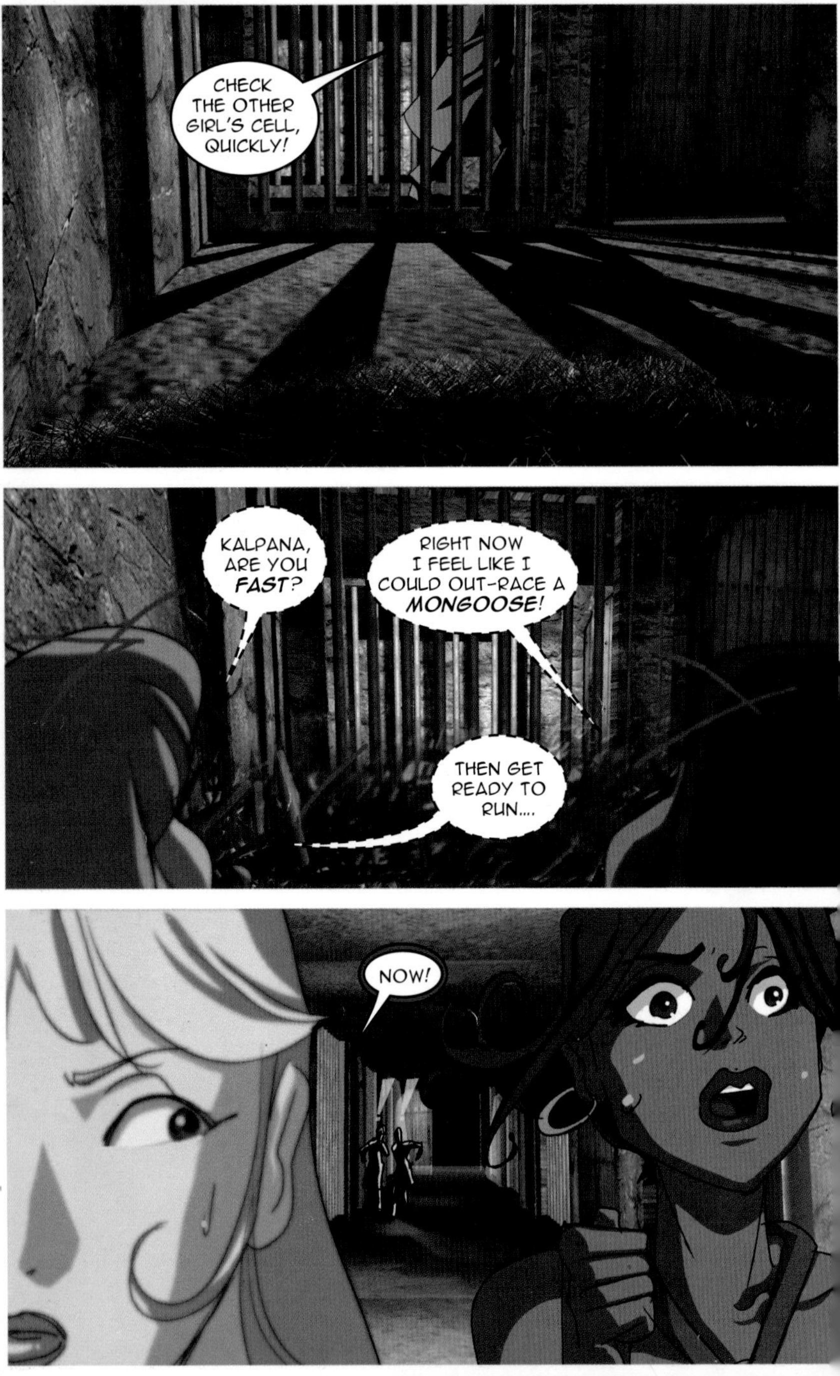
CHECK THE OTHER GIRL'S CELL, QUICKLY!
KALPANA, ARE YOU FAST?
RIGHT NOW I FEEL LIKE I COULD OUT-RACE A MONGOOSE!
THEN GET READY TO RUN....
NOW!

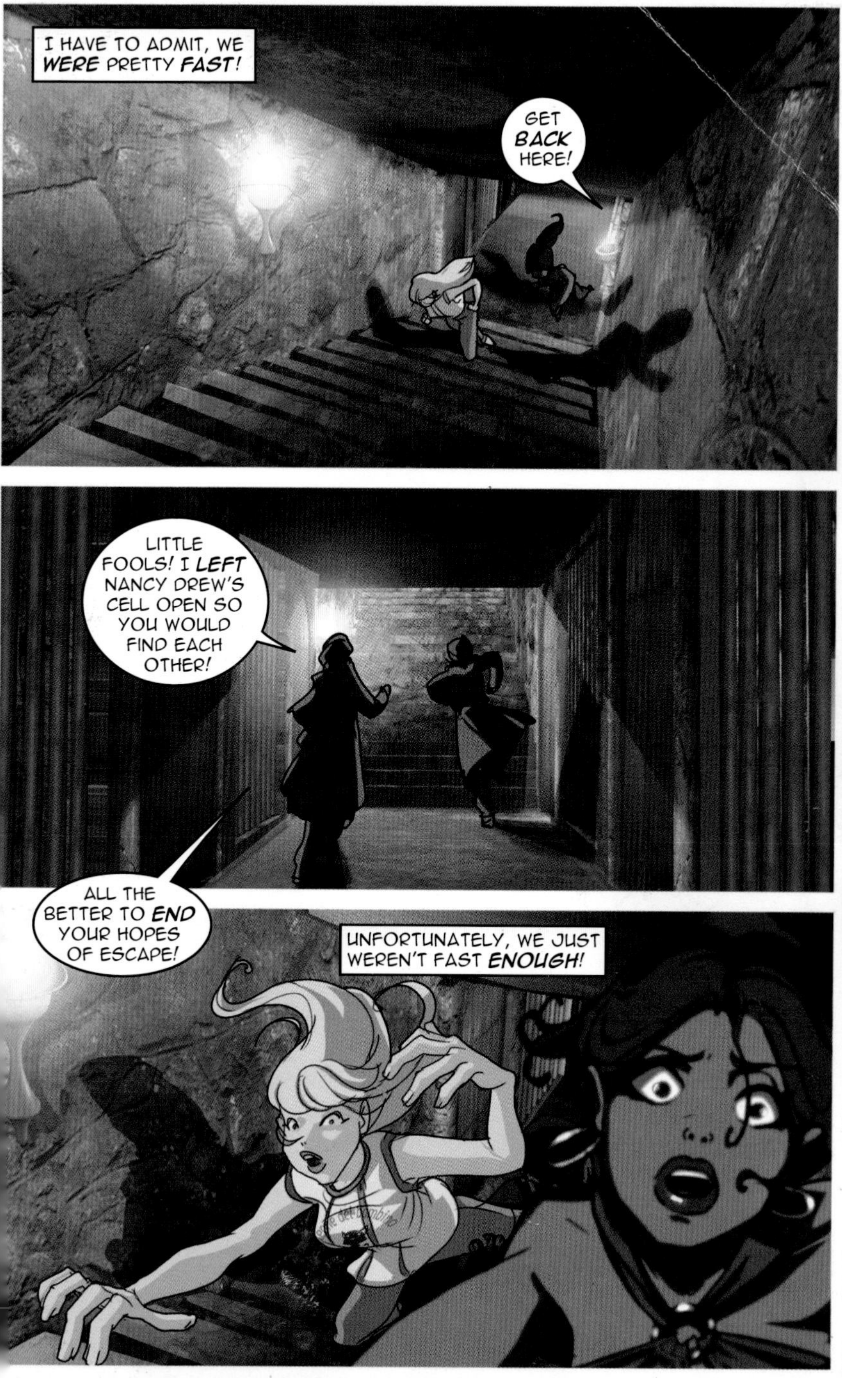

I HAVE TO ADMIT, WE WERE PRETTY FAST!
GET BACK HERE!
LITTLE FOOLS! I LEFT NANCY DREW'S CELL OPEN SO YOU WOULD FIND EACH OTHER!
ALL THE BETTER TO END YOUR HOPES OF ESCAPE!
UNFORTUNATELY, WE JUST WEREN'T FAST ENOUGH!

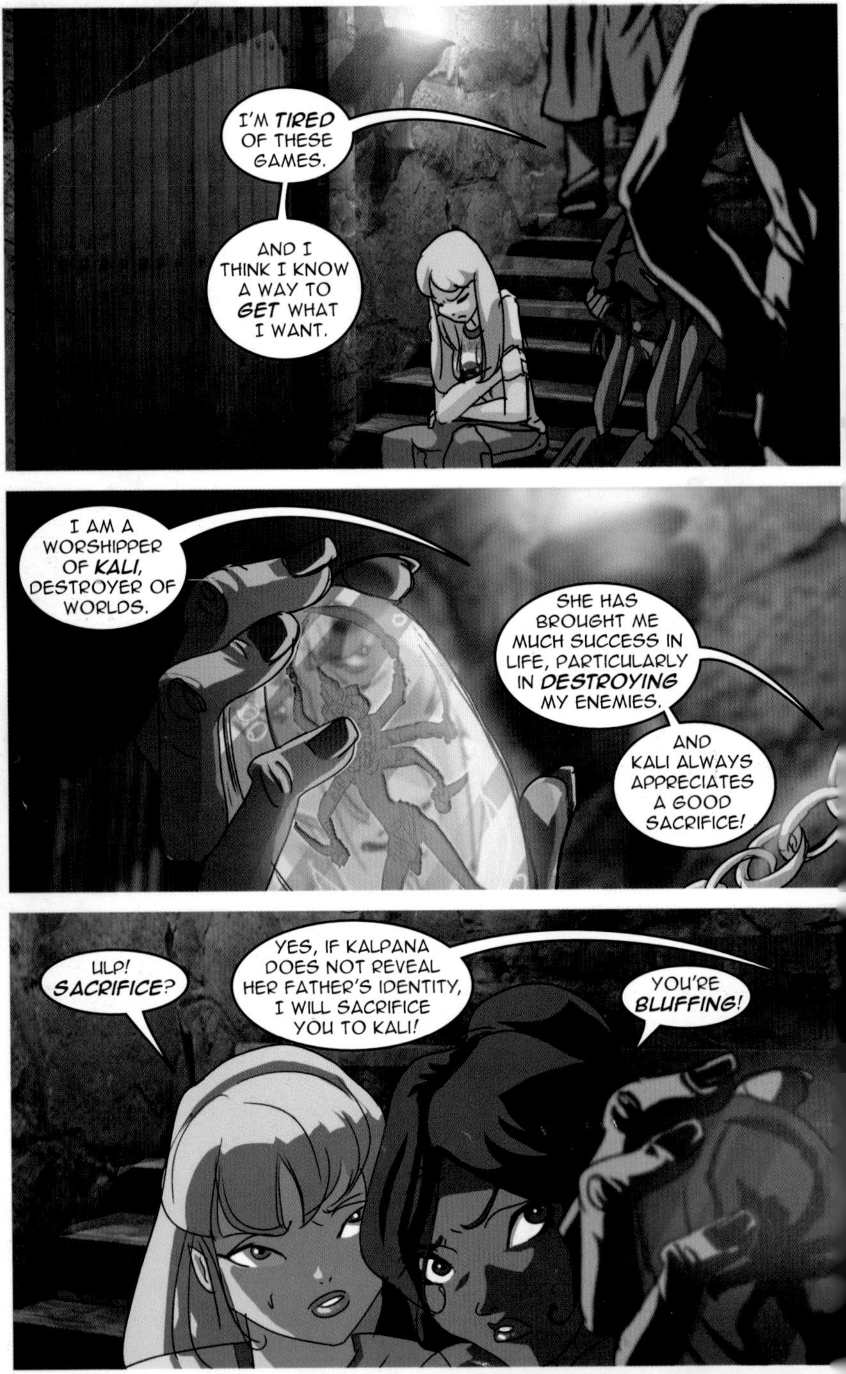
I'M TIRED OF THESE GAMES.
AND I THINK I KNOW A WAY TO GET WHAT I WANT.
I AM A WORSHIPPER OF KALI, DESTROYER OF WORLDS.
SHE HAS BROUGHT ME MUCH SUCCESS IN LIFE, PARTICULARLY IN DESTROYING MY ENEMIES.
AND KALI ALWAYS APPRECIATES A GOOD SACRIFICE!
ULP! SACRIFICE?
YES, IF KALPANA DOES NOT REVEAL HER FATHER'S IDENTITY, I WILL SACRIFICE YOU TO KALI!
YOU'RE BLUFFING!

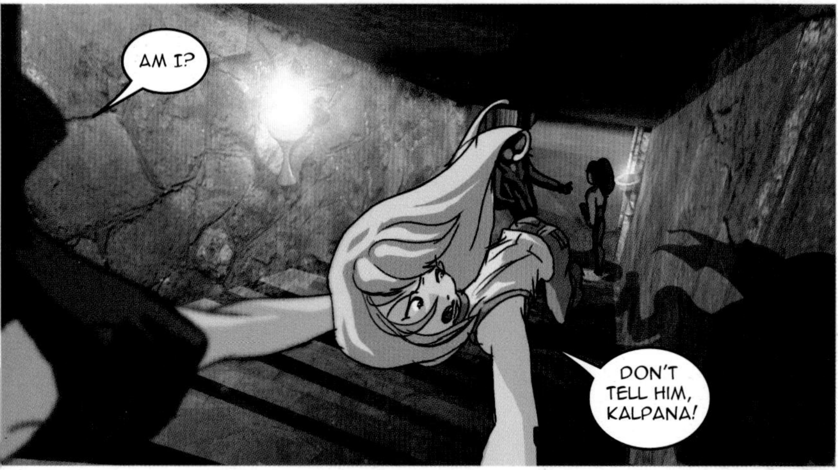
AM I?
DON'T TELL HIM, KALPANA!

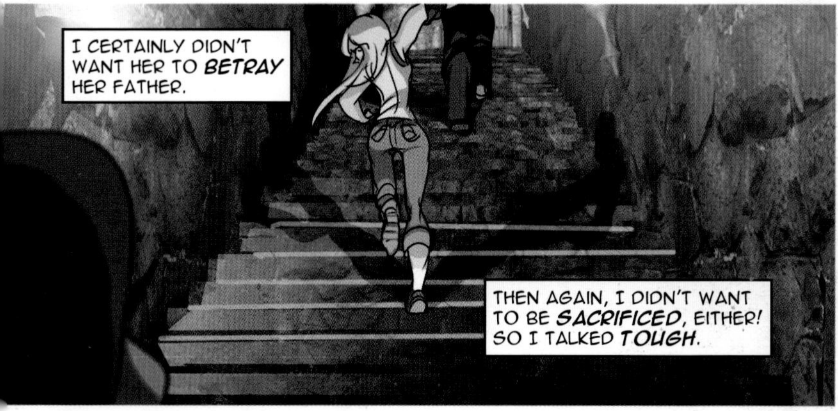
I CERTAINLY DIDN'T WANT HER TO ***BETRAY*** HER FATHER.
THEN AGAIN, I DIDN'T WANT TO BE ***SACRIFICED***, EITHER! SO I TALKED ***TOUGH***.

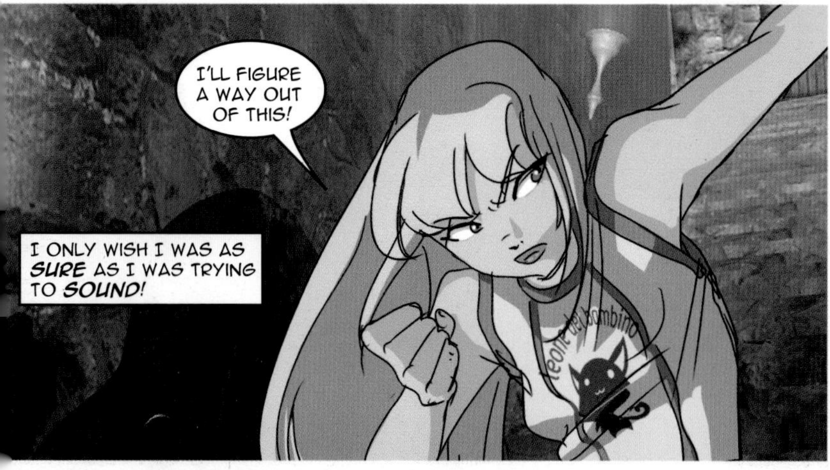
I'LL FIGURE A WAY OUT OF THIS!
I ONLY WISH I WAS AS ***SURE*** AS I WAS TRYING TO ***SOUND***!

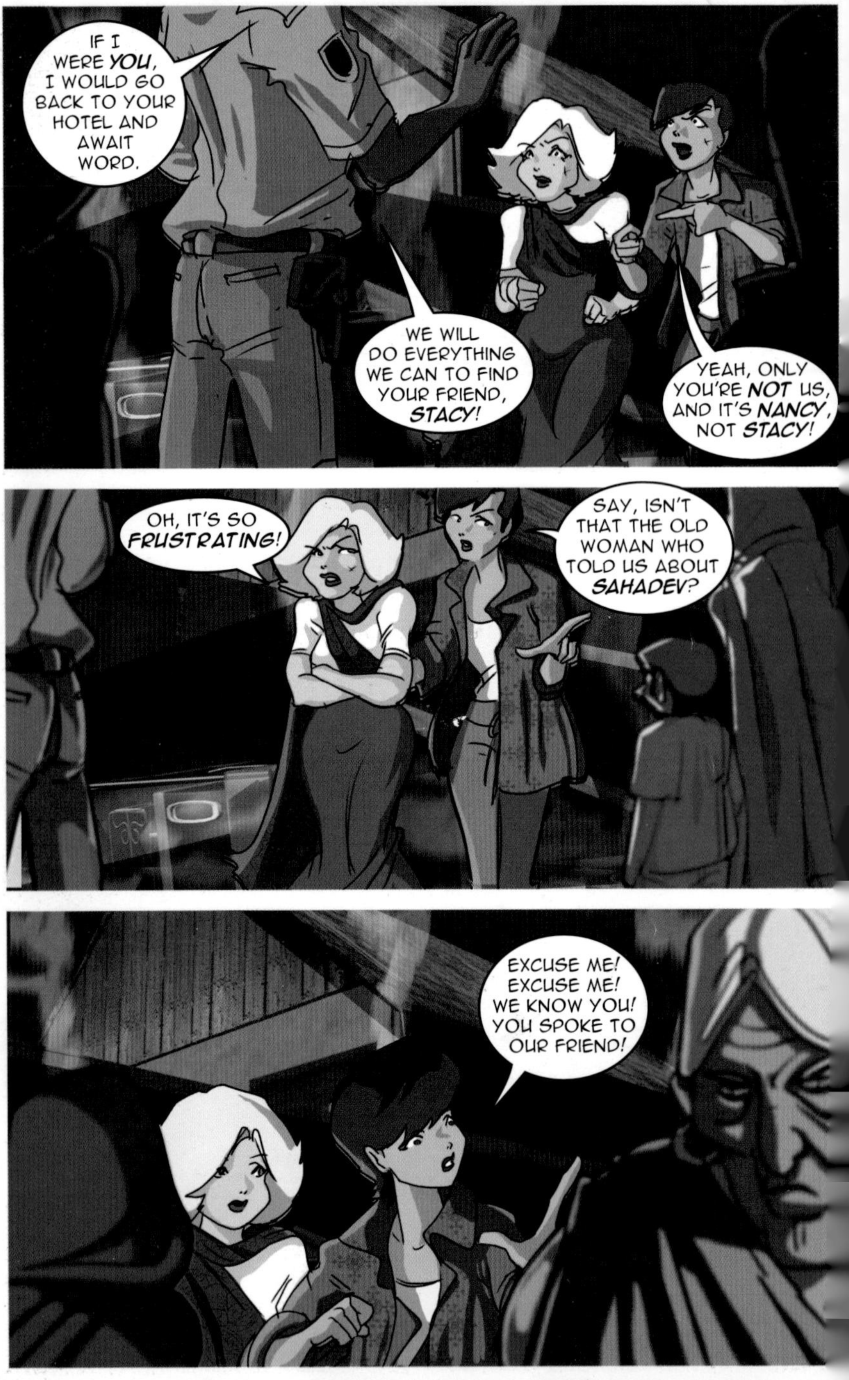
IF I WERE YOU, I WOULD GO BACK TO YOUR HOTEL AND AWAIT WORD.
WE WILL DO EVERYTHING WE CAN TO FIND YOUR FRIEND, STACY!
YEAH, ONLY YOU'RE NOT US, AND IT'S NANCY, NOT STACY!
OH, IT'S SO FRUSTRATING!
SAY, ISN'T THAT THE OLD WOMAN WHO TOLD US ABOUT SAHADEV?
EXCUSE ME! EXCUSE ME! WE KNOW YOU! YOU SPOKE TO OUR FRIEND!

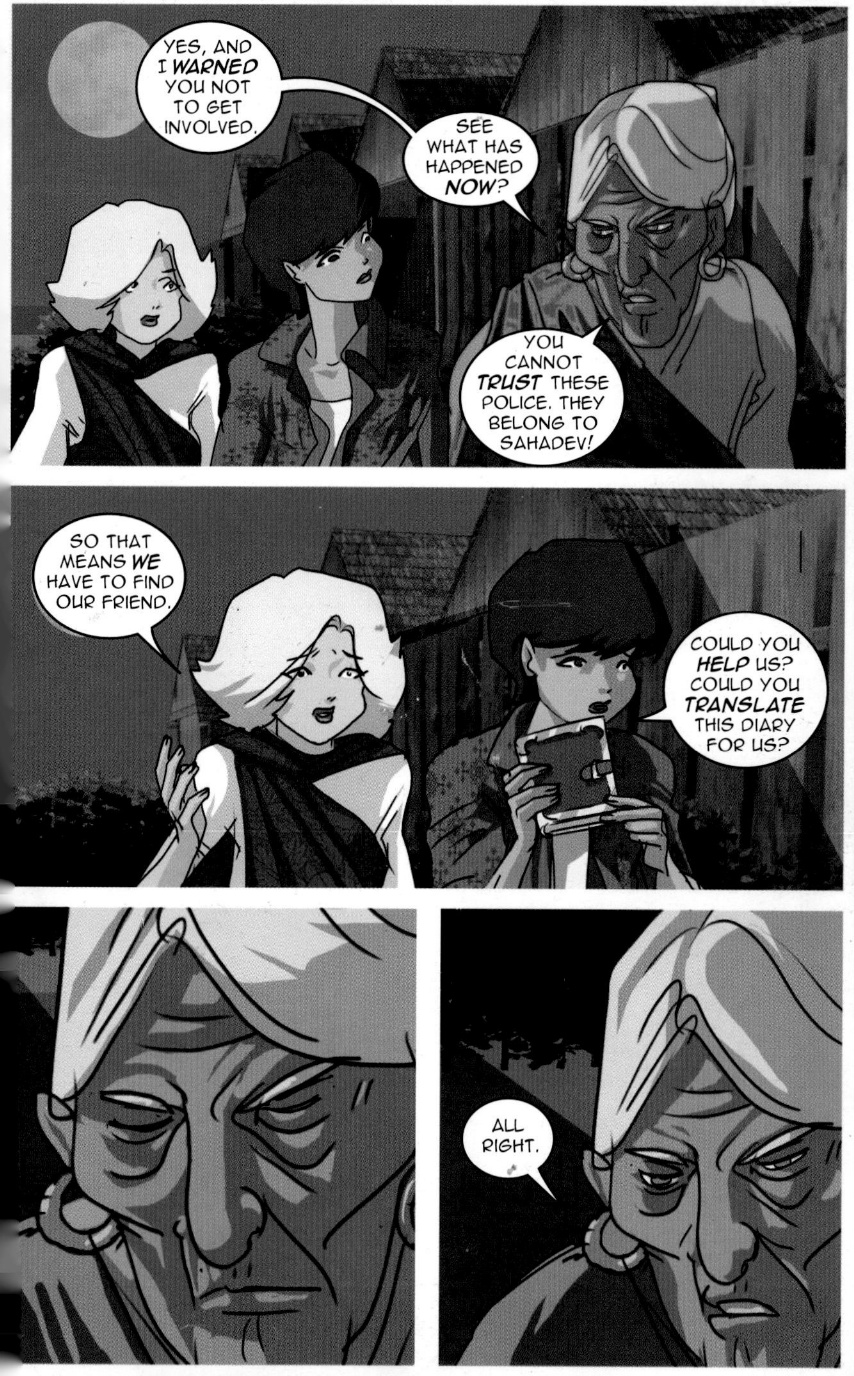
YES, AND I WARNED YOU NOT TO GET INVOLVED.
SEE WHAT HAS HAPPENED NOW?
YOU CANNOT TRUST THESE POLICE. THEY BELONG TO SAHADEV!
SO THAT MEANS WE HAVE TO FIND OUR FRIEND.
COULD YOU HELP US? COULD YOU TRANSLATE THIS DIARY FOR US?
ALL RIGHT.

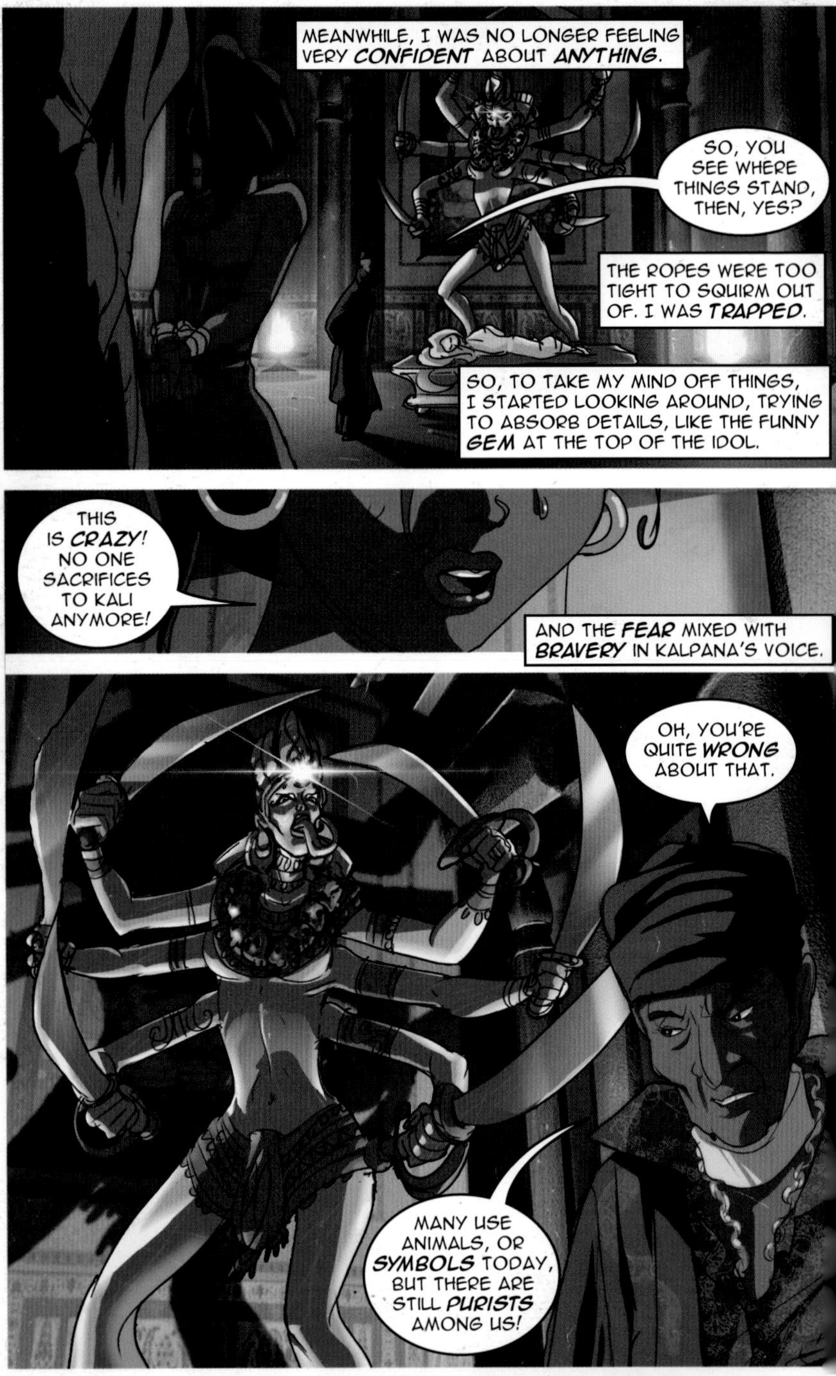
MEANWHILE, I WAS NO LONGER FEELING VERY CONFIDENT ABOUT ANYTHING.
SO, YOU SEE WHERE THINGS STAND, THEN, YES?
THE ROPES WERE TOO TIGHT TO SQUIRM OUT OF. I WAS TRAPPED.
SO, TO TAKE MY MIND OFF THINGS, I STARTED LOOKING AROUND, TRYING TO ABSORB DETAILS, LIKE THE FUNNY GEM AT THE TOP OF THE IDOL.
THIS IS CRAZY! NO ONE SACRIFICES TO KALI ANYMORE!
AND THE FEAR MIXED WITH BRAVERY IN KALPANA'S VOICE.
OH, YOU'RE QUITE WRONG ABOUT THAT.
MANY USE ANIMALS, OR SYMBOLS TODAY, BUT THERE ARE STILL PURISTS AMONG US!

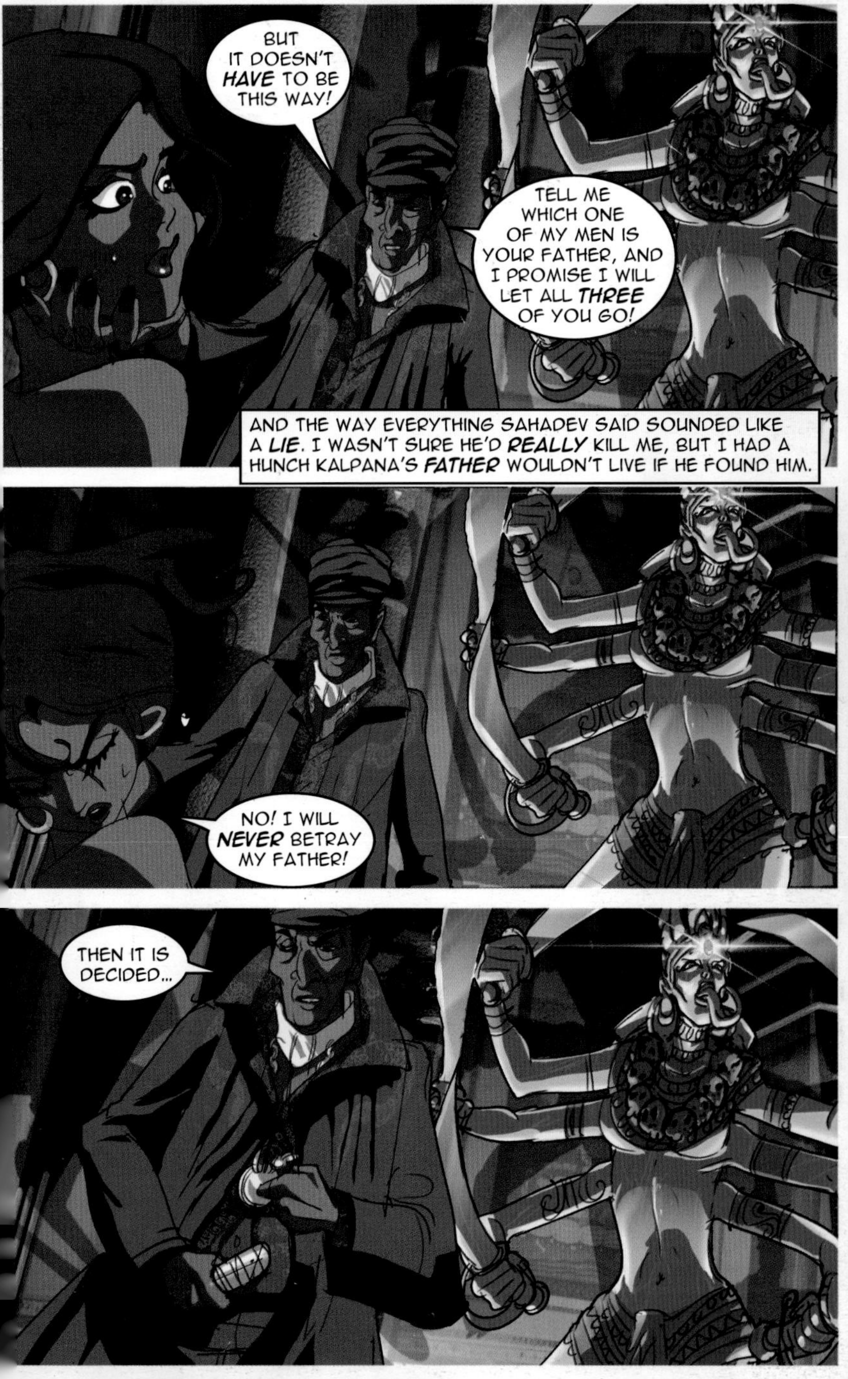
BUT IT DOESN'T HAVE TO BE THIS WAY!
TELL ME WHICH ONE OF MY MEN IS YOUR FATHER, AND I PROMISE I WILL LET ALL THREE OF YOU GO!
AND THE WAY EVERYTHING SAHADEV SAID SOUNDED LIKE A LIE. I WASN'T SURE HE'D REALLY KILL ME, BUT I HAD A HUNCH KALPANA'S FATHER WOULDN'T LIVE IF HE FOUND HIM.
NO! I WILL NEVER BETRAY MY FATHER!
THEN IT IS DECIDED...

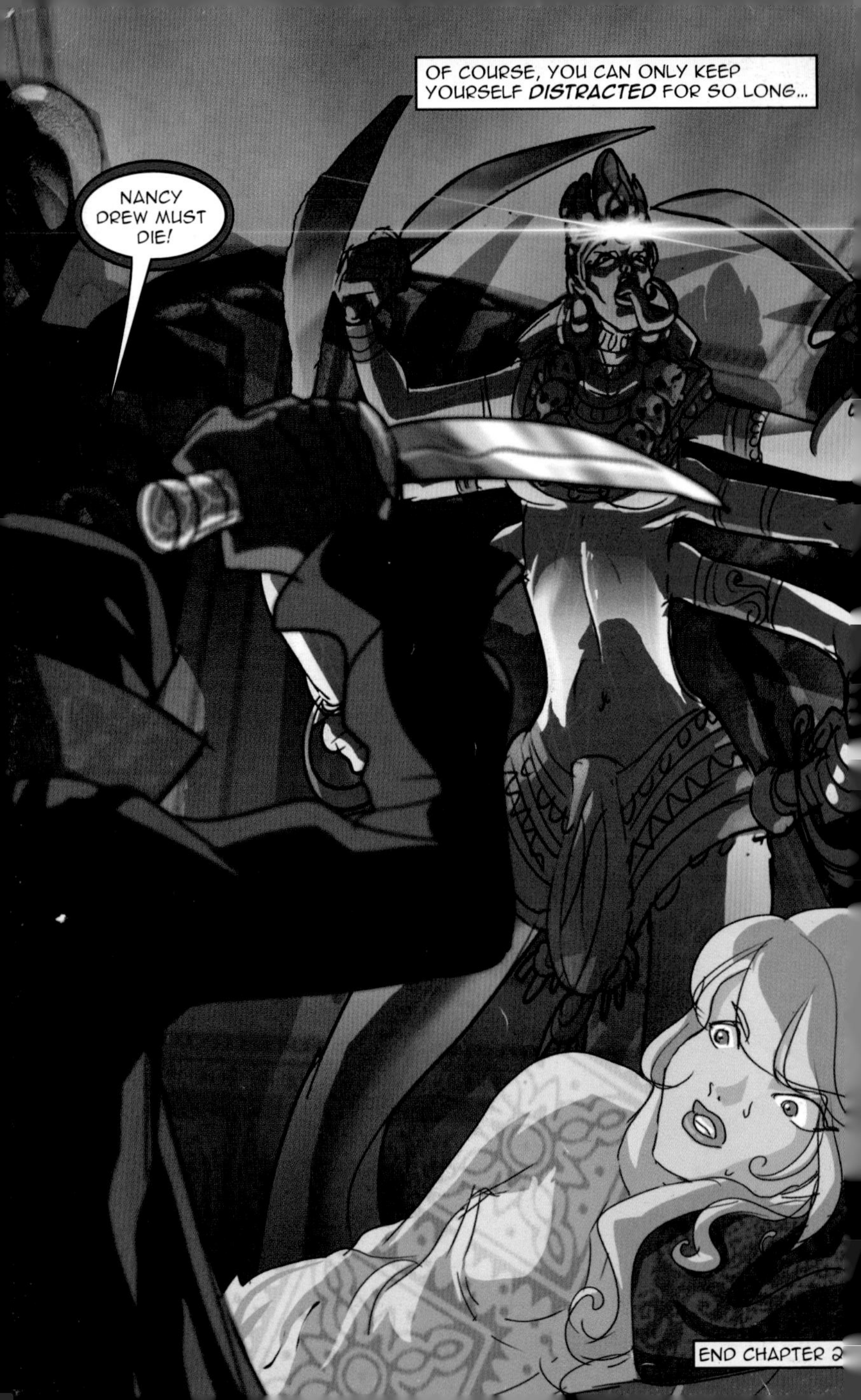
OF COURSE, YOU CAN ONLY KEEP YOURSELF DISTRACTED FOR SO LONG...
NANCY DREW MUST DIE!
END CHAPTER 2

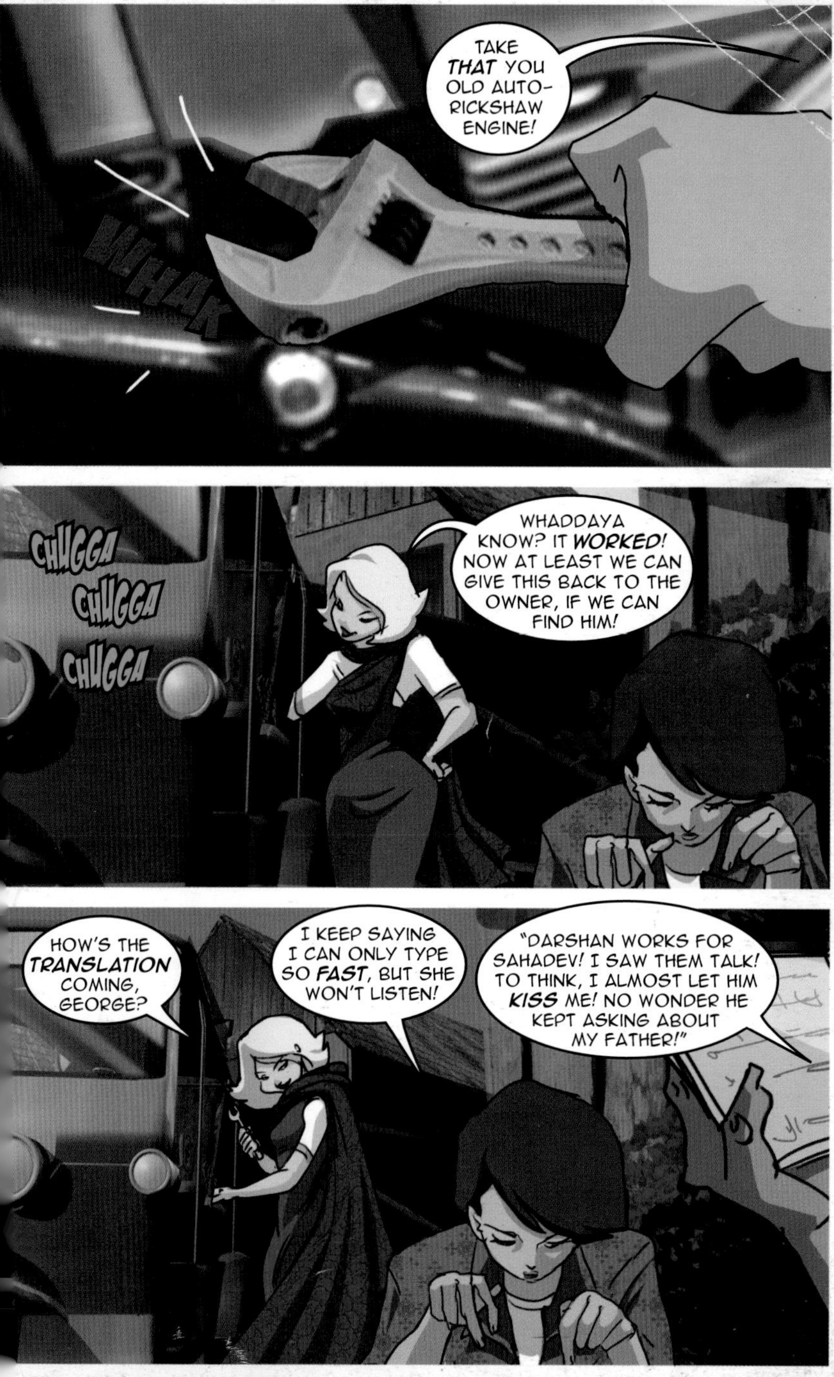
TAKE THAT YOU OLD AUTO-RICKSHAW ENGINE!
WHHAK
CHUGGA CHUGGA CHUGGA
WHADDAYA KNOW? IT WORKED! NOW AT LEAST WE CAN GIVE THIS BACK TO THE OWNER, IF WE CAN FIND HIM!
HOW'S THE TRANSLATION COMING, GEORGE?
I KEEP SAYING I CAN ONLY TYPE SO FAST, BUT SHE WON'T LISTEN!
"DARSHAN WORKS FOR SAHADEV! I SAW THEM TALK! TO THINK, I ALMOST LET HIM KISS ME! NO WONDER HE KEPT ASKING ABOUT MY FATHER!"

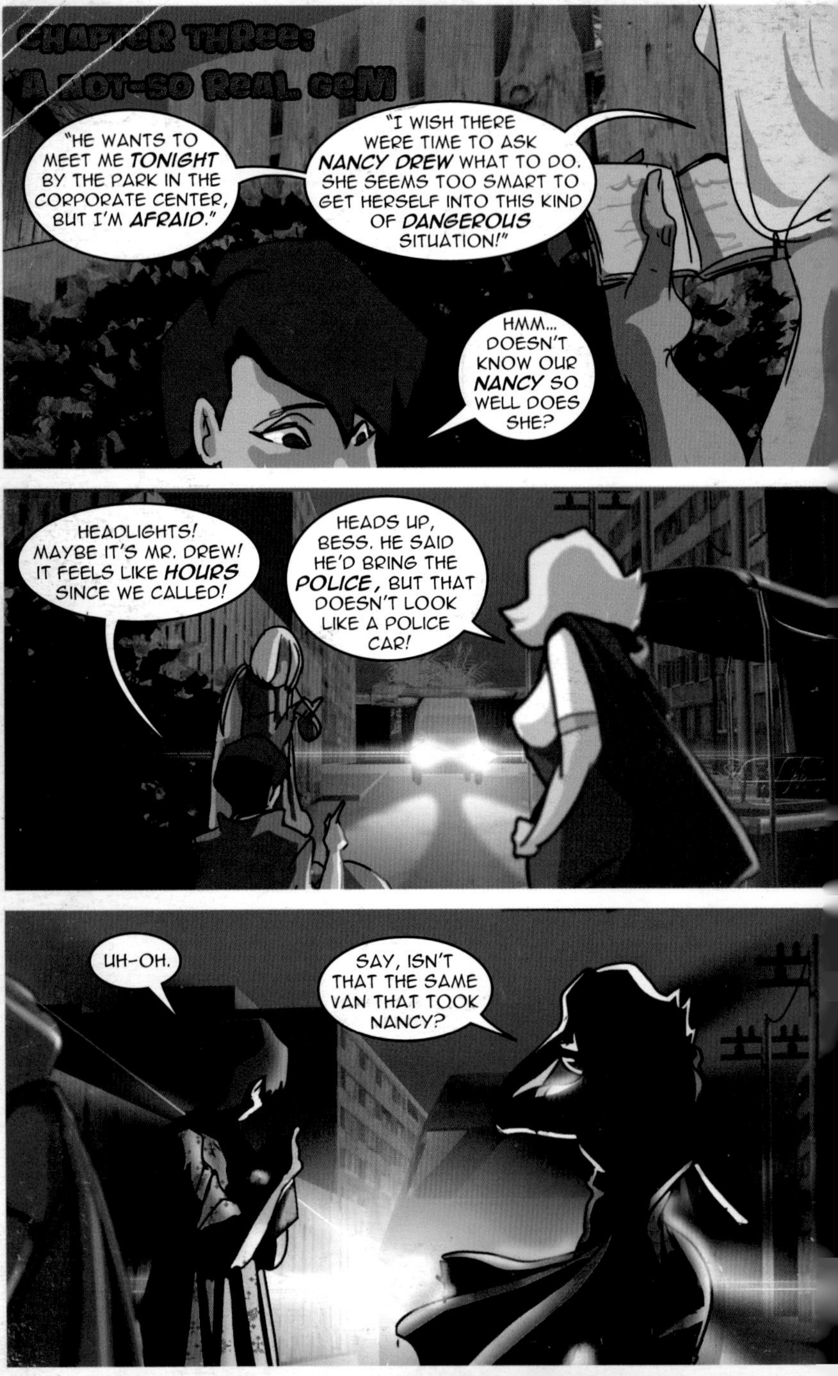

CHAPTER THREE:
A NOT-SO REAL GEM
"HE WANTS TO MEET ME TONIGHT BY THE PARK IN THE CORPORATE CENTER, BUT I'M AFRAID."
"I WISH THERE WERE TIME TO ASK NANCY DREW WHAT TO DO. SHE SEEMS TOO SMART TO GET HERSELF INTO THIS KIND OF DANGEROUS SITUATION!"
HMM... DOESN'T KNOW OUR NANCY SO WELL DOES SHE?
HEADLIGHTS! MAYBE IT'S MR. DREW! IT FEELS LIKE HOURS SINCE WE CALLED!
HEADS UP, BESS. HE SAID HE'D BRING THE POLICE, BUT THAT DOESN'T LOOK LIKE A POLICE CAR!
UH-OH.
SAY, ISN'T THAT THE SAME VAN THAT TOOK NANCY?

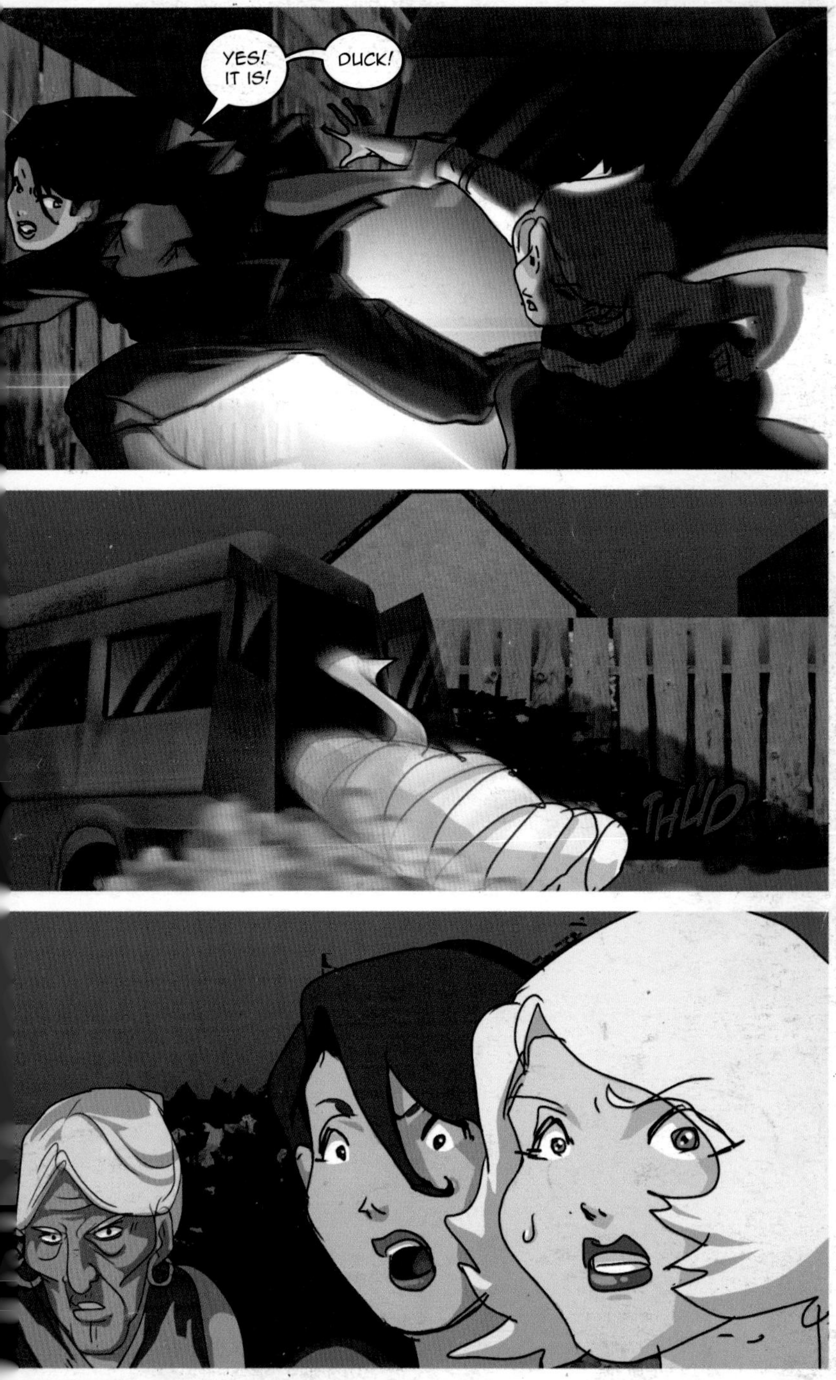
YES! IT IS!
DUCK!
THUD

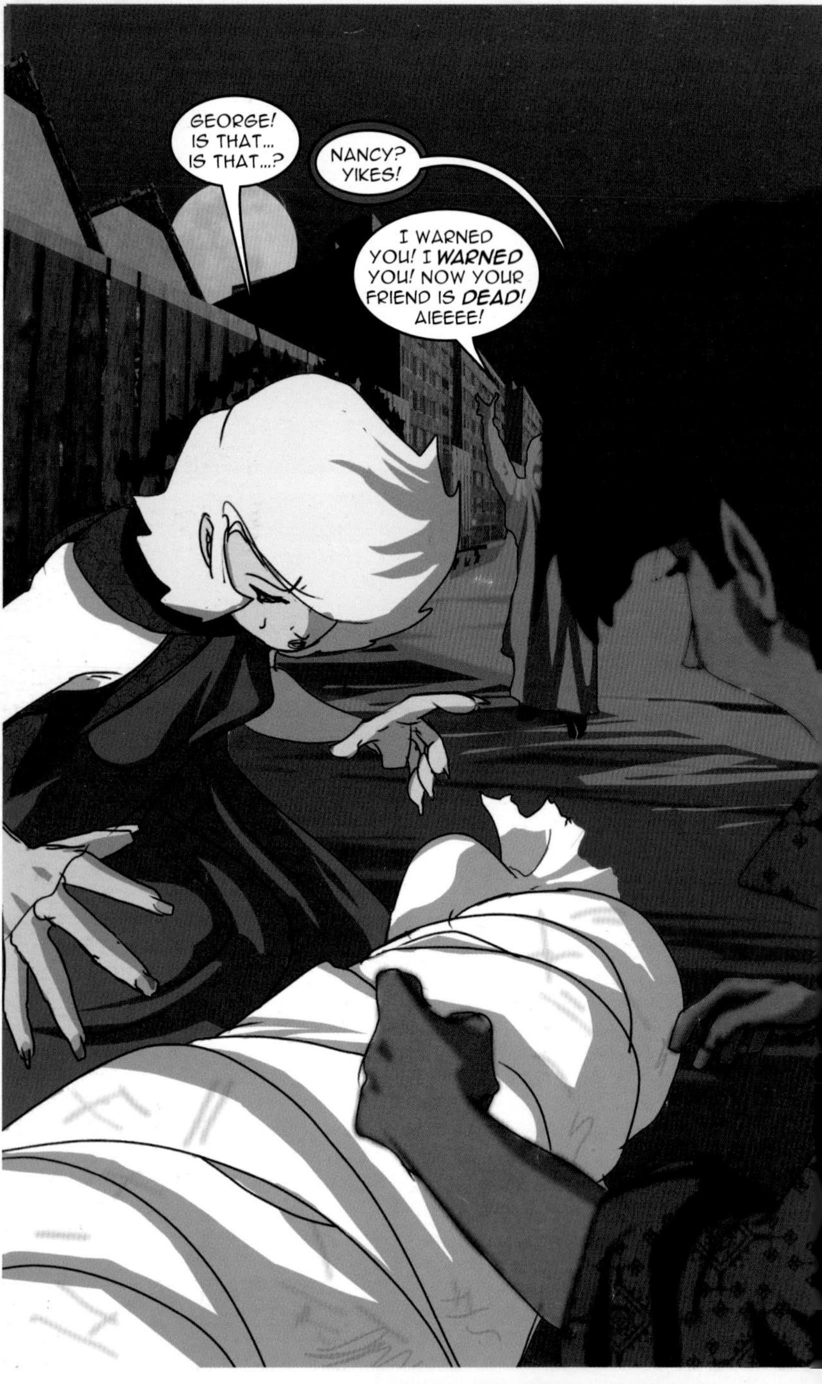
GEORGE! IS THAT... IS THAT...?
NANCY? YIKES!
I WARNED YOU! I WARNED YOU! NOW YOUR FRIEND IS DEAD! AIEEEE!

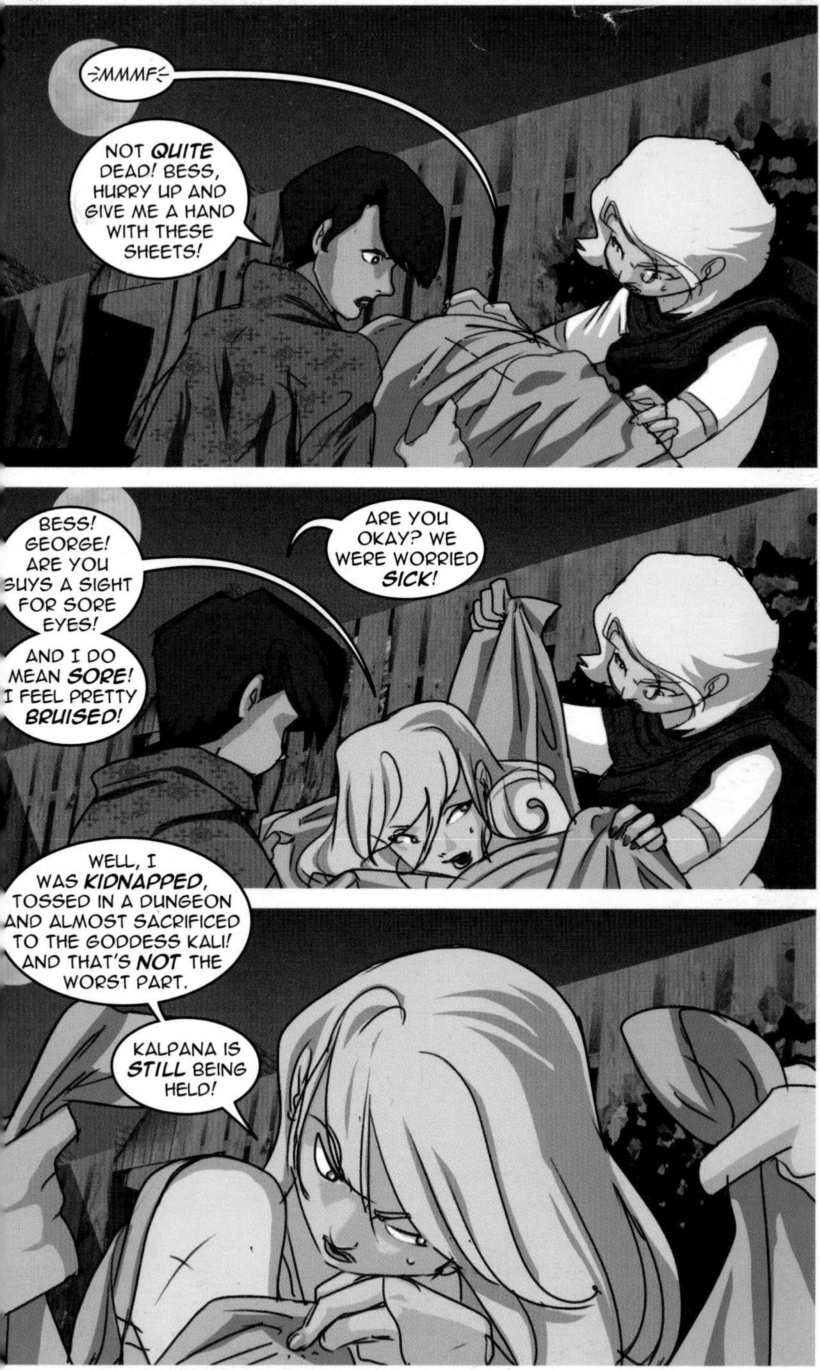
MMMF
NOT QUITE DEAD! BESS, HURRY UP AND GIVE ME A HAND WITH THESE SHEETS!
BESS! GEORGE! ARE YOU GUYS A SIGHT FOR SORE EYES!
AND I DO MEAN SORE! I FEEL PRETTY BRUISED!
ARE YOU OKAY? WE WERE WORRIED SICK!
WELL, I WAS KIDNAPPED, TOSSED IN A DUNGEON AND ALMOST SACRIFICED TO THE GODDESS KALI! AND THAT'S NOT THE WORST PART.
KALPANA IS STILL BEING HELD!

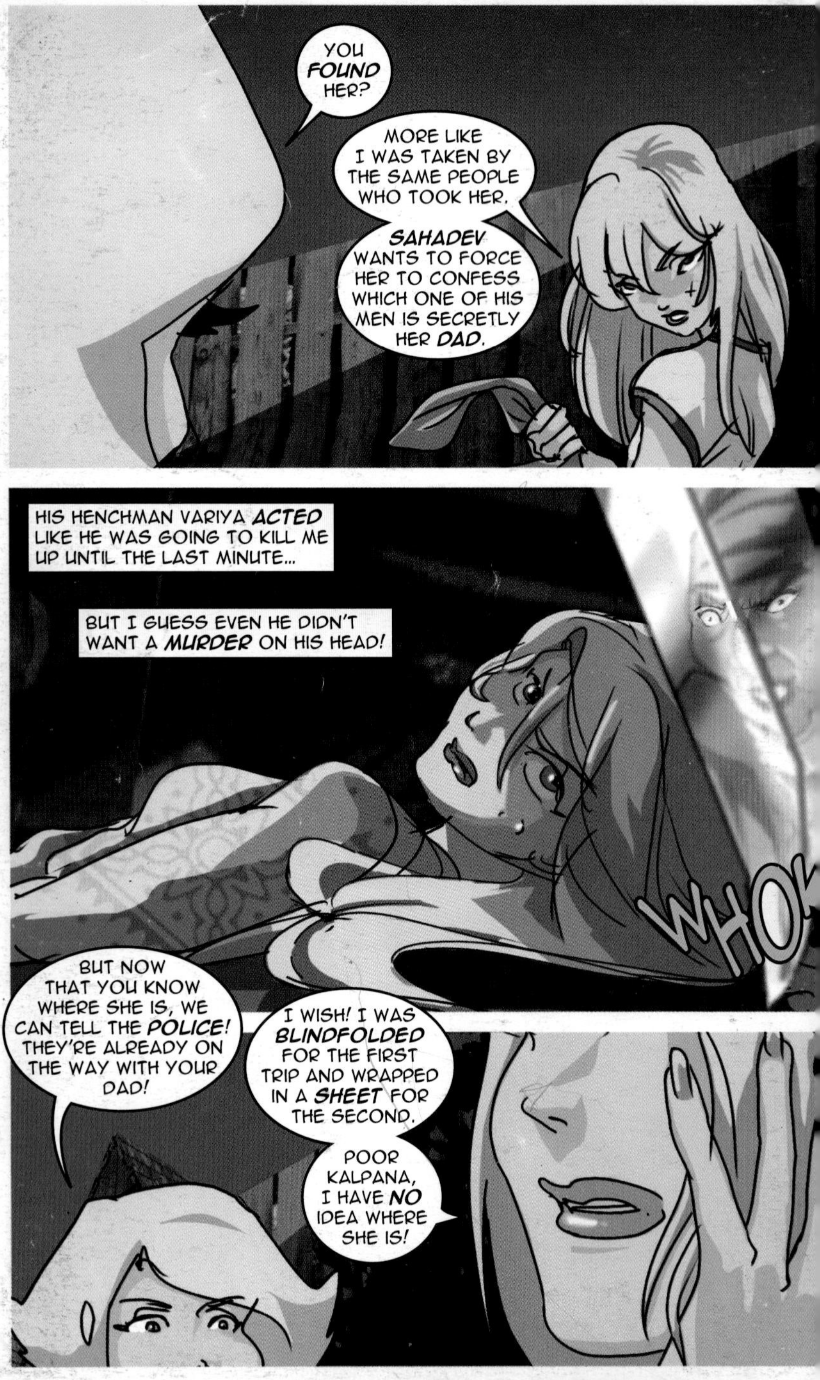

YOU FOUND HER?
MORE LIKE I WAS TAKEN BY THE SAME PEOPLE WHO TOOK HER.
SAHADEV WANTS TO FORCE HER TO CONFESS WHICH ONE OF HIS MEN IS SECRETLY HER DAD.
HIS HENCHMAN VARIYA ACTED LIKE HE WAS GOING TO KILL ME UP UNTIL THE LAST MINUTE...
BUT I GUESS EVEN HE DIDN'T WANT A MURDER ON HIS HEAD!
WHOK
BUT NOW THAT YOU KNOW WHERE SHE IS, WE CAN TELL THE POLICE! THEY'RE ALREADY ON THE WAY WITH YOUR DAD!
I WISH! I WAS BLINDFOLDED FOR THE FIRST TRIP AND WRAPPED IN A SHEET FOR THE SECOND.
POOR KALPANA, I HAVE NO IDEA WHERE SHE IS!

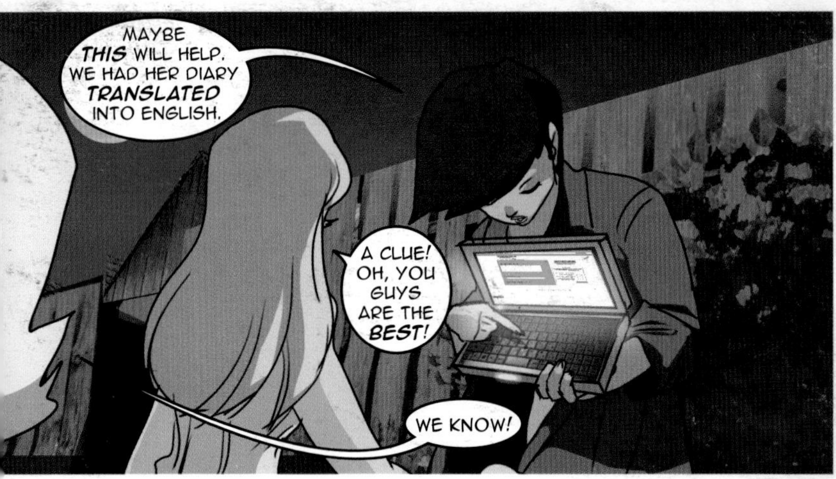
MAYBE **THIS** WILL HELP. WE HAD HER DIARY **TRANSLATED** INTO ENGLISH.
A CLUE! OH, YOU GUYS ARE THE **BEST**!
WE KNOW!

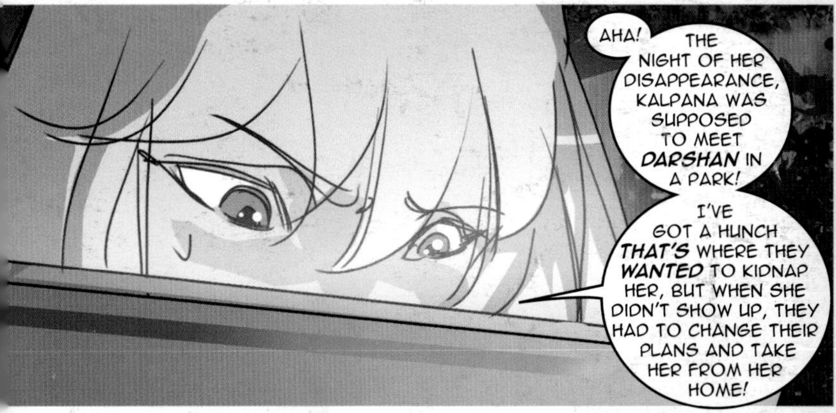
AHA!
THE NIGHT OF HER DISAPPEARANCE, KALPANA WAS SUPPOSED TO MEET **DARSHAN** IN A PARK!
I'VE GOT A HUNCH **THAT'S** WHERE THEY **WANTED** TO KIDNAP HER, BUT WHEN SHE DIDN'T SHOW UP, THEY HAD TO CHANGE THEIR PLANS AND TAKE HER FROM HER HOME!

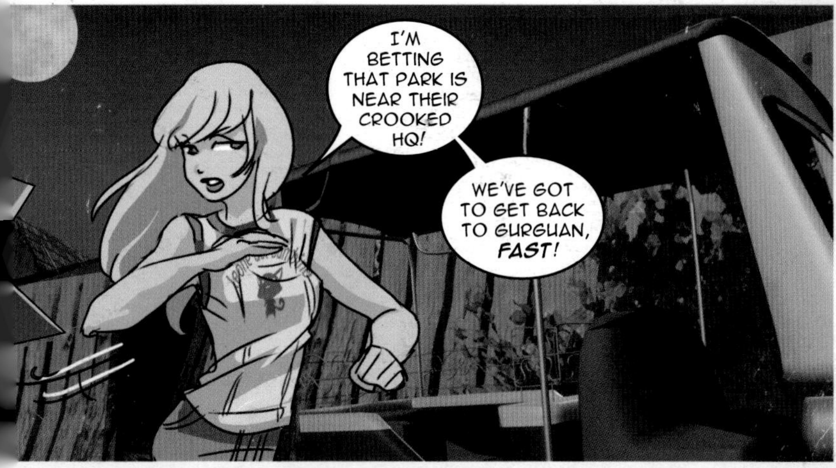
I'M BETTING THAT PARK IS NEAR THEIR CROOKED HQ!
WE'VE GOT TO GET BACK TO GURGUAN, **FAST**!

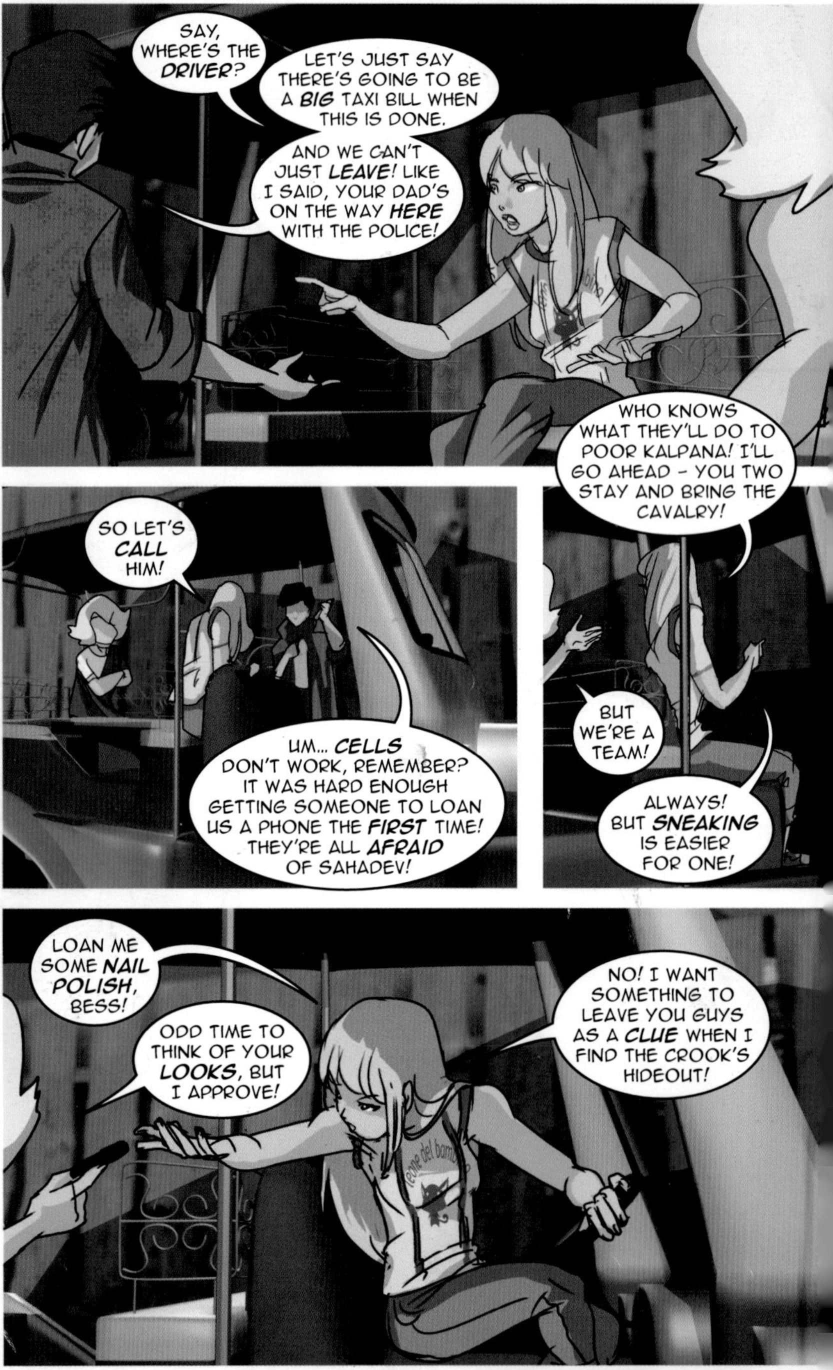
SAY, WHERE'S THE DRIVER?
LET'S JUST SAY THERE'S GOING TO BE A BIG TAXI BILL WHEN THIS IS DONE.
AND WE CAN'T JUST LEAVE! LIKE I SAID, YOUR DAD'S ON THE WAY HERE WITH THE POLICE!
SO LET'S CALL HIM!
UM... CELLS DON'T WORK, REMEMBER? IT WAS HARD ENOUGH GETTING SOMEONE TO LOAN US A PHONE THE FIRST TIME! THEY'RE ALL AFRAID OF SAHADEV!
WHO KNOWS WHAT THEY'LL DO TO POOR KALPANA! I'LL GO AHEAD - YOU TWO STAY AND BRING THE CAVALRY!
BUT WE'RE A TEAM!
ALWAYS! BUT SNEAKING IS EASIER FOR ONE!
LOAN ME SOME NAIL POLISH, BESS!
ODD TIME TO THINK OF YOUR LOOKS, BUT I APPROVE!
NO! I WANT SOMETHING TO LEAVE YOU GUYS AS A CLUE WHEN I FIND THE CROOK'S HIDEOUT!

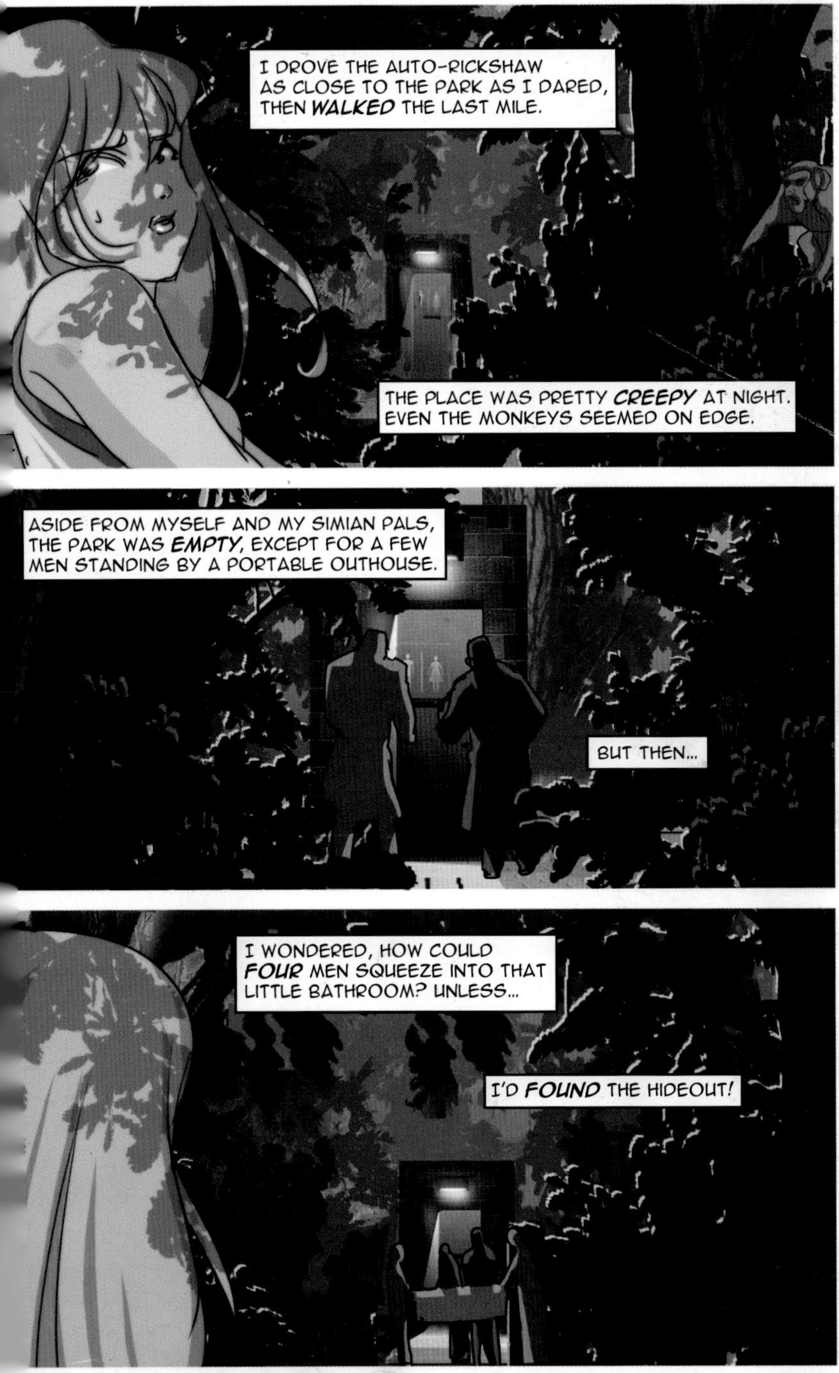
I DROVE THE AUTO-RICKSHAW AS CLOSE TO THE PARK AS I DARED, THEN WALKED THE LAST MILE.
THE PLACE WAS PRETTY CREEPY AT NIGHT. EVEN THE MONKEYS SEEMED ON EDGE.
ASIDE FROM MYSELF AND MY SIMIAN PALS, THE PARK WAS EMPTY, EXCEPT FOR A FEW MEN STANDING BY A PORTABLE OUTHOUSE.
BUT THEN...
I WONDERED, HOW COULD FOUR MEN SQUEEZE INTO THAT LITTLE BATHROOM? UNLESS...
I'D FOUND THE HIDEOUT!

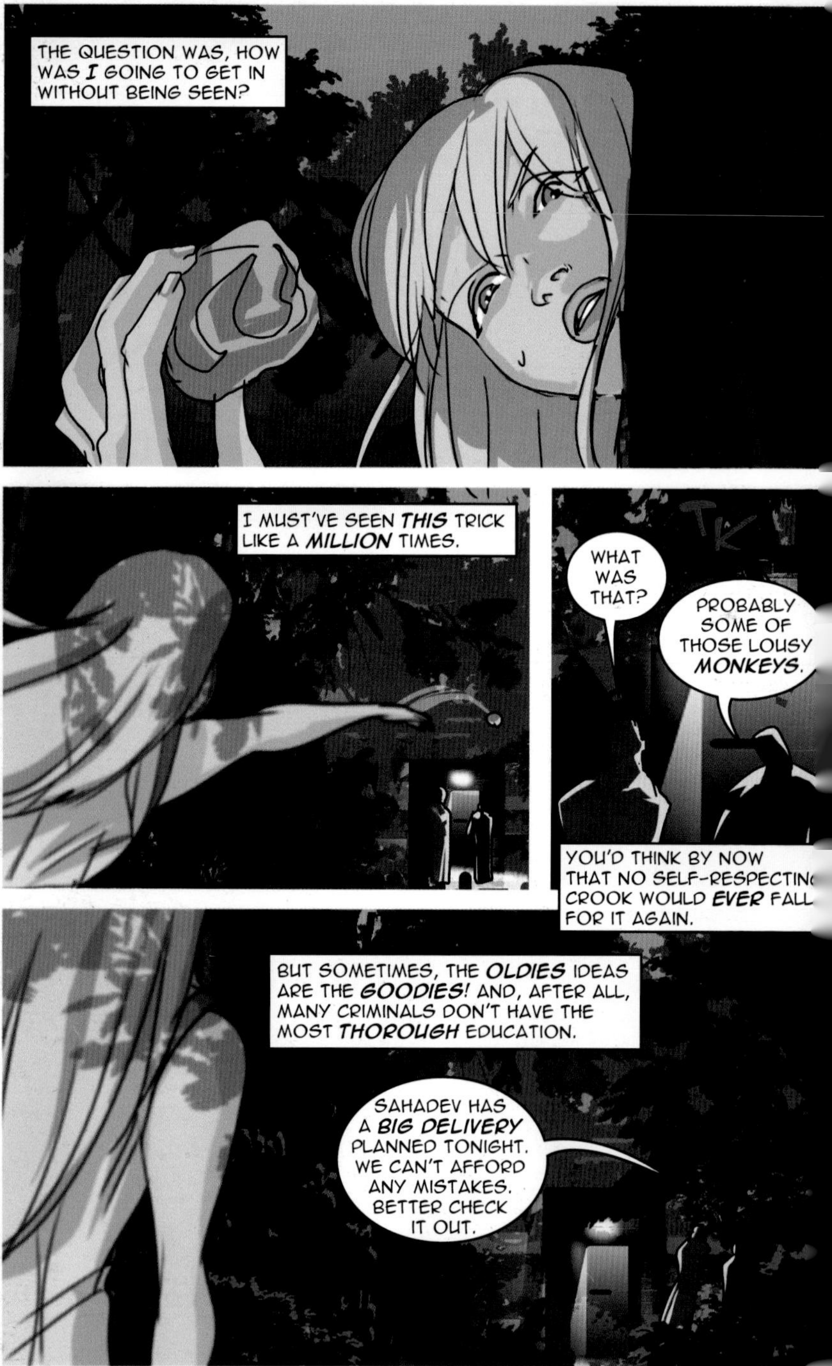
THE QUESTION WAS, HOW WAS *I* GOING TO GET IN WITHOUT BEING SEEN?
I MUST'VE SEEN ***THIS*** TRICK LIKE A ***MILLION*** TIMES.
TK
WHAT WAS THAT?
PROBABLY SOME OF THOSE LOUSY ***MONKEYS***.
YOU'D THINK BY NOW THAT NO SELF-RESPECTIN
CROOK WOULD ***EVER*** FALL
FOR IT AGAIN.
BUT SOMETIMES, THE ***OLDIES*** IDEAS ARE THE ***GOODIES***! AND, AFTER ALL, MANY CRIMINALS DON'T HAVE THE MOST ***THOROUGH*** EDUCATION.
SAHADEV HAS A ***BIG DELIVERY*** PLANNED TONIGHT. WE CAN'T AFFORD ANY MISTAKES. BETTER CHECK IT OUT.

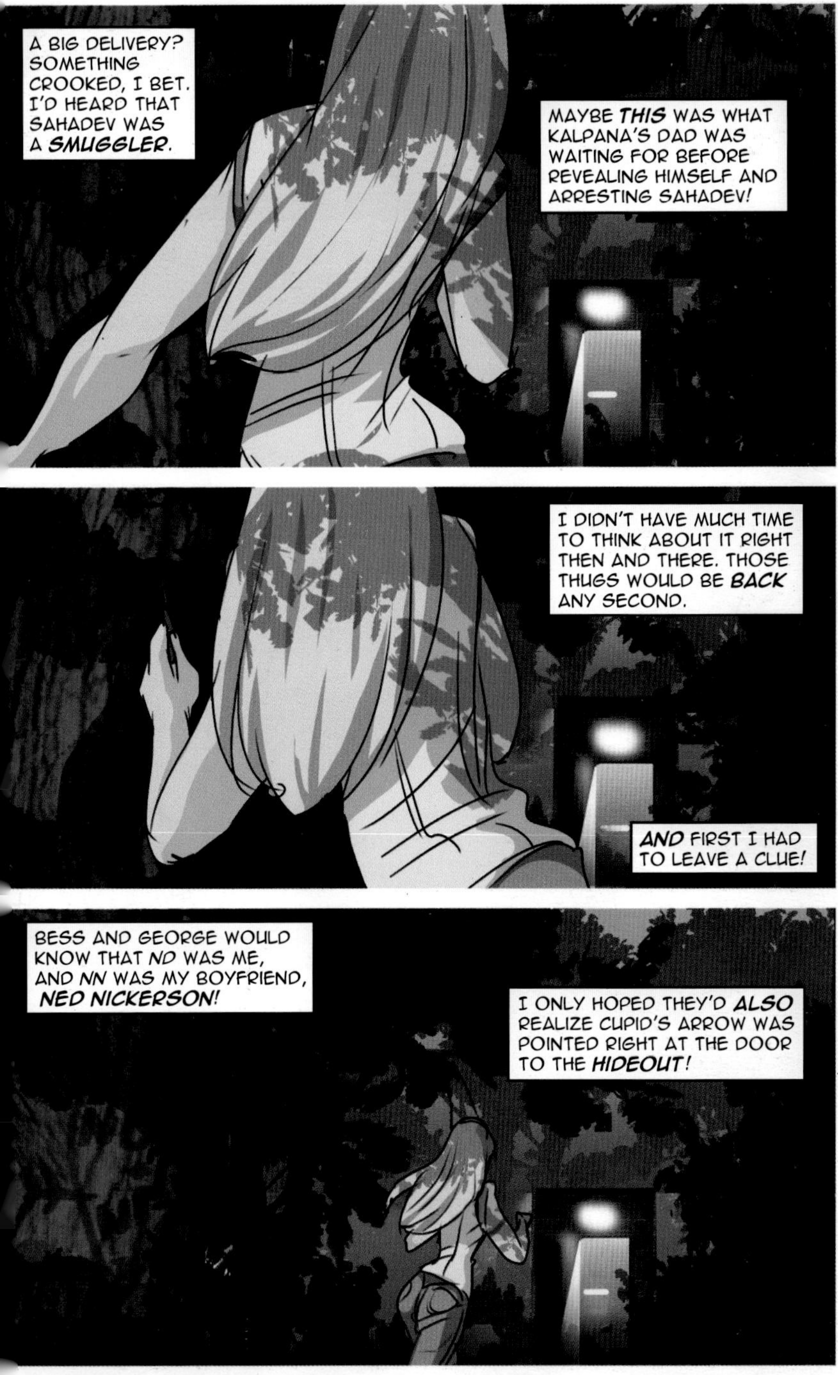
A BIG DELIVERY? SOMETHING CROOKED, I BET. I'D HEARD THAT SAHADEV WAS A SMUGGLER.
MAYBE THIS WAS WHAT KALPANA'S DAD WAS WAITING FOR BEFORE REVEALING HIMSELF AND ARRESTING SAHADEV!
I DIDN'T HAVE MUCH TIME TO THINK ABOUT IT RIGHT THEN AND THERE. THOSE THUGS WOULD BE BACK ANY SECOND.
AND FIRST I HAD TO LEAVE A CLUE!
BESS AND GEORGE WOULD KNOW THAT ND WAS ME, AND NN WAS MY BOYFRIEND, NED NICKERSON!
I ONLY HOPED THEY'D ALSO REALIZE CUPID'S ARROW WAS POINTED RIGHT AT THE DOOR TO THE HIDEOUT!

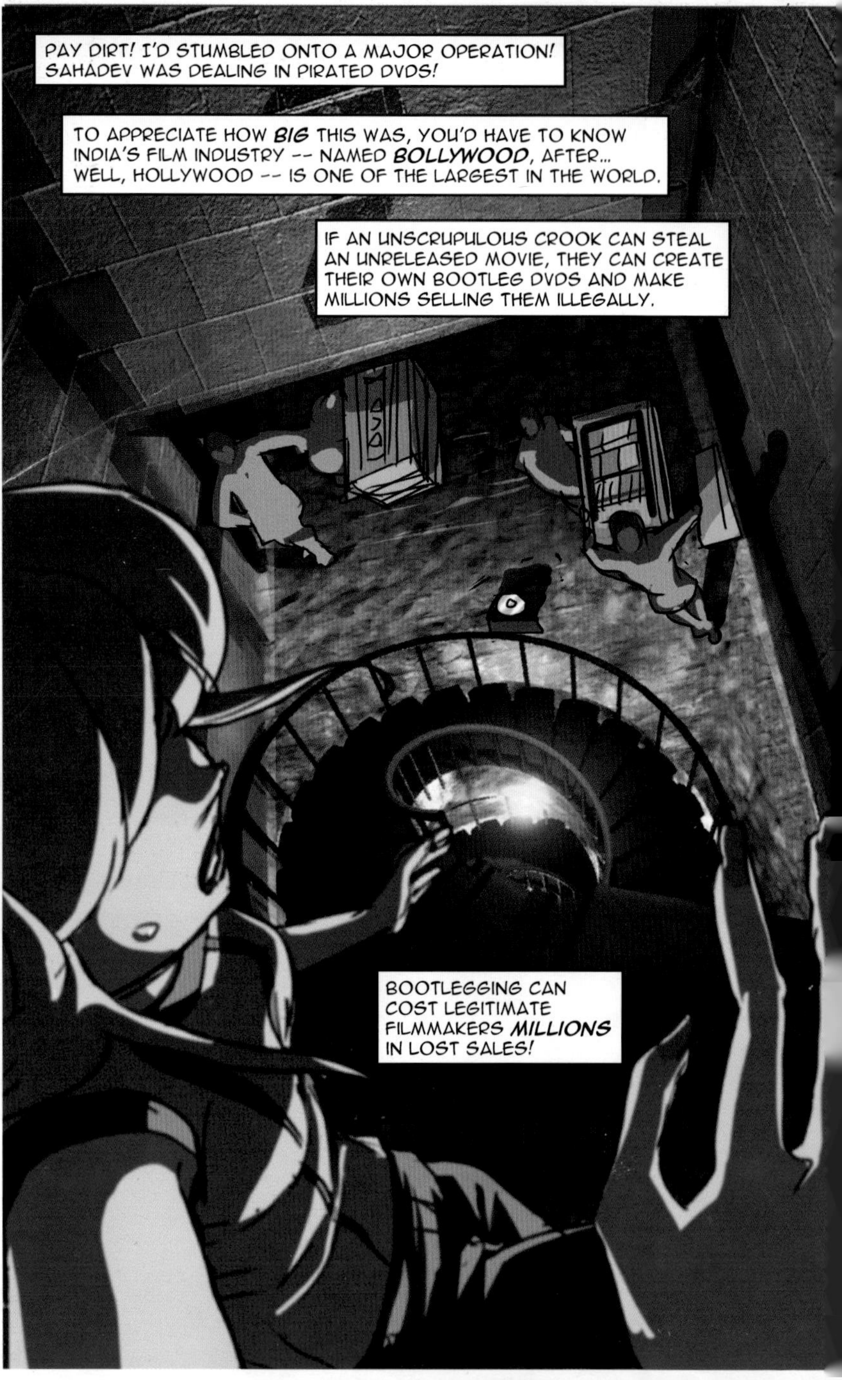
PAY DIRT! I'D STUMBLED ONTO A MAJOR OPERATION! SAHADEV WAS DEALING IN PIRATED DVDS!
TO APPRECIATE HOW BIG THIS WAS, YOU'D HAVE TO KNOW INDIA'S FILM INDUSTRY -- NAMED BOLLYWOOD, AFTER... WELL, HOLLYWOOD -- IS ONE OF THE LARGEST IN THE WORLD.
IF AN UNSCRUPULOUS CROOK CAN STEAL AN UNRELEASED MOVIE, THEY CAN CREATE THEIR OWN BOOTLEG DVDS AND MAKE MILLIONS SELLING THEM ILLEGALLY.
BOOTLEGGING CAN COST LEGITIMATE FILMMAKERS MILLIONS IN LOST SALES!

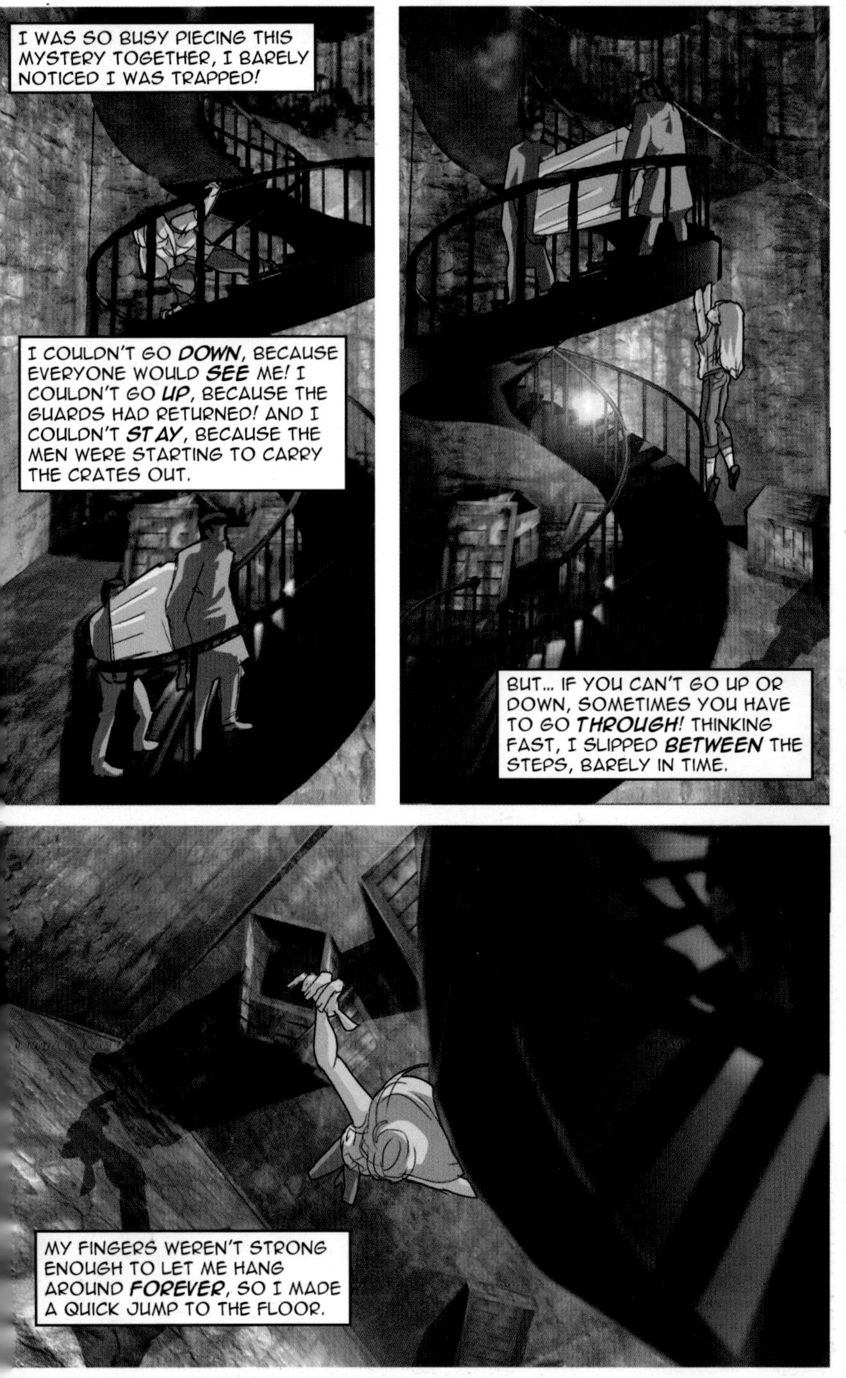
I WAS SO BUSY PIECING THIS MYSTERY TOGETHER, I BARELY NOTICED I WAS TRAPPED!
I COULDN'T GO DOWN, BECAUSE EVERYONE WOULD SEE ME! I COULDN'T GO UP, BECAUSE THE GUARDS HAD RETURNED! AND I COULDN'T STAY, BECAUSE THE MEN WERE STARTING TO CARRY THE CRATES OUT.
BUT... IF YOU CAN'T GO UP OR DOWN, SOMETIMES YOU HAVE TO GO THROUGH! THINKING FAST, I SLIPPED BETWEEN THE STEPS, BARELY IN TIME.
MY FINGERS WEREN'T STRONG ENOUGH TO LET ME HANG AROUND FOREVER, SO I MADE A QUICK JUMP TO THE FLOOR.

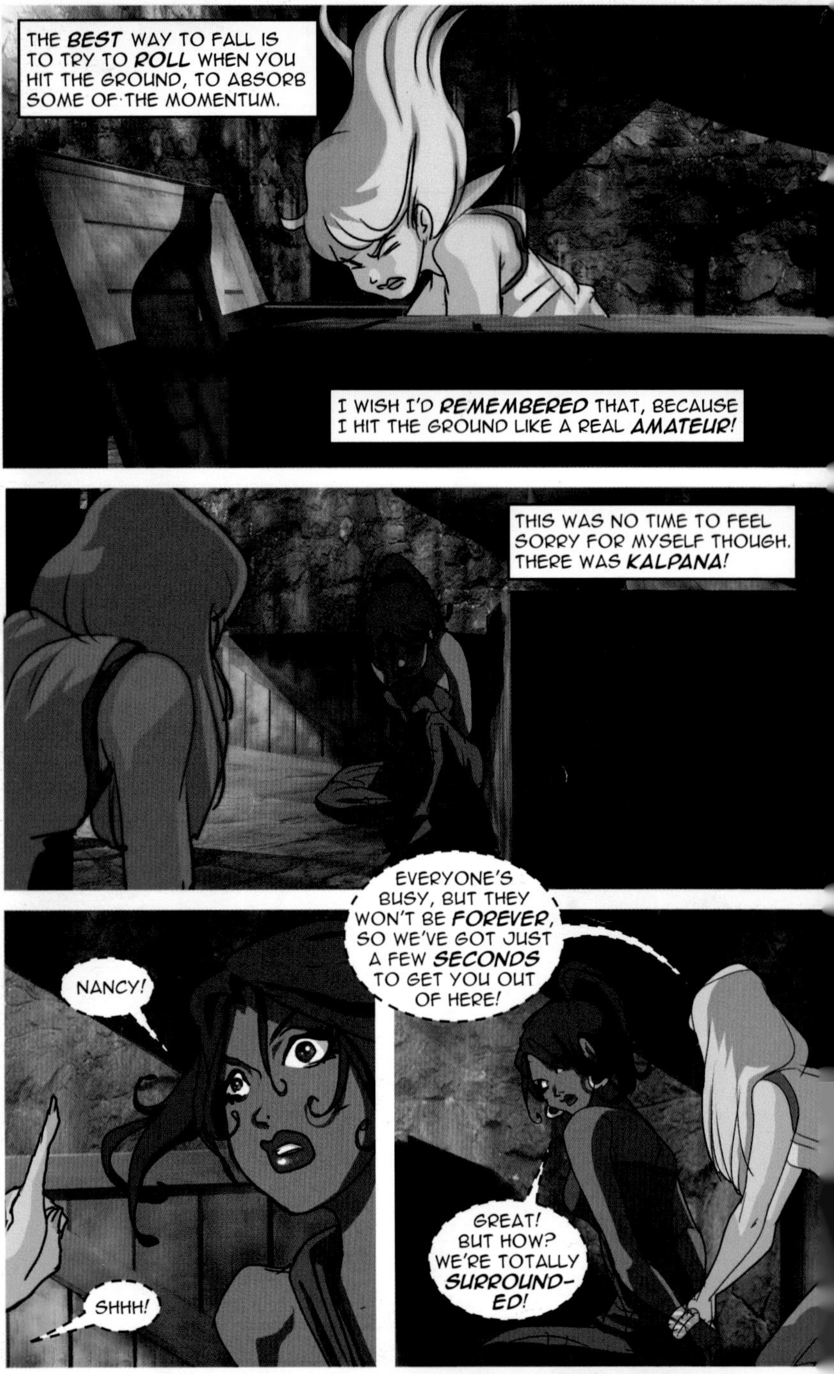
THE BEST WAY TO FALL IS TO TRY TO ROLL WHEN YOU HIT THE GROUND, TO ABSORB SOME OF THE MOMENTUM.
I WISH I'D REMEMBERED THAT, BECAUSE I HIT THE GROUND LIKE A REAL AMATEUR!
THIS WAS NO TIME TO FEEL SORRY FOR MYSELF THOUGH. THERE WAS KALPANA!
NANCY!
SHHH!
EVERYONE'S BUSY, BUT THEY WON'T BE FOREVER, SO WE'VE GOT JUST A FEW SECONDS TO GET YOU OUT OF HERE!
GREAT! BUT HOW? WE'RE TOTALLY SURROUND-ED!

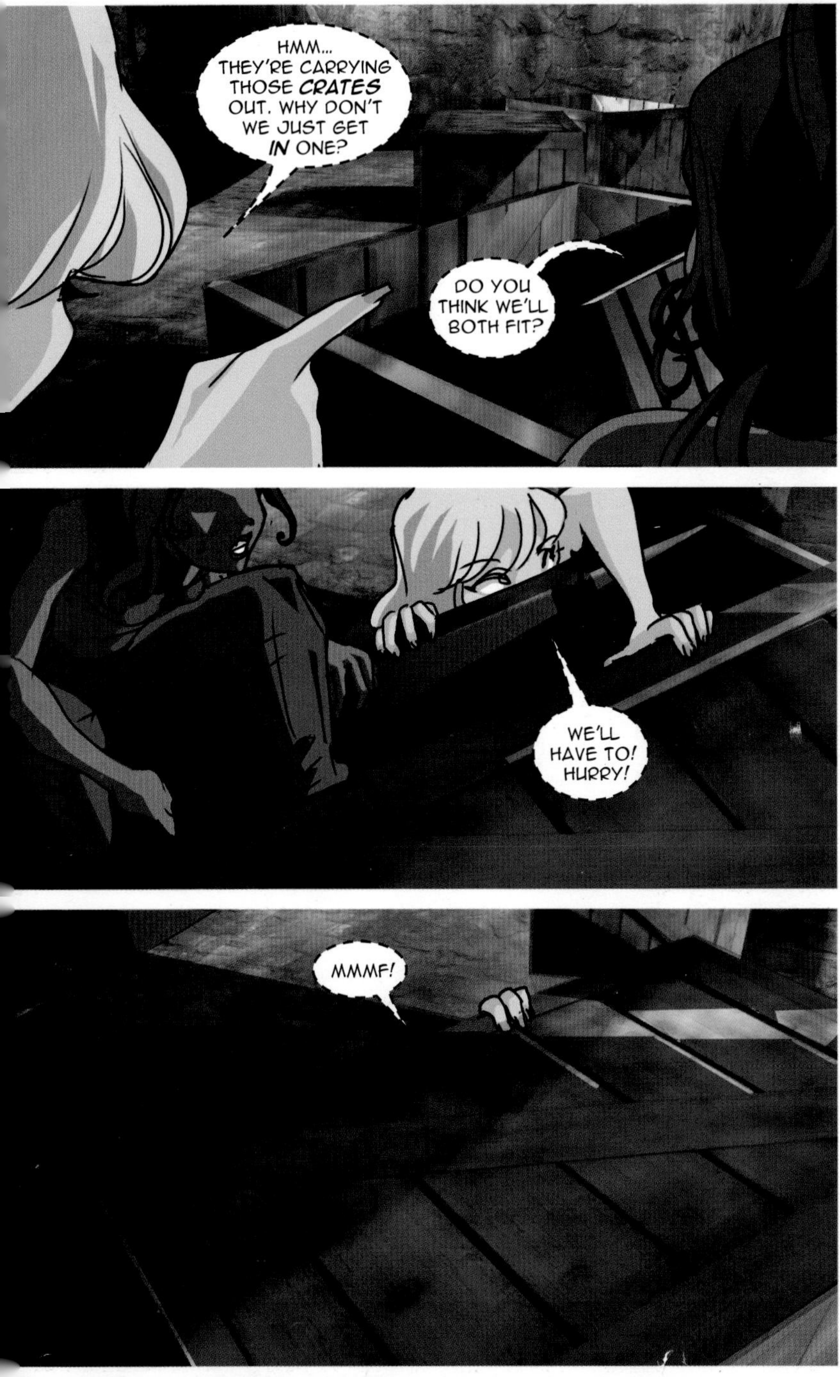
HMM... THEY'RE CARRYING THOSE CRATES OUT. WHY DON'T WE JUST GET IN ONE?
DO YOU THINK WE'LL BOTH FIT?
WE'LL HAVE TO! HURRY!
MMMF!

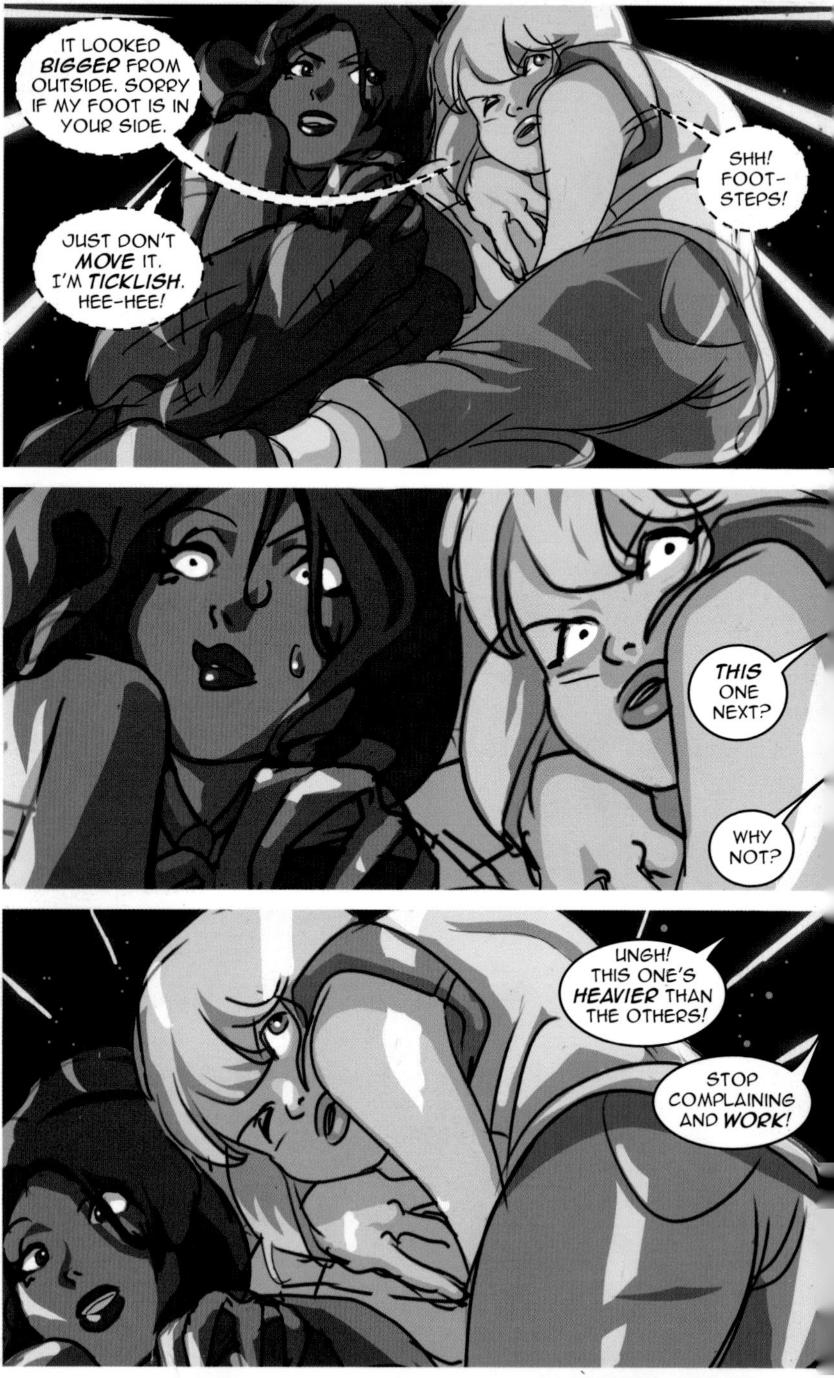
IT LOOKED BIGGER FROM OUTSIDE. SORRY IF MY FOOT IS IN YOUR SIDE.
JUST DON'T MOVE IT. I'M TICKLISH. HEE-HEE!
SHH! FOOT-STEPS!
THIS ONE NEXT?
WHY NOT?
UNGH! THIS ONE'S HEAVIER THAN THE OTHERS!
STOP COMPLAINING AND WORK!

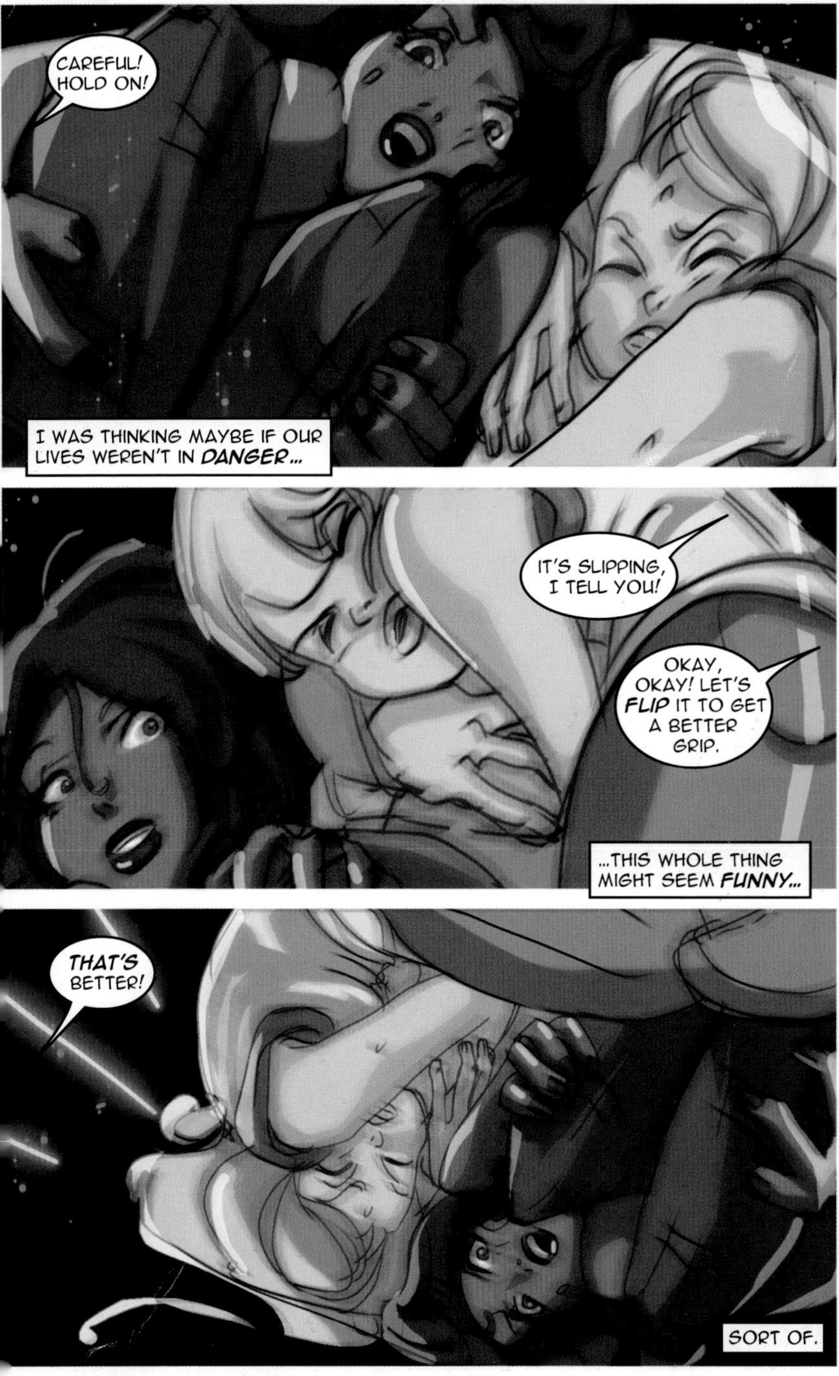
CAREFUL! HOLD ON!
I WAS THINKING MAYBE IF OUR LIVES WEREN'T IN DANGER...
IT'S SLIPPING, I TELL YOU!
OKAY, OKAY! LET'S FLIP IT TO GET A BETTER GRIP.
...THIS WHOLE THING MIGHT SEEM FUNNY...
THAT'S BETTER!
SORT OF.

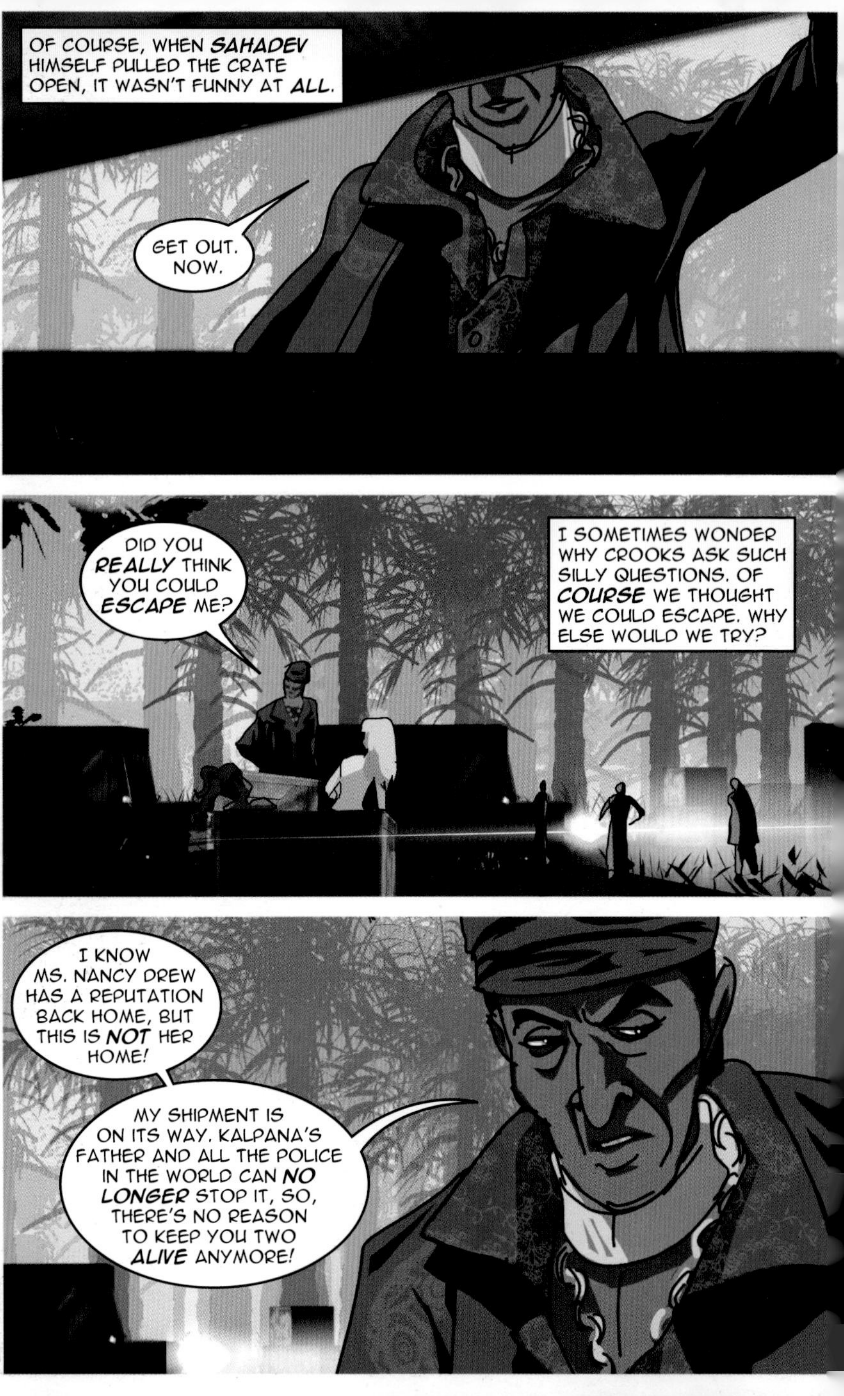

OF COURSE, WHEN SAHADEV HIMSELF PULLED THE CRATE OPEN, IT WASN'T FUNNY AT ALL.
GET OUT. NOW.
DID YOU REALLY THINK YOU COULD ESCAPE ME?
I SOMETIMES WONDER WHY CROOKS ASK SUCH SILLY QUESTIONS. OF COURSE WE THOUGHT WE COULD ESCAPE. WHY ELSE WOULD WE TRY?
I KNOW MS. NANCY DREW HAS A REPUTATION BACK HOME, BUT THIS IS NOT HER HOME!
MY SHIPMENT IS ON ITS WAY. KALPANA'S FATHER AND ALL THE POLICE IN THE WORLD CAN NO LONGER STOP IT, SO, THERE'S NO REASON TO KEEP YOU TWO ALIVE ANYMORE!

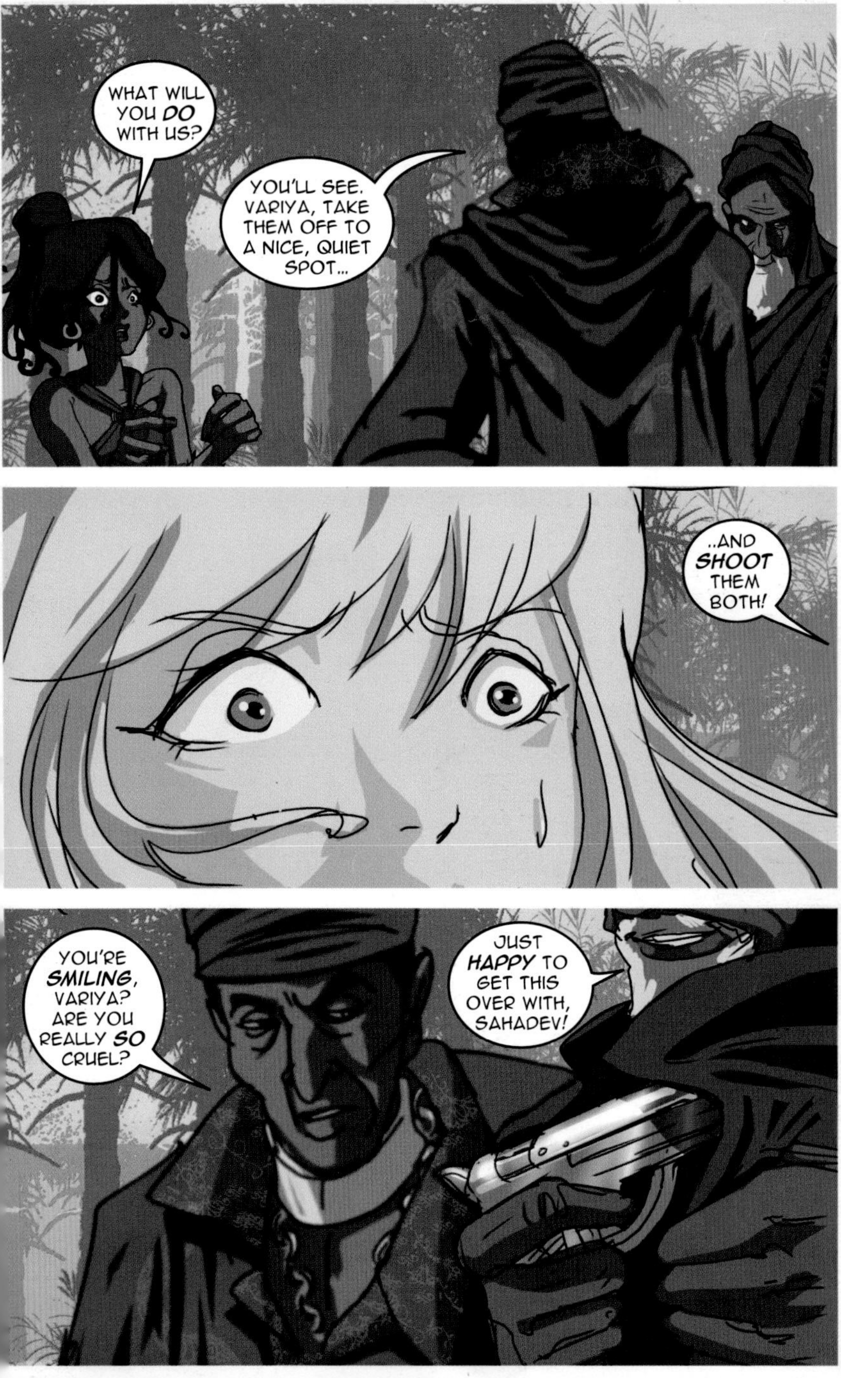
WHAT WILL YOU DO WITH US?
YOU'LL SEE. VARIYA, TAKE THEM OFF TO A NICE, QUIET SPOT...
..AND SHOOT THEM BOTH!
YOU'RE SMILING, VARIYA? ARE YOU REALLY SO CRUEL?
JUST HAPPY TO GET THIS OVER WITH, SAHADEV!

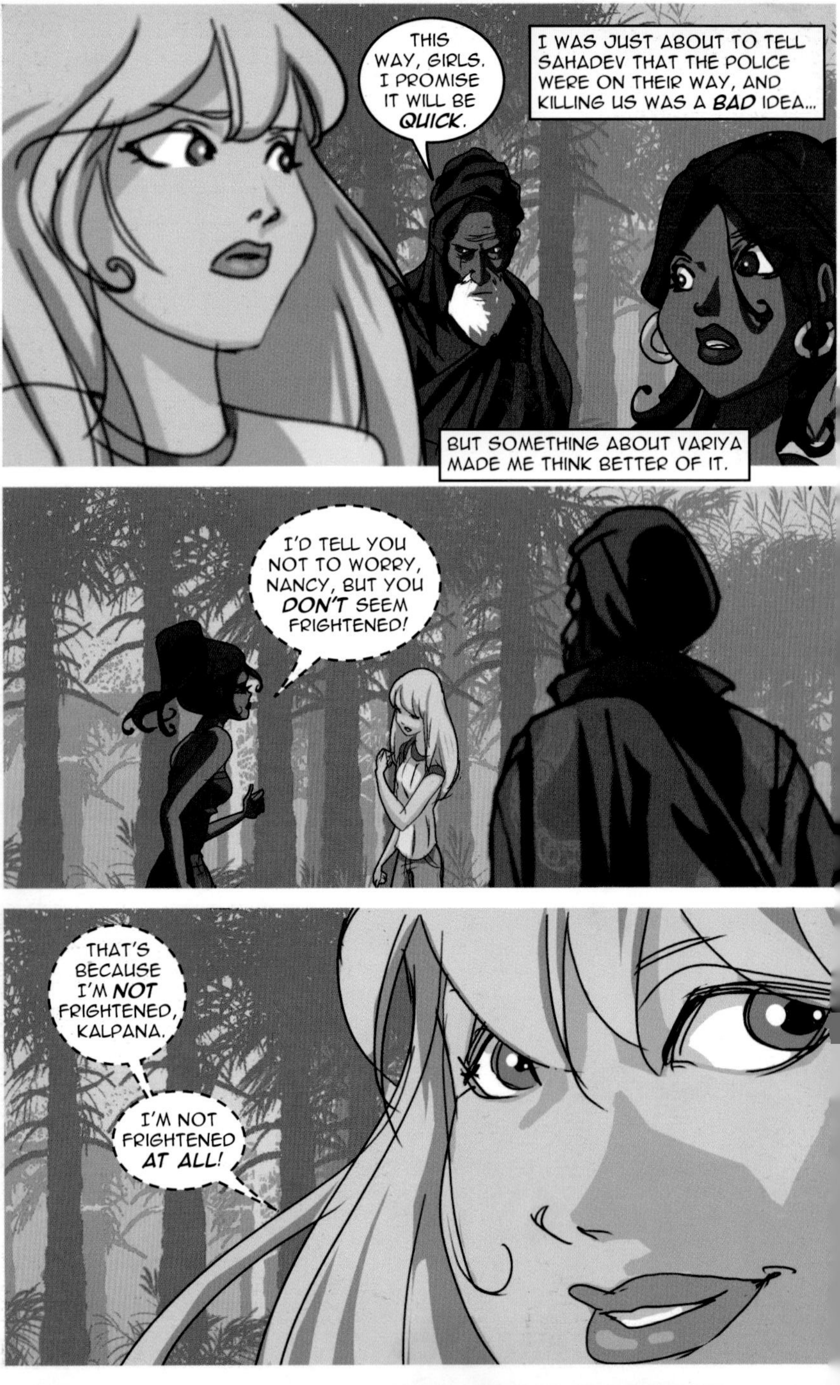
THIS WAY, GIRLS. I PROMISE IT WILL BE QUICK.
I WAS JUST ABOUT TO TELL SAHADEV THAT THE POLICE WERE ON THEIR WAY, AND KILLING US WAS A BAD IDEA...
BUT SOMETHING ABOUT VARIYA MADE ME THINK BETTER OF IT.
I'D TELL YOU NOT TO WORRY, NANCY, BUT YOU DON'T SEEM FRIGHTENED!
THAT'S BECAUSE I'M NOT FRIGHTENED, KALPANA.
I'M NOT FRIGHTENED AT ALL!

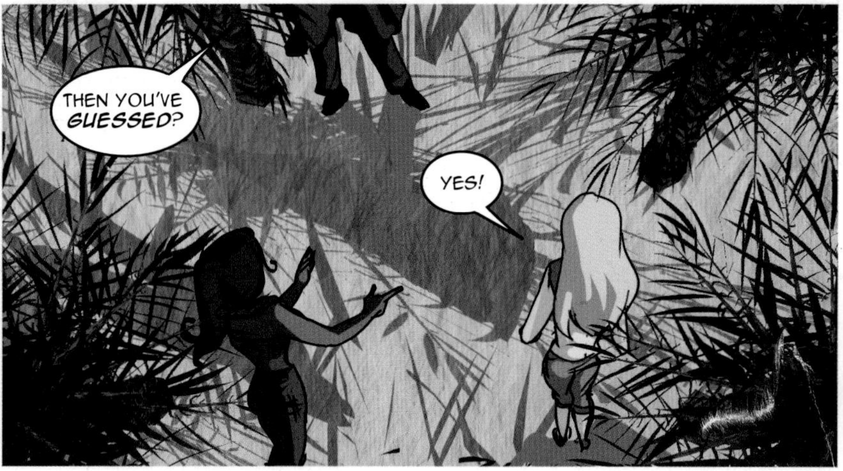
THEN YOU'VE *GUESSED*?
YES!

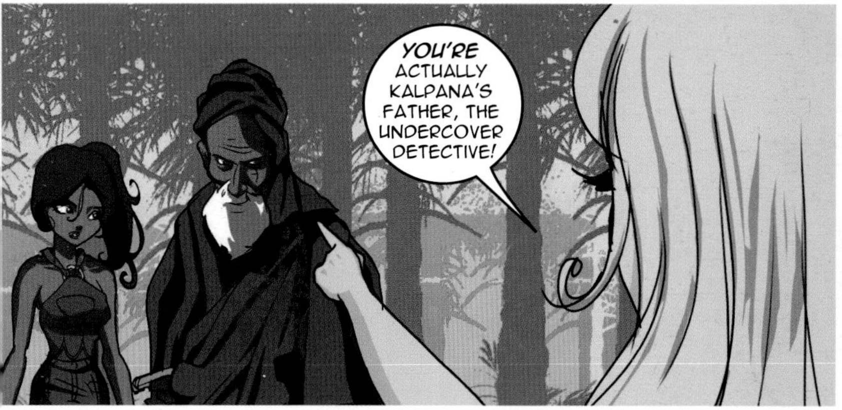
YOU'RE ACTUALLY KALPANA'S FATHER, THE UNDERCOVER DETECTIVE!

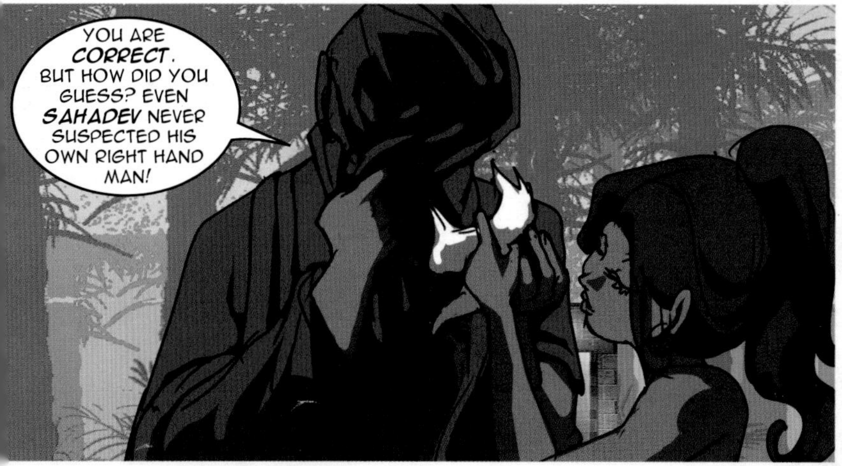
YOU ARE **CORRECT**. BUT HOW DID YOU GUESS? EVEN ***SAHADEV*** NEVER SUSPECTED HIS OWN RIGHT HAND MAN!

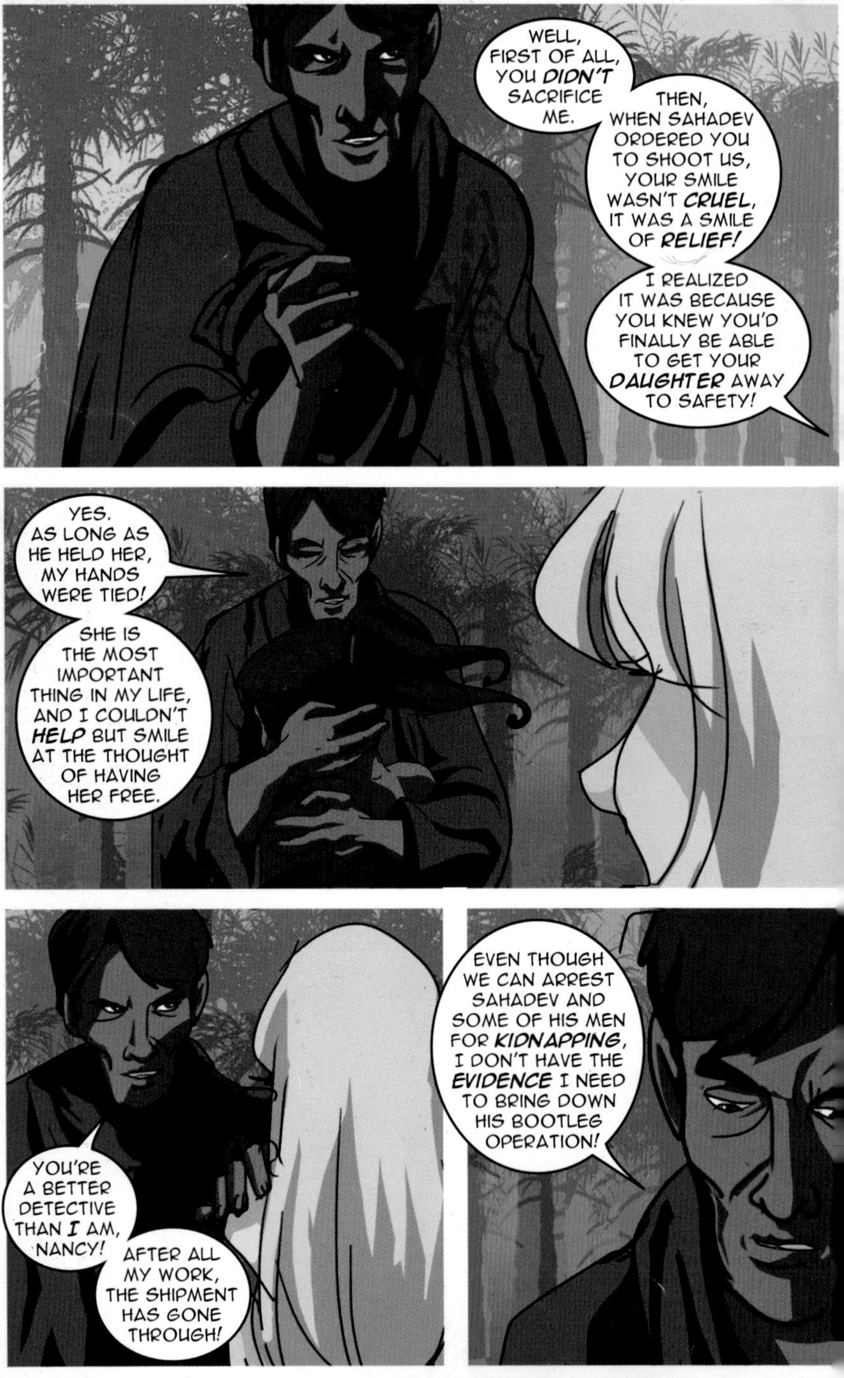
WELL, FIRST OF ALL, YOU DIDN'T SACRIFICE ME.
THEN, WHEN SAHADEV ORDERED YOU TO SHOOT US, YOUR SMILE WASN'T CRUEL, IT WAS A SMILE OF RELIEF!
I REALIZED IT WAS BECAUSE YOU KNEW YOU'D FINALLY BE ABLE TO GET YOUR DAUGHTER AWAY TO SAFETY!
YES. AS LONG AS HE HELD HER, MY HANDS WERE TIED!
SHE IS THE MOST IMPORTANT THING IN MY LIFE, AND I COULDN'T HELP BUT SMILE AT THE THOUGHT OF HAVING HER FREE.
YOU'RE A BETTER DETECTIVE THAN I AM, NANCY!
AFTER ALL MY WORK, THE SHIPMENT HAS GONE THROUGH!
EVEN THOUGH WE CAN ARREST SAHADEV AND SOME OF HIS MEN FOR KIDNAPPING, I DON'T HAVE THE EVIDENCE I NEED TO BRING DOWN HIS BOOTLEG OPERATION!

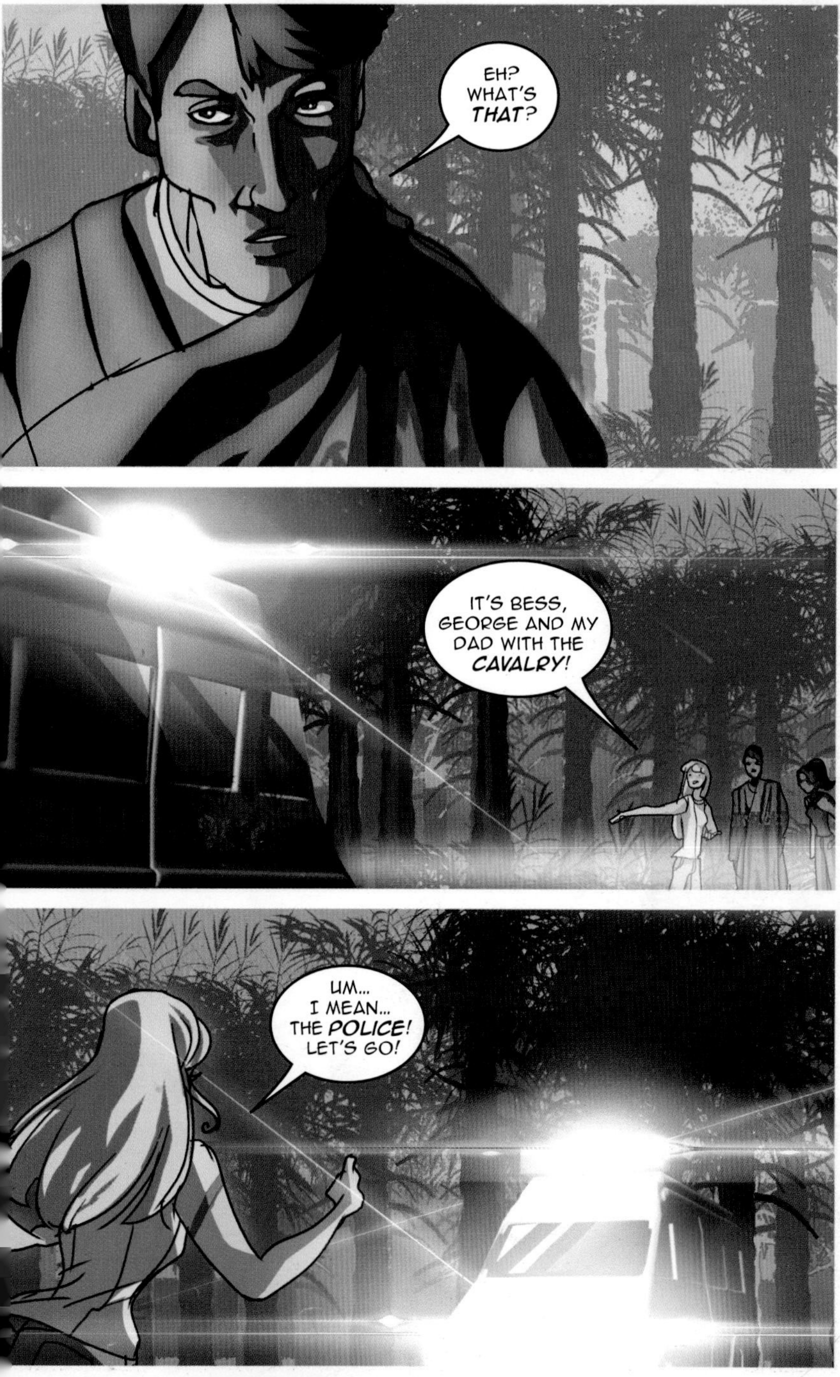
EH? WHAT'S *THAT*?
IT'S BESS, GEORGE AND MY DAD WITH THE *CAVALRY*!
UM... I MEAN... THE *POLICE*! LET'S GO!

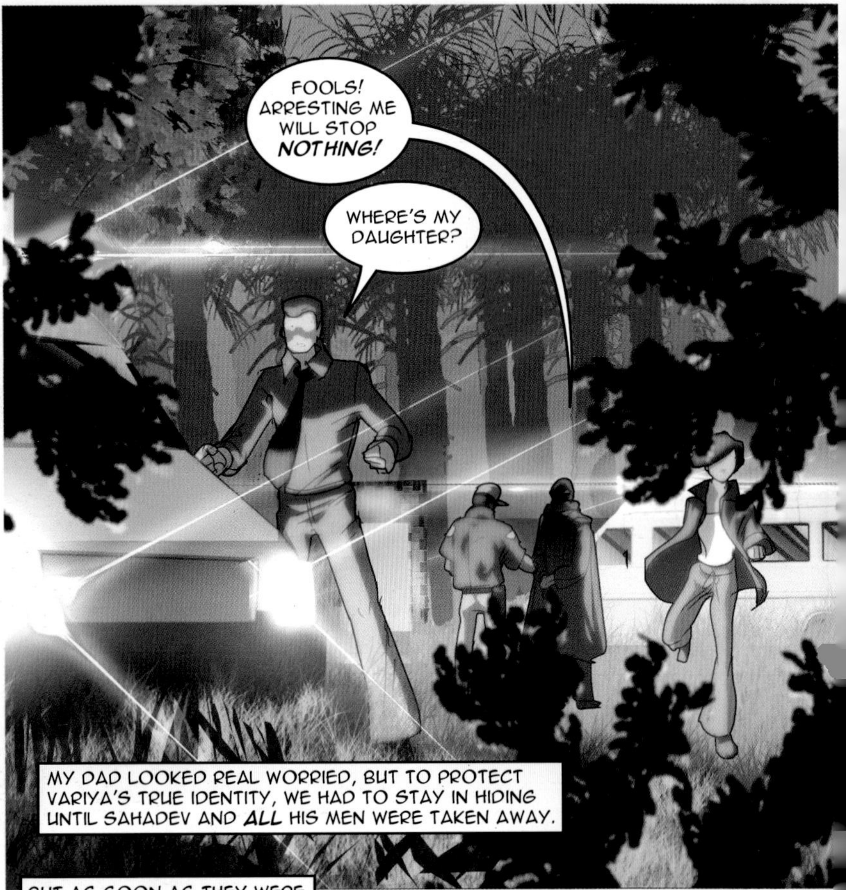
FOOLS! ARRESTING ME WILL STOP NOTHING!
WHERE'S MY DAUGHTER?
MY DAD LOOKED REAL WORRIED, BUT TO PROTECT VARIYA'S TRUE IDENTITY, WE HAD TO STAY IN HIDING UNTIL SAHADEV AND ALL HIS MEN WERE TAKEN AWAY.

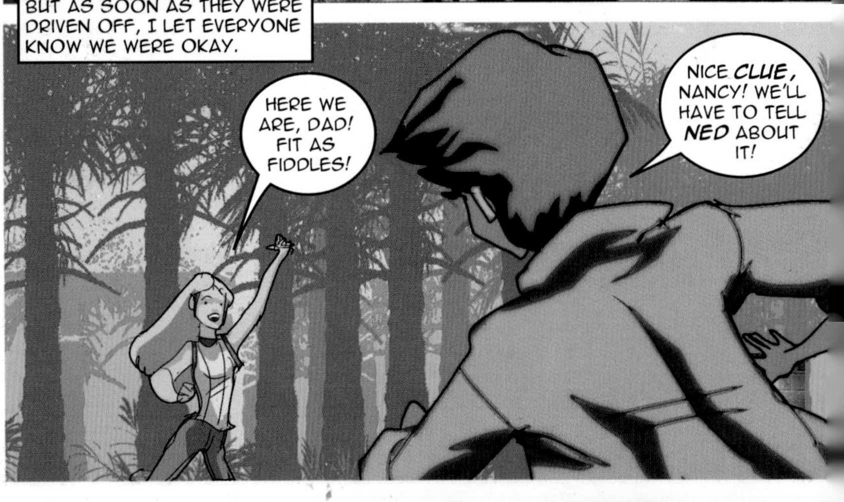
BUT AS SOON AS THEY WERE DRIVEN OFF, I LET EVERYONE KNOW WE WERE OKAY.
HERE WE ARE, DAD! FIT AS FIDDLES!
NICE CLUE, NANCY! WE'LL HAVE TO TELL NED ABOUT IT!

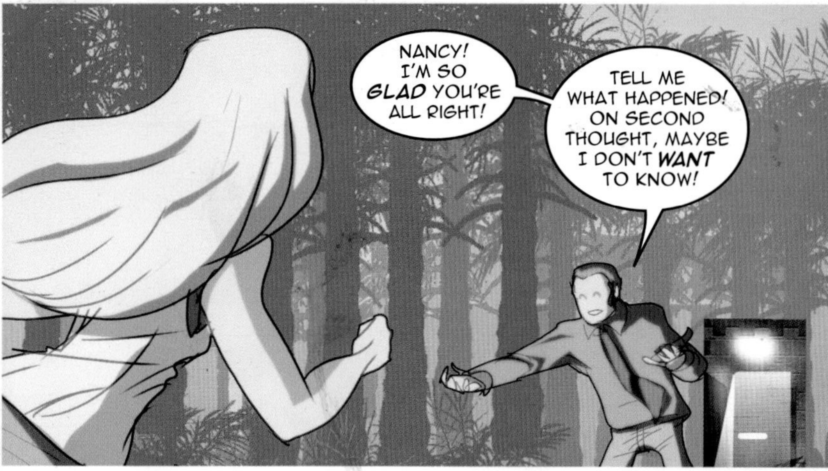
NANCY! I'M SO GLAD YOU'RE ALL RIGHT!
TELL ME WHAT HAPPENED! ON SECOND THOUGHT, MAYBE I DON'T WANT TO KNOW!

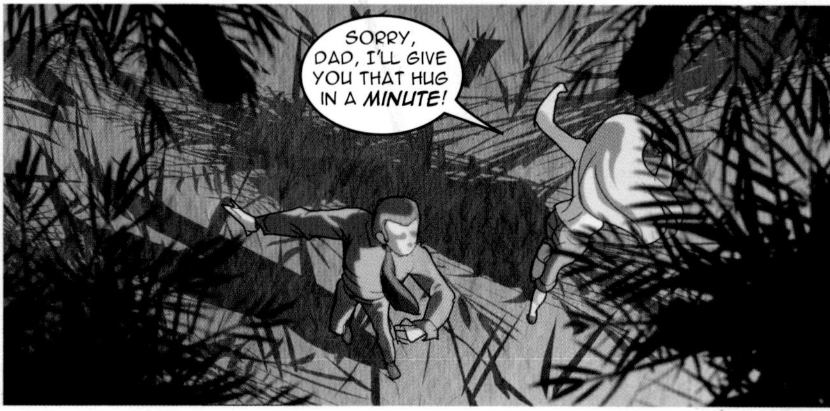
SORRY, DAD, I'LL GIVE YOU THAT HUG IN A MINUTE!

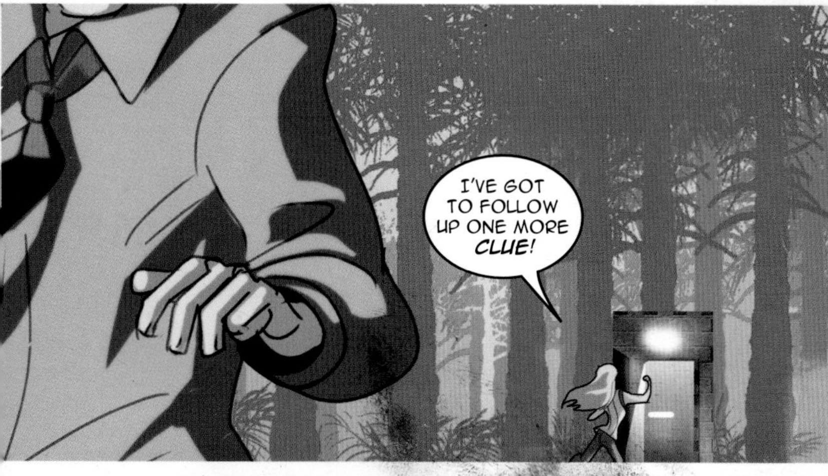
I'VE GOT TO FOLLOW UP ONE MORE CLUE!

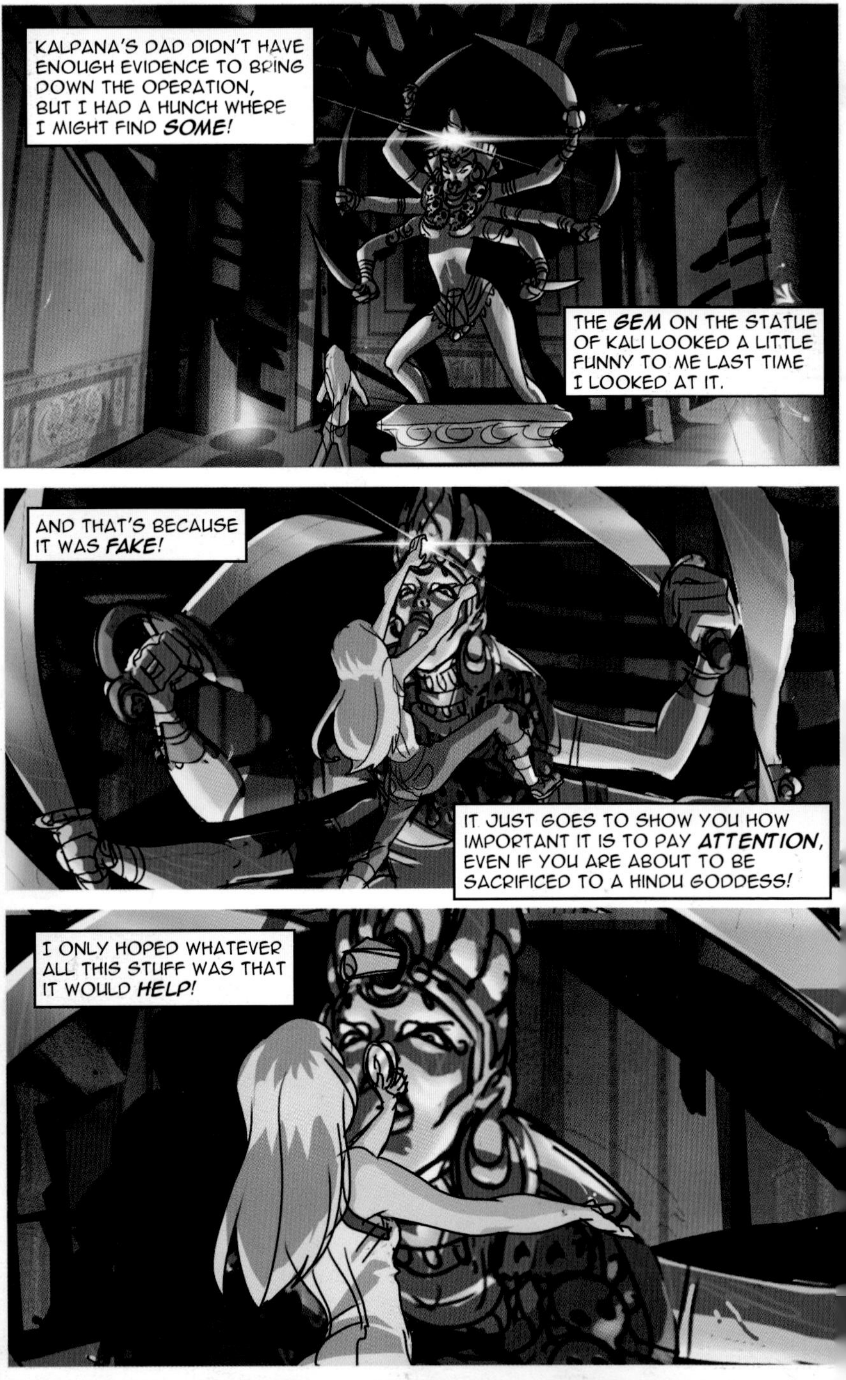
KALPANA'S DAD DIDN'T HAVE ENOUGH EVIDENCE TO BRING DOWN THE OPERATION, BUT I HAD A HUNCH WHERE I MIGHT FIND SOME!
THE GEM ON THE STATUE OF KALI LOOKED A LITTLE FUNNY TO ME LAST TIME I LOOKED AT IT.
AND THAT'S BECAUSE IT WAS FAKE!
IT JUST GOES TO SHOW YOU HOW IMPORTANT IT IS TO PAY ATTENTION, EVEN IF YOU ARE ABOUT TO BE SACRIFICED TO A HINDU GODDESS!
I ONLY HOPED WHATEVER ALL THIS STUFF WAS THAT IT WOULD HELP!

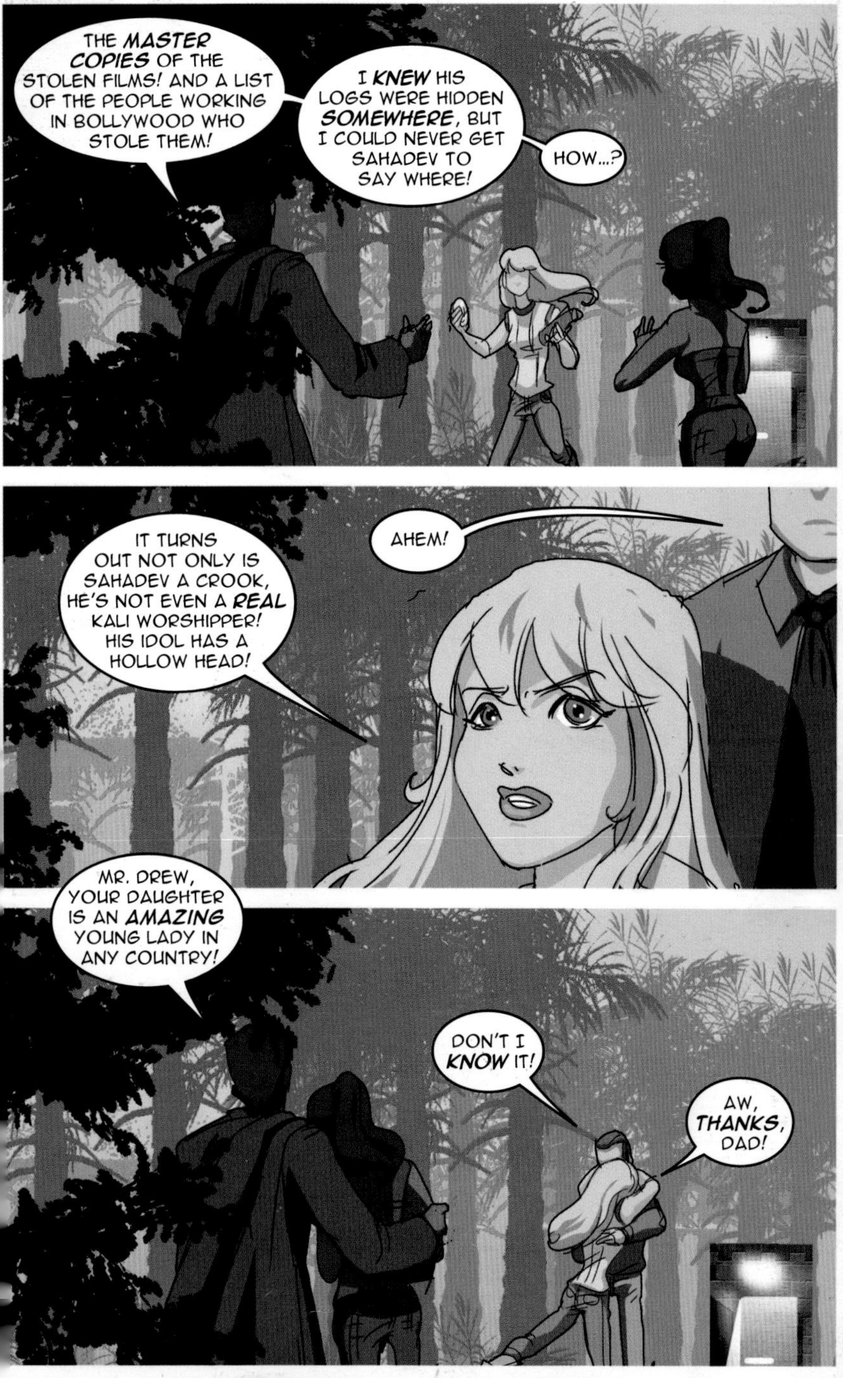
THE MASTER COPIES OF THE STOLEN FILMS! AND A LIST OF THE PEOPLE WORKING IN BOLLYWOOD WHO STOLE THEM!
I KNEW HIS LOGS WERE HIDDEN SOMEWHERE, BUT I COULD NEVER GET SAHADEV TO SAY WHERE!
HOW...?
IT TURNS OUT NOT ONLY IS SAHADEV A CROOK, HE'S NOT EVEN A REAL KALI WORSHIPPER! HIS IDOL HAS A HOLLOW HEAD!
AHEM!
MR. DREW, YOUR DAUGHTER IS AN AMAZING YOUNG LADY IN ANY COUNTRY!
DON'T I KNOW IT!
AW, THANKS, DAD!

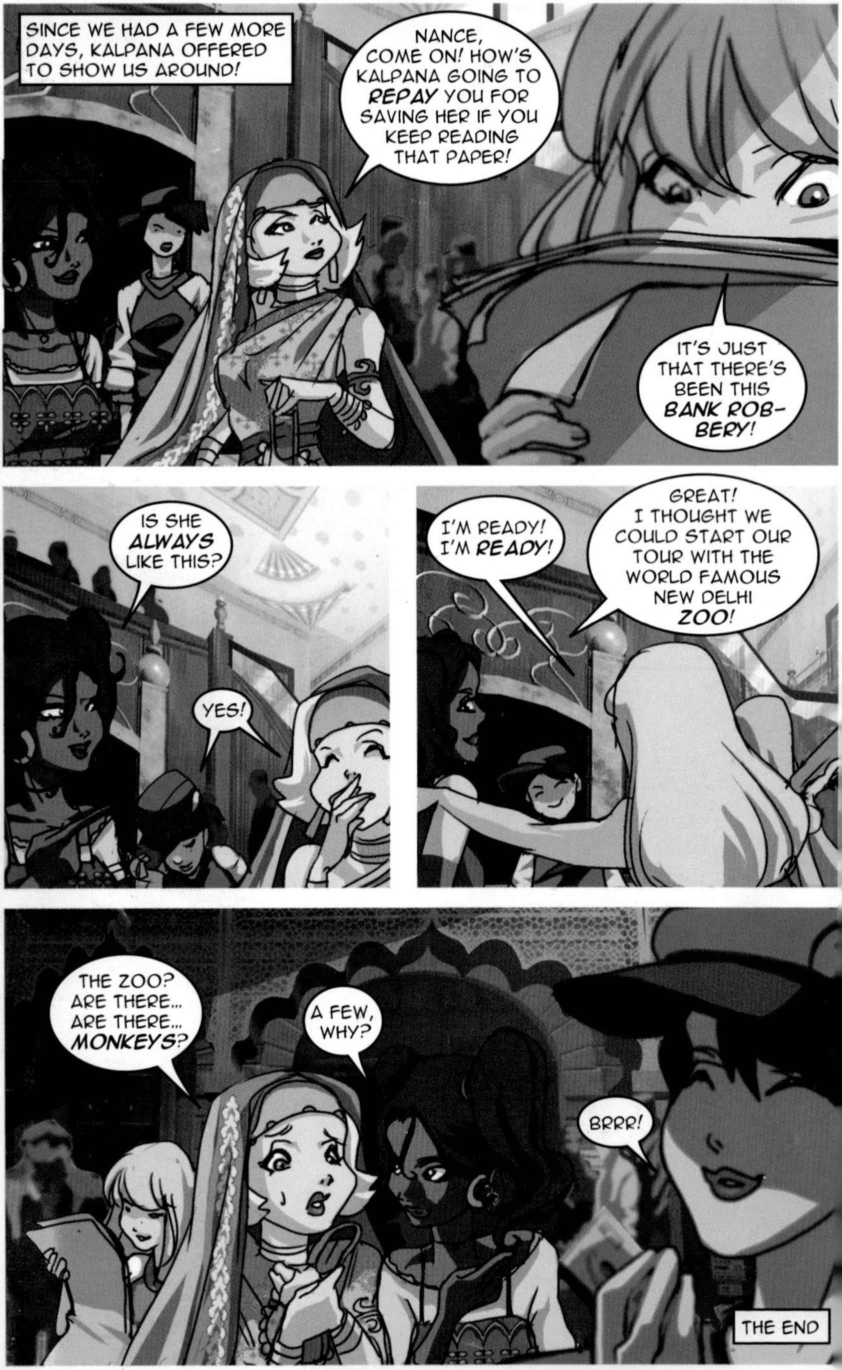
SINCE WE HAD A FEW MORE DAYS, KALPANA OFFERED TO SHOW US AROUND!
NANCE, COME ON! HOW'S KALPANA GOING TO REPAY YOU FOR SAVING HER IF YOU KEEP READING THAT PAPER!
IT'S JUST THAT THERE'S BEEN THIS BANK ROBBERY!
IS SHE ALWAYS LIKE THIS?
YES!
I'M READY! I'M READY!
GREAT! I THOUGHT WE COULD START OUR TOUR WITH THE WORLD FAMOUS NEW DELHI ZOO!
THE ZOO? ARE THERE... ARE THERE... MONKEYS?
A FEW, WHY?
BRRR!
THE END

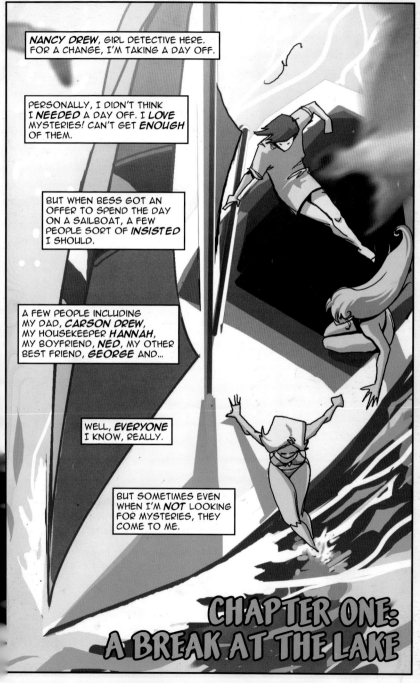

NANCY DREW, GIRL DETECTIVE HERE. FOR A CHANGE, I'M TAKING A DAY OFF.

PERSONALLY, I DIDN'T THINK I **NEEDED** A DAY OFF. I **LOVE** MYSTERIES! CAN'T GET **ENOUGH** OF THEM.

BUT WHEN BESS GOT AN OFFER TO SPEND THE DAY ON A SAILBOAT, A FEW PEOPLE SORT OF **INSISTED** I SHOULD.

A FEW PEOPLE INCLUDING MY DAD, **CARSON DREW**, MY HOUSEKEEPER **HANNAH**, MY BOYFRIEND, **NED**, MY OTHER BEST FRIEND, **GEORGE** AND...

WELL, **EVERYONE** I KNOW, REALLY.

BUT SOMETIMES EVEN WHEN I'M **NOT** LOOKING FOR MYSTERIES, THEY COME TO ME.

CHAPTER ONE:
A BREAK AT THE LAKE

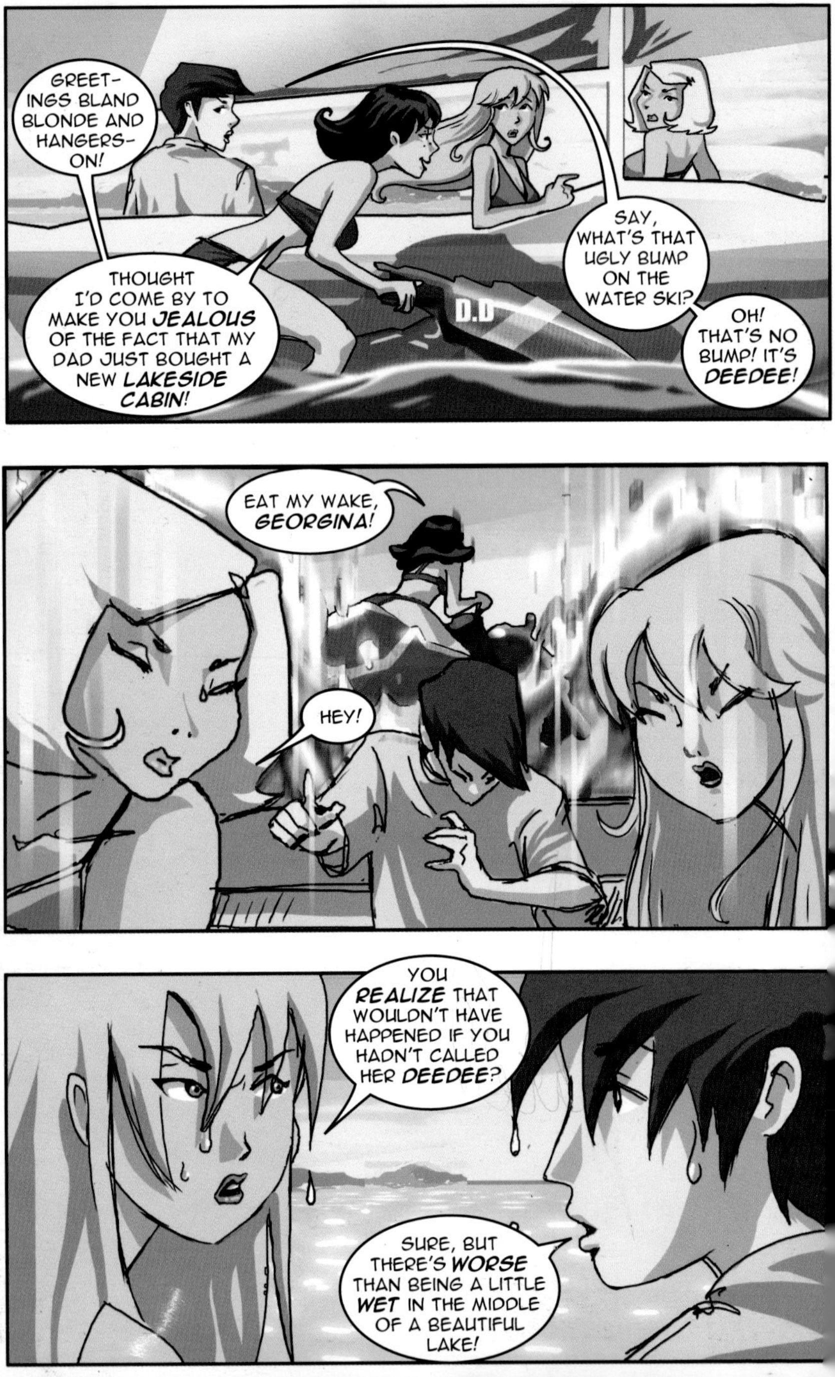

GREET-INGS BLAND BLONDE AND HANGERS-ON!
THOUGHT I'D COME BY TO MAKE YOU JEALOUS OF THE FACT THAT MY DAD JUST BOUGHT A NEW LAKESIDE CABIN!
SAY, WHAT'S THAT UGLY BUMP ON THE WATER SKI?
OH! THAT'S NO BUMP! IT'S DEEDEE!
D.D
EAT MY WAKE, GEORGINA!
HEY!
YOU REALIZE THAT WOULDN'T HAVE HAPPENED IF YOU HADN'T CALLED HER DEEDEE?
SURE, BUT THERE'S WORSE THAN BEING A LITTLE WET IN THE MIDDLE OF A BEAUTIFUL LAKE!

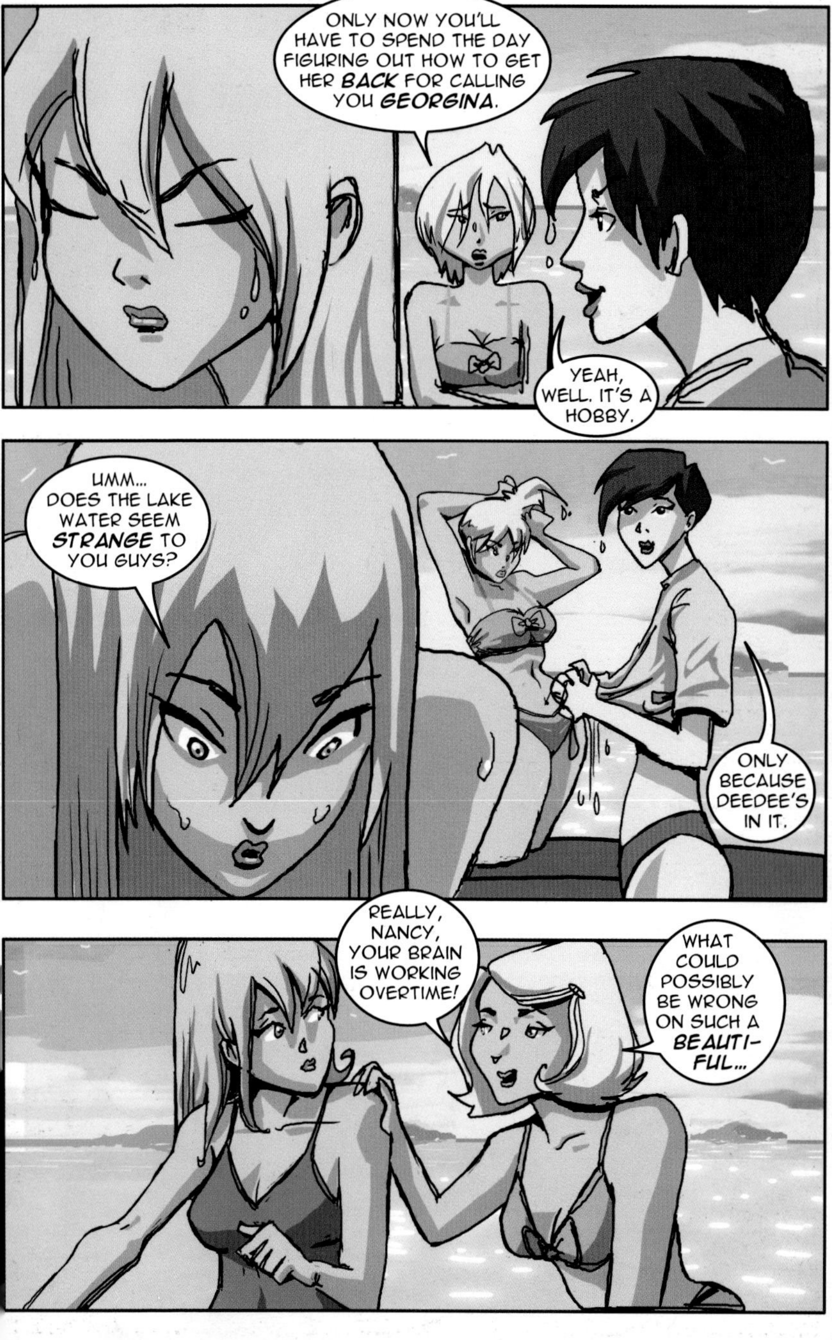
ONLY NOW YOU'LL HAVE TO SPEND THE DAY FIGURING OUT HOW TO GET HER BACK FOR CALLING YOU GEORGINA.
YEAH, WELL. IT'S A HOBBY.
UMM... DOES THE LAKE WATER SEEM STRANGE TO YOU GUYS?
ONLY BECAUSE DEEDEE'S IN IT.
REALLY, NANCY, YOUR BRAIN IS WORKING OVERTIME!
WHAT COULD POSSIBLY BE WRONG ON SUCH A BEAUTI-FUL...

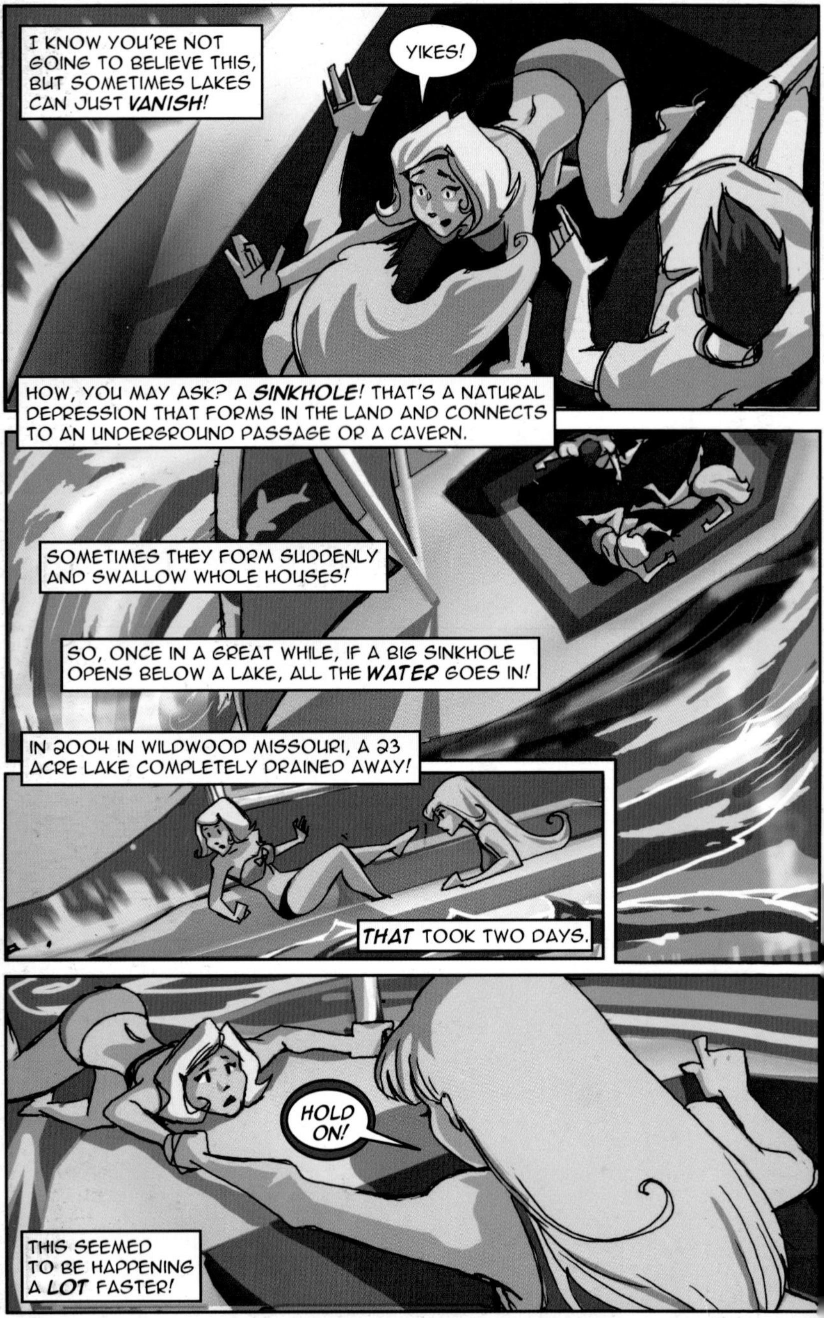
I KNOW YOU'RE NOT GOING TO BELIEVE THIS, BUT SOMETIMES LAKES CAN JUST VANISH!
YIKES!
HOW, YOU MAY ASK? A SINKHOLE! THAT'S A NATURAL DEPRESSION THAT FORMS IN THE LAND AND CONNECTS TO AN UNDERGROUND PASSAGE OR A CAVERN.
SOMETIMES THEY FORM SUDDENLY AND SWALLOW WHOLE HOUSES!
SO, ONCE IN A GREAT WHILE, IF A BIG SINKHOLE OPENS BELOW A LAKE, ALL THE WATER GOES IN!
IN 2004 IN WILDWOOD MISSOURI, A 23 ACRE LAKE COMPLETELY DRAINED AWAY!
THAT TOOK TWO DAYS.
HOLD ON!
THIS SEEMED TO BE HAPPENING A LOT FASTER!